CLOSE TO SHINING

CLOSE TO SHINING

Carolyn Bell Young Hisel

COLUMBUS PRESS

Columbus Press

Revised and Developed by
BRAD PAUQUETTE

Edited by
JOSHUA ENO

Cover Design by
JESSICA OSTRANDER

LCCN: 2021949381

Print ISBN: 978-1-63337-565-9
E-book ISBN: 978-1-63337-566-6

Author Photo by Lucy Massie Phenix

This book is a work of fiction and the product of the author's imagination. Any resemblance to real people, places, or events is coincidental.

PART ONE
CHAPTER ONE: GOT A NAME?

"Got a name?"

When the eighteen-wheeler turned up the ramp, slow as a terrapin, it took Jake real effort to lift his arm and raise his thumb. The big rig pulled over, and, desperate for this ride, he forced himself to move his legs. He grabbed the door handle, slung the duffle onto the floor, and hauled himself up into the seat. As he pulled the door shut and shoved his hands into the pockets of his scuffed leather jacket, he addressed the question.

"It's Jake. And thanks for the lift, man."

"You bet." The driver released the air brakes, and the semi rumbled back onto the grade and headed north on I-65. "Where you headed to before the crack of dawn?"

"Louisville?"

"My first stop. You can keep me awake." The driver shot him a grin. But the grin faded, and he reached to flip on the dome light. "What the hell happened to your face?"

Jake's hand trembled as he brushed aside his dark, chin-length hair from high cheekbones gutting beneath his honeyed skin and touched his nose. The question had kindness in it, and tears burned behind his eyes. "Aw, I, uh, lost an argument with my steering wheel."

"Oh yeah?" A chuckle. "Too many toss-backs?"

"Maybe. Probably." Jake's voice came in low and slow.

"You total it?"

"Yes sir. I did. Yes." In the silence that descended between them, Jake stared ahead, but what he saw was his car sinking beneath the black waters of the quarry.

"Bummer." The man's eyes crinkled at the corners. "But you're alive. It's almost morning and going to be a real pretty day."

Jake glanced at the belly rolling like a barrel over the black belt and the arms straining against rolled-up shirt sleeves. He saw a smile peek out at the road as the driver shifted gears. "Ah, well, I sure thank you for the ride . . ."

The driver frowned and looked at Jake. "That's an ugly bruise under your eyes. I bet your nose is broke. Shouldn't you be getting yourself seen to, instead of hitching?"

"Nah—I'll be fine." Jake had, in fact, forgotten to think what he looked like, and unless he leaned forward, causing the blood to pound into the bruises, he was mostly numb to the pain across his nose and cheekbone. "You been driving all night?" he asked, trying for a casual tone.

"Nope. Live in Nashville and picked up this load about three, but it's always these hours around six that make me want to nod off."

"Yeah." Jake turned his head and watched the sun begin to slide between the trees. It was mid-November, and in Kentucky the red maples were losing the last of their brilliant leaves—drops of blood falling through the air. Jake returned his gaze to the road ahead. He was desperate for sleep, and oblivion, but he understood he had made a kind of pact with the man at the wheel: for one ride north, provide conversation. His eyes found the pictures taped above the windshield.

"Your kids?"

"Yep." The driver's face broke into a proud grin. "Five good reasons to keep this rig on the road. You got kids?"

"No—none I know of anyway." Jake tried to share a grin but felt his facial muscles resist.

"Ah. Well, enjoy your freedom while you can, buddy."

Northward, sunrise lit the road unrolling ahead of them and Jake, squinting, shrank from the oncoming day.

A mile or two clipped by before the man said, "What happened? The wreck, I mean."

"Well . . ." Jake wished he had planned for this conversation. He could have said it was a fight. He should have cleaned himself up—thought how to explain it—but his practiced skill with the extemporaneous lie came to his rescue. He shrugged. "I don't remember much—lost control. Hit a fence."

"Anybody else hurt?"

The question caught Jake like a bat behind the knees. He could feel blood rush into his banged-up face.

"What? Oh no. Uh, I got stood up, so I was by myself." That part, at least, was true.

"Well, that was lucky, huh?"

"Yeah."

Silence. Jake struggled to pay attention, to change the subject. Finally, noting the man's royal-blue ball cap with a *K* on the front, he asked, "How you like the Wildcats' chances this year?"

"Whoa! Did you see that game last night?" The driver didn't look to see Jake's head shake. He just went on. "I'd say our chances are great. Final Four, here come the Cats!"

And so they found their way into the familiar, favorite territory of conversation in Kentucky: basketball.

§

When the driver of the Freightliner let Jake off at a bus stop, he leaned sideways to say, "Good luck to you, son. I'll be praying for you."

Jake turned his bruised face upward to look at the guy, too surprised to answer before the door swung closed and the eighteen wheels rolled away down Broadway.

An hour later, he had found his mother's street and her building without much trouble, but when Jake lifted his fisted hand to knock on the door, he hesitated, frowning. He heard a baby crying behind the door. *What the hell—a baby?*

He drew back to check the apartment number, and though the black number two was broken and hanging from one nail, a clean space outlined the number clearly: two thirteen—the number he remembered from her letter of a year ago. He looked up and down the littered hallway, listening to the crying as it escalated to shrieks.

He hadn't been to this apartment before. They'd had an apartment in another part of town when she was sentenced to three years in Pee Wee Valley Correctional, and he remembered the shock of that day in frightening detail.

He often thought his good memory was a curse, and as this one burst in his mind, it scorched him all over again.

§

It had been a school day, late spring of tenth grade, and Jake was sixteen unhappy years old. It had been no better or worse than most school days, but when Jake opened the door to the apartment, his mother was sitting at the table with her jacket on. He remembered it was her court day—and now she was waiting for him. Not a good sign, and his heart fell. They surveyed each other warily. A full ashtray sat in front of her, and with the two fingers that held her cigarette aloft, she gestured at the chair across from her.

She'd had other scrapes and short stays in jail, but the look on her face this time was different—frightened, frightening him.

"Sit down, Jakey."

He remained in the doorway, looking at her from beneath heavy eyelids. After a beat, he dropped his backpack and leaned one shoulder against the frame, crossed his feet, and folded his arms across his chest.

Light from the television set flickered in the corner, but his mother, KatieLyn, had thumbed the mute button. The room seemed to be waiting on them.

"What," he finally spoke—coldly, without inflection or curiosity.

"I said come on over here and sit down, smart mouth. Drop the attitude and pay attention. There's been a change of plans."

He rolled his chewing gum around to the other cheek, shrugged, and finally slouched his way to the chair and dropped into it with an exaggerated sigh.

KatieLyn stubbed out her smoke. "It looks bad this time. They gave me Judge Richards again."

"So?" He kept chewing, trying hard to hide his fear.

She looked down at her hands fiddling with the pack of Winstons. "Yeah, well, he won't let me do drug court again. Looks like I'll get the book thrown at me this time around. My lawyer ain't doing squat for me, and it . . ." She shrugged. "It don't look good."

Jake stared at her.

"Sentencing is next week."

"So what the fuck? You going to jail again?"

"No. This time I go to prison, and he can give me three to five years over there." Her eyes shone with tears.

Jake continued to stare at her and he swallowed hard.

She brushed the tears away and looked down at the table, picked up the pack, and started to shake out another smoke, but laid them back down on the table with a trembling hand. Then she looked directly at him. "So I called your dad."

"What?" His face went dead white. "My what?"

Her eyes fell away from him. "Yeah. So okay, Jakey, I lied. Your dad ain't dead. He lives down in Bedford Green. He just don't want to know us. He sends a little money ever month, but he don't want to hear or know a thing about us. That's the deal—been the deal since you were little tiny."

Jake's face flushed a livid red as he jumped up from the table, heading for the bathroom. After water ran for a while, he came back in the room, dry eyed and angry. He flung himself into a chair across the table, staring at her with burning coals for eyes.

"Liar." The word was low and knife edged. "Why should I believe this story? I've asked you about him plenty of times and he was always— *always*—dead."

KatieLyn sat still with her head hung low, her lank hair falling forward over one eye. When she spoke, her voice was trembling. "It was kind of true—he was dead to *us* is why I told you that." She leaned toward him and pushed her folded hands across the table. "Listen, I know I'm not a great mom—but I always kept you fed, Jakey, and clothes on your back. That's no small thing, you know." Self-pity was running the tears now, dragging mascara down her gaunt cheeks.

In spite of himself, Jake's anger began to dissipate, rinsed away by her low voice and her appearance of abject defeat. He laid his head down on his arms, but when she reached to stroke his hair, he jerked upright again and stared off at the television, where people laughed and applauded hysterically and silently.

After a few minutes, KatieLyn's voice came again, "He said you can come live with him."

Jake's head jerked toward her. "I don't want to go live with a father who don't want to know me! Shit, I don't even know his name."

"Wait, Jake! Listen. It's a good deal for you. His name is Roger Wright, and he's set up real good down there. My friend Mary Beth sees him sometimes, so she keeps me up to speed about him. She says he goes to her AA meetings, so he's joined up with the straight world—and I know he makes steady money now, because your support check comes real regular."

Jake waited, his face closed hard against her.

"He says he won't put up with no trouble, and I said that was good, because he wouldn't have any, since you're a good kid." She reached her hand to him. "And that's the truth—you are a good kid."

"Why can't I go live with Aunt Nell and Ebenezer?"

KatieLyn's face plummeted from false cheer to genuine sadness. She shook her head. "We haven't been over to Union Gate in ages, and we didn't exactly make a good impression on our last visit, you know."

"What. I don't remember nothing." Jake let his gaze fall to the floor.

"No, you wouldn't. I think you were stoned or something. You didn't act like you knew where you were. Anyway, I've used up all the credit I had with your great-aunt Nell, and I still owe her money. I can't call her again. Got that?"

Minutes ticked by and finally Jake lifted his head to look at her, his face frozen and his eyes masked, withdrawn. "'Good kid.' You got no fucking idea, Mama-san, because you don't pay attention."

KatieLyn looked stunned.

"I tried out your painkillers and your booze. None of it helped. None of it kept me from being afraid of what was going to happen next—who was going to come in and beat us up, or which boyfriend might try to fuck with me." His voice was grim and hard, striking out at her like rocks lobbed at an old factory window. "I don't smoke pot or take pills like candy because *you* do. If I'm a 'good kid,' it's because I don't want to be like *you*."

The blows struck home, and her eyes filled up and spilled over with real pain. He slumped down in the chair and didn't say anything more.

After a few minutes and no sympathy, she wiped her eyes and blew her nose. "Okay, Reverend, you may think you've got it all figured out, but trust me on this—you do not want to be a ward of the state, or some bum by the side of a railroad track."

She paused and he said nothing.

"Bedford Green's a good high school. You're smart, and your dad can help you. He's smart too. It's time you get to know your father, so get packed. You're going, and that's an end of it."

§

It was not the end of it. In fact, as Jake looked back over the years with Roger, he knew it was just a different kind of rough patch in his life. Maybe staying with his father was not quite as bad as the years with his mother, but still, plenty of ugly went down. Now here he was, back on her doorstep again—

He knocked, and the baby's cries mingled with voices as a woman and a man wrangled over answering the door. While he waited, Jake found himself thinking about the truck driver. *"I'll be praying for you." What does that mean?*

The door flew open in the hand of a stranger. Clearly just out of bed, he stood there scratching a swollen, pale belly, his eyes squinting into the dark hallway at the bunged-up, skinny guy half hidden in the gloom. His eyes finally rested on the duffel bag at Jake's feet.

"Hell, KatieLyn, who's this?" he growled.

Tangled dark hair massed around her white face as she approached the door with the baby. Her lips were slack and her eyes were almost swollen together with sleep. She was fumbling with a bottle, trying to get it lodged in the infant's mouth, and when she looked up finally at Jake, she seemed to stagger with shock.

"Hello, Mother."

CHAPTER TWO: THE TRAILER

Nell stopped mid-wipe and glared through crooked glasses at the ringing telephone. Partly hidden under the clutter on the kitchen counter, it was an old cradle phone connected to the wall box. Nell did not find cell phones to her liking. Landlines either, for that matter.

"Damn!" She had just gotten Eb settled into his old recliner for *Wheel of Fortune* and warmed dinner for herself, and she was tired. It had been a long day—and she did not need whatever aggravation was calling her. She willed silence from the phone.

Rinng.

She smacked the dented saucepan onto the dishes stacked in the drainer and tossed the empty can of Campbell's cream of mushroom soup at the pile of garbage spilling over the pail by the door. As it bounced off and hit the floor, the phone rang again.

Rinng.

Ebenezer was oblivious as he stared transfixed at the TV screen, a smile curving his open lips, drooling a little. Nell knew it was the repetition, the familiarity of the show, that pleased him, but still she liked to imagine that somewhere in her brother's severely malfunctioning brain, there were flickers of understanding. Who knew? Perhaps he was figuring out the phrases faster than the competitors.

Rinng.

Finally she gave up with a sigh and reached over the pile of coupons and unopened mail to free the phone and raise the receiver to her ear.

"What."

"Aunt Nell?" The woman's voice was all too familiar and superficially cheerful.

Nell's head dropped and she sat down on the barstool. "Yeah?"

The television audience clapped and cheered as a competitor was introduced.

"Oh—you got company?"

"Yeah. Vanna White. What's the problem this time, KatieLyn?"

There was a pause, then the caller's voice was more tentative. "Well . . . how are you all? How's Uncle Eb?"

"We're about the same, but you got to speak up. Eb don't like to miss his program."

"Well, listen, Aunt Nell. I know you're mad. I been meaning to call you and explain. I mean to return your money. I don't want you to think I've forgotten. It's just been real hard around here lately, and you know, with the baby and all . . ." The forced cheer tapered out of the voice as KatieLyn spoke more directly—with a measure of sincerity. "I appreciate you helping me out like you did."

Nell picked up the remote and hit the mute button. "Baby? What baby?" She waited, her lips set tight.

"Oh, I forgot you don't know. Skinny and I have a baby. His name is Samuel."

Silence met this news.

"Okay, well, Aunt Nell, listen, this isn't about me. I'm calling about Jakey."

"*Jakey?*" Nell's heart lurched. "You talking about the kid on crack . . . or meth or whatever the hell it was last time I saw him?"

"No ma'am. Truth is, he quit all that. He finished high school and everything. I got out of women's just in time to see him graduate. I was really proud of him. He did so good in math and stuff, he got a scholarship to college. How about that? I should have called to tell you." KatieLyn's voice died away.

This time the silence dragged into eternity and back.

Ebenezer began to moan, rocking against the chair back, miserable without the familiar game show sounds, so Nell thumbed the mute button. When the noisy, clapping crowd filled the trailer with its artificial delight, the large man slowed his motion and stopped, absorbed once more in the spinning wheel.

"Yeah, well . . ." KatieLyn took a breath and, hearing the TV, she raised her voice and blurted, "Aunt Nell, I wouldn't have called you, but Jake asked me to. He wants to come down and stay with you awhile. He says he won't be any trouble."

The shock landed in her gut. "Wants to stay *here*—with *us*? Why in holy hell . . ." her voice thickened and she coughed. When she caught her breath, she croaked, "I thought you said he was in college!"

"Well, he dropped out. He won't tell me why." The voice whined on, "I also don't know why he won't stay here with us." A burst of clapping from the TV filled a sudden silence in the receiver. "I guess he don't like Skinny much."

"Who?"

"My boyfriend." A sharp exhale whispered over the line. "The feeling's mutual, I guess."

"Aw hell, KatieLyn, you know there ain't hardly room for me and Eb in this old trailer as it is, and I absolutely can't feed another mouth on our disability checks. What in the world are you thinking?"

"I know. I *know*, but he said he'd find a job, sleep on the couch, and help out all he could. He's turned out a good boy, Aunt Nell. He is."

"Yeah, shit for promises. I've heard ever damn one of them—too many times." She started to cough again, the rattle deep.

An old electric clock sat on the stove, and while Nell watched the second hand click forward, and forward, she knew she would give in—*again*.

CHAPTER THREE: REMEMBERING HOPE

Jake's head rested against the cold window of the Greyhound bus as it hummed southeast through the falling dark. It felt good—the coolness and the vibration—until the cold began to seep down his neck. He pulled his sweatshirt hood up and settled once more against the window.

Going to Great-aunt Nell's—his plan to disappear for a while in her small town in central Kentucky—helped him slow his breathing. The panic lifted.

He stared at the patterned fabric on the seat in front of him, thinking about the future he had planned for himself—the future that now lay in bits and pieces all around him. He began to fixate on Mr. Phillips, and Algebra II.

When he had gotten to Bedford Green High School as a sophomore, he had tested into the upper-level math classes. However, the counselor had threatened him with remedial English if he didn't work harder. So he worked harder. Although, unlike math, where he could see the numbers fitting together to make exact and perfect wholes, he couldn't see the point of studying English. Tammy, Becky—none of them cared if he used good grammar.

That day he had been sitting in the back of the classroom with his arm slung behind him, staring out the window, thinking lazily of everything but algebra, until he realized the classroom had hushed, waiting. And his hand was raised.

All the kids and the heavyset Mr. Phillips were looking at him. This was a first: the silent guy in back had his hand up.

"Zero." It was barely audible, but he was heard.

There was a pause—then, "How did you get to that conclusion, Mr. Wright?" Mr. Phillips, who rarely smiled, was suddenly alert, his curly eyebrows lifted above his glasses. "Come to the board and show us how to do it."

Jake looked out the window again. When he looked back at Mr. Phillips and his grease-spotted tie, he saw the challenge in his eyes.

With a shrug, he rose and walked to the front, picked up the chalk, and sent white marks flying across the board. Checked it. Replaced the chalk. Walked back to his desk. Sat down and looked out the window at the red trees.

Students and teacher sat like spooked deer, the silence broken only by a fly buzzing against a windowpane.

"See me after class, Jake."

After the kids filed out—the girls whispering and glancing at him over their shoulders, the boys looking everywhere but at him—Mr. Phillips gestured to a desk in the first row, near his own desk, where he sat down and leaned forward until his wrinkled shirt brushed the worn wood. Jake slouched into the seat and looked at the floor.

Mr. Phillips put his hands together, with his thumbs forming the base of a triangle, and surveyed Jake. "So . . . it would seem we have a genius among us?"

Jake said nothing.

"I threw the class a curve with that problem," Mr. Phillips said. "I wanted to knock a little humility into this know-it-all bunch."

No comment.

"*I* would have had trouble working that problem at your age, Jake. Did you read it somewhere?"

Jake looked at him with surprise. "Where can you read that?"

Mr. Phillips chuckled. "Yeah, exactly. So you got it all by yourself. You just got it."

Jake shrugged, puzzled. "Sure. Wasn't that hard."

"Oh yeah? Well, my young friend, it seems to me we have all been underestimating the boy who says nothing."

Jake said nothing but held the gaze of his teacher's eyes, steady and bright.

"You know what the kids call you?"

Jake jerked his head back and frowned. "They call me something?"

"Yeah: Major Mystery." Mr. Phillips smiled.

Jake huffed a short laugh into the dark bus. That hadn't seemed too bad. In fact, he kind of liked it. Then he remembered what else Mr. Phillips had said: "They wish you'd join Math Club, and I do too. I've been watching you since you showed up in my class this year, and I think you might have a future in math, Mr. Mystery. If you want it. There are a lot of math-related fields that would open up to you. You'd need a couple of graduate degrees, but you sure have the brain power to do it."

"With no money?"

"Now, wait. People will help a bright mind like yours—scholarships now, grants later. I think you should start planning on it."

Jake stared at him, his mind spinning.

Mr. Phillips dipped his head, looking at him closely over his glasses. "Has no one ever mentioned college to you?"

College. Career.

Jake shook his head and let it flop back against the seat. No, no one had ever mentioned those two words.

He had dreamed of college from that day on.

Jake shook himself and turned again to the dark window, watching the streetlights jitter past in the rain. *I should have known it wouldn't work out.* His gut burned and cramped with disappointment.

CHAPTER FOUR: PICKUP

It was after ten. A dark November drizzle spattered the windshield of the old Dodge as Nell turned into the Greyhound parking lot. She pulled into a corner space and turned off the engine. Through the dust-edged rivulets that meandered down the glass, she watched the lighted platform.

She had stopped at the Walmart and picked up a twelve-pack of Bud Light, some toilet paper, and Twinkies for breakfast. These she pitched onto the heap of stuff in the back seat, and as she made the turn off Mill Street, she heard the thump of the beer sliding onto the floor.

While she waited, she wrestled a pack of Marlboro Lights from the pocket of her faded pants, shook one out, and lit it from the stub still smoldering in her mouth, then laid her head back against the broken headrest and blew smoke at the dark ceiling with a long sigh.

"Shit fire and damnation," she groaned to herself. "What in hell have I opened the door for this time?"

She could've used a Bud, but when she thought of having to get out into the drizzle and root around in the pile of old clothes, Styrofoam boxes from Arby's, and other crap that had no doubt slid off the seat with the beer, she decided she could do without.

The raindrops hit now in big, slow plops and she cranked the window down some to let out the smoke.

"Where's the damn bus? Poor old Eb, tied to his chair. What if he has to pee again? That diaper will only hold so much . . . O Lord, Lord. He'll be a mess to clean when I get home. Sure, Charlie's watching him, but he ain't gonna clean." She tapped the wheel in front of her and thought about Katie-Lyn, her sister's beautiful daughter—Pride of Oldham County, Queen of this and that—now reduced to skin and bones, whoring for drugs in the big city.

Not that she herself had amounted to much. But she'd never prostituted herself. *Don't know what you'd call what I did, but never that—at least not for money. And I never started with drugs either.* "Oh hooray for old Nell." She shook her head ruefully and blew smoke rings.

Not that KatieLyn had exactly chosen her lot in life. It was more like she just loved a party and finally got onto one slope too steep for her.

Finally Nell heard air brakes squeal, and she watched the big bus rock up over the curb as it turned in, laboring over the wet and littered lot to nose into the slot against the walkway. After a long, hissing sigh, the door slammed back and the driver appeared, swung himself down to the walk, and gestured to his passengers to dismount.

Nell watched from the safe distance of her parking place as though she might change her mind, take off, leave this baggage unclaimed. But she couldn't do it. He was just a kid—what, twenty-one, twenty-two? She had last seen him maybe six, seven years ago, and back then he was a sullen youngster covered with pimples and bad attitude, sweating and shaky with whatever he was high on. Could you call that high? Looked like he was awful low on something.

She recognized the cashier from the dollar store stepping awkwardly off the bus steps. Her big black purse snagged on the door hinge and nearly pulled her backward off her feet. Nell chuckled as the heavy woman unhooked herself with an angry jerk and walked off, stiff legged, into the night.

Then several others appeared and disappeared before a man leaned out and, holding his duffle in front of him, stepped down onto the curb. His face was pale and bony, and largely hidden by sunglasses. As she watched, he pulled a dark hood up from under his leather jacket and drew it over his hair. The shades turned slightly back and forth as he checked out the parking lot. At this distance Nell didn't recognize the slump-shouldered, thin-lipped man, but no one else was getting off.

She studied him with a frown, realizing there was something vaguely familiar about him. He stood there, a motionless, bent figure, the turned-up collar of his jacket loose behind his drooping, hooded head. He looked like a windup toy at the end of its performance.

Finally he seemed to pull himself together, and as he took another quick survey of the parking lot, Nell realized it was Jake—or a not-quite Jake. He looked at least forty years old. His face was gaunt with planes that didn't quite fit together, as though he was broken somehow, and his blank expression did not invite interpretation. He shrugged the rain off and turned to go into the bus station. Nell honked her horn. He glanced over his shoulder but couldn't see her behind the streaked windshield, and she had to get out and shout his name before he changed direction to make his way around the standing water to her car.

She withdrew inside, watching him from behind the wheel, where she didn't have to shake his hand, much less welcome him with a hug, and when he opened the passenger door, she leaned over and handed him the keys, gruffly telling him to dump the duffle in the trunk.

He obeyed and then folded himself into the front seat, shutting the door and enclosing the two of them in the dank space. He looked over at her, passing her the keys without smiling.

"Jacob."

"Aunt Nell." His voice was low and quiet. "Thanks. I really thank you for letting me come."

His deep voice threw her off. This young man was nothing like the one she had imagined, the one she was expecting.

She spoke the first words that came into her head. "Want a beer?"

"Yeah, that'd be good."

"Mind rootin' in the back floor? They fell off the seat. Get two."

When he had set himself back down in the dim light of the front seat and cracked the two open, he handed one to her, and they both drank a few swallows without speaking, looking out at the rain, which was dropping faster now, little beads dancing all over the windshield.

"Didn't hardly recognize you," she finally said.

"No."

"You look awful growed up to still be living with your mom."

The sunglasses turned toward her. "I haven't been living with her for— well, since she went to prison. I was sixteen, I guess. Didn't you know that?"

"Honey, I don't talk to my niece any more than I have to, and she sure as hell didn't call me to say 'Hey, Aunt Nell, I get to go to prison!'" After a pause to swallow another sip, she said, "I thought since she called to ask me if . . ."

"Yeah, well, I had to go back to her place to figure out how to find you. She didn't want to call you. Wanted me to stay with her." His voice trailed off and a tractor-trailer shushed by on the wet street behind them.

Another bus pulled in before she asked, "It's been a long time. Why here, Jake?"

It was her turn to listen to empty space. She drank the rest of her beer and stubbed out her cigarette while he stared through his sunglasses at the red taillights of the Greyhound, watching as they fractured into shards that melted and slid down the windshield. She sighed and started the car.

CHAPTER FIVE: ARRIVAL

The trailer park was very dark. Most of the security lights were out, as usual.

Jake carried the twelve-pack, less two, as well as his duffle as he followed Nell around the round concrete table and up the stoop. In the drizzling dark he stumbled over a broken concrete step. At the door, Nell set her plastic Walmart bag down on the wet concrete. It sagged and rustled like a live thing while she dug in her pocket for the key.

They heard the "UNH, UNH!" greeting from inside, and when they entered, Nell stepped aside.

"Look who it is, Ebenezer!"

Eb stopped rocking against the back of his recliner next to the couch and stared at the newcomer, his mouth slack and drooling, his small eyes startled wide, and dully curious.

A slight, jockey-sized man stood from a rocker on the other end of the couch from Ebenezer and tried to make his way behind Jake toward the door as if he would disappear without a sound, but Nell caught his arm. "Here now, Charlie, you got to meet my great-nephew Jake." The two men stared at the floor as Nell persisted. "Here you go, Charlie, now you take these," she said as she pulled a couple of Buds from the twelve-pack and pressed them into his hands, "and I'll fix fried chicken for your supper tomorrow night, okay? Jake'll bring you a plate over."

"Yeah, sure, Nell," came the gravelly voice. "But, you know, any time . . ."

"Yeah, I know. Thanks, Charlie!"

The small man made his escape, and Jake turned his attention to Ebenezer, whose gaze had never left him.

Jake went over to Eb and sat on the edge of the couch next to his recliner. "Hey, old man!"

Eb's face broke into his slow, angelic smile and Jake grinned beneath his sunglasses.

"Look at that! I think he remembers me!" He looked around at Nell. "Can you tell if he does, for sure?"

"Sure he does," she said, glancing at her younger brother. "Those are his happy sounds. Wipe his mouth for him with the rag on the chair arm, okay? He drools a lot if he's excited."

She swung the plastic bag to the kitchen counter—the ten square inches that were free of unopened mail and grocery coupons—and turned to watch.

As a kid, Jake had felt a deep affection for the big man with Down syndrome, climbing into his lap to watch TV, chattering to him while he played with cars on the arm of Eb's chair. The misery chiseled into Jake's face softened, and Eb broke into a wider grin.

"You've gotten *big*!" Jake said, looking him over, and Eb nodded eagerly, pushing his hands high over his head and smiling broadly in blissful innocence. His size, though, surprised Jake. Uncle Eb looked twice the size he had been—what was it?—eight years ago when he'd last been here. The man must have grown to weigh over three hundred pounds.

Jake glanced over at Nell with a guarded question in his eyes. She caught his look and threw it back with a hard glare. Jake felt an apology rise in his mouth, but he said nothing and shrugged half-heartedly. He needed her. He needed this place to hide in.

The last time he saw Nell and Eb, the visit had ended badly. He was fourteen years old and so full of himself nobody could stand him. A punk. Hated school. Hated his mother and had taken some kind of crap he'd found in her dresser drawer just to prove what a tough guy he was. Swallowed it down before he knew she wanted to go to Aunt Nell's. He didn't remember most of the visit.

Nell continued putting things away with crisp movements and hard little slams of the cabinet doors.

Jake made an effort to smooth things over by talking to Ebenezer. "I used to come stay with you and Aunt Nell when I was a little boy. Do you remember?"

Eb nodded.

"Aunt Nell used to take care of me sometimes, and you and me, we'd play cars."

Ebenezer's smile broadened and his close-set eyes lit up. "Cahs!" he said and rocked himself back and forth, his excitement rising. "Pay cahs. *Jakey!*"

"That's good, Eb!" Nell broke in, her voice calming, soothing. "You're right, it's Jakey! You can play cars with him later. Now, do you want some ice cream?"

He swung his heavy round shoulders toward her, nodding and smiling. "Yes, ice c'eam. Jakey. Yes, ice c'eam."

"Do you want some, Jake? It's chocolate ripple." Nell held up the carton.

"Sure." Jake patted Eb on the shoulder and stood up. "Come on, Uncle Eb, it's ice cream time!"

"Leave him be, Jake. He can eat in his chair."

Jake sat down again, next to Eb.

While she scooped, Jake's eyes roamed around the room. The worn old furnishings somehow calmed him, distracting him from the ever-present pain in his face and the suffering in his soul. The carpet was old and beaten down from the same feet moving back and forth over the same paths. Once a greenish gold, the color was gone except for under the furniture edges, and the area in front of Ebenezer was almost worn through.

He remembered the old maroon couch—nubby, frayed at the corners, and sagging at one end, bookended by hard pillows in bright floral patterns.

Ebenezer's La-Z-Boy still stood to one side of the couch, with the cushioned rocker on the other, all crowded together to face the television set, everything pretty much the same as it used to be.

Jake's throat constricted as he craned his neck and noticed the paint-by-numbers picture of a wild mustang rearing against a sunset over Western mountains. He had been around nine when he painted that. He had sat there at the kitchen table and worked on it for a long time. Did a good job with those little round pots of paint and the thin brush. *I'll be damned.* Aunt Nell had put it in a wood frame and hung it over the couch.

Maybe that was my best day ever.

Nell brought Eb's bowl to him and then went back to get theirs. She beckoned to Jake with a bowl, inviting him to sit with her at the round table, and she sat down with a heavy sigh. Jake got up and joined her.

They ate without speaking. Eb spooned his ice cream into his mouth without taking his eyes off the television screen. *Beauty and the Beast* had been on when they came in, and it was toward the end, the Beast sitting by the window, grieving for Belle. Eb and the Beast looked eerily alike: the soft mountain of a man and the sad Beast.

When she finished, Nell pushed her bowl away and looked at Jake. He laid his spoon on the table and waited.

"Any idea how long you'll stay?"

"No ma'am." His eyes searched hers and then glanced away. "First thing I need to do is find me a job. I mean to pay for my keep—if you'll let me stay a while."

"What's under them sunglasses you wear in the dark?"

He drew in a deep breath, took them off, and laid them carefully down. He blew his hair off his forehead through narrowed lips and looked at Nell with an unreadable expression. Nell stared at him. It was the first time she had taken a good look at his face in the light, and he saw her eyes widen as she took in the swollen cheek, the bruises around his eyes, and the cut on his nose.

"You been in a fight?"

"No," he said, "I had an accident back in Bedford Green, ended up with a broken nose. Left there with some real bad memories . . ." He picked up the spoon and began bouncing it noiselessly against his fist balled up on the table in front of him. "I thought if I could come stay with you a little while, earn some money . . . I'd just like a chance to start over." His voice and his courage petered out about the same time.

Nell's face softened slightly. "Well, Jake, it's kind of like this: as you can see, the quarters are pretty tight for three grown folks. My room's in back, and the other room is Eb's, so I'm afraid you'll have to make do with the old couch—meaning that you are stuck with our TV shows and our routines until we go to bed every night at ten o'clock."

Jake nodded, watching her eyes for a hint of her feeling. "That's fine. That'll suit me fine."

"Well, I can't much imagine it would suit the kid I used to know—having to go to bed at ten, and having to watch Eb's TV shows."

Jake looked at her without comment.

"See, Eb can't tolerate much excitement. I have to make sure the television doesn't get him too riled up. We don't watch *CSI* or *True Crime* and such in this house. So mostly after the game shows, we watch Disney movies."

Jake nodded and said, "Sure. That's okay by me." He smiled a soft smile and said, "I'm not too keen on getting riled up myself anymore. Sounds real peaceful."

Nell stared at him in bafflement, a little frown creasing her forehead over her glasses. The clock on the back of the stove ticked away. She said, "You're not running away from the cops, are you, Jake?"

"Nah." But his eyes were on the floor. "From myself maybe. That's all."

§

Jake jarred awake—lurching, crying out. A man was walking through the dark, walking toward him, closer and closer. Suddenly he burst into flames and people were screaming and the fire was hot. Jake felt his skin burning, and then he reared awake, thrashing at the covers. He threw off the blanket and sat up, dragging himself back to consciousness over the rough upholstery of the couch cushions. Folding his body over his legs, he put his chin on his knees and locked his hands behind his neck, stifling a groan that rose in his throat.

The space heater ticked on, glowing red in the dark.

"Hell. This is hell and I'm in it," he muttered through his teeth. "Hell don't wait for a person to get there. It's right here in this world just waiting for you to make a mistake."

There was a sound and Jake jumped to his feet, his heart pounding.

A figure loomed in the doorway, filling the frame, and Jake realized it was Eb.

"Aw, sorry, Uncle Eb. It's okay. Just a bad dream." He stood and went to him, put his arm around his shoulder, and turned him around. "You go back to sleep. I'm okay." He guided the big man back into his room, Ebenezer's thick tongue roaming his wet lower lip and worry folding his brow. Jake tucked him back in and Eb, reassured, smiled up at the young man, turned on his side, and closed his eyes.

Jake went back to the small front room. Caged, with little room to pace, he went to the window and stared out into the night.

"I'll be praying for you."

Funny how those words seemed to linger around the edges of his thoughts and insert themselves persistently into all that was so muddy and painful.

What does that mean exactly? That old fat truck driver seemed to believe it was important for me to know he was going to "pray" for me.

Jake smiled a little to himself. He was a nice guy though—easy to talk to. *He was driving all over the country, had five kids at home . . . Why would it even cross his mind to pray for me, of all people? Did I look so pitiful? The driver would never have said that if he knew . . .*

Jake shook his head. He folded his arms on the window frame and leaned his forehead against the cold glass. He sighed, then raised his eyes and found the Big Dipper winking at him across unimaginable space.

Yeah, well, if you ARE something real out there, be nice to the guy in the truck, right?

§

Jake had left the trailer by the time Nell got up. Ebenezer always woke early, but he was usually content to lie in his bed and talk to himself. Today, though, he began to grunt and huff pretty loudly. Nell fumbled into her old robe and hurried in. As she helped him dress, she wondered if he was agitated because he remembered Jake's arrival last night, but when there was no sign of him in the front room, Eb didn't seem to notice.

She saw that Jake had folded the worn blanket she had given him and stowed it over his duffle in a corner. She was grateful for the small courtesy, but still she frowned at the empty room. She turned to eye the box of Twinkies she'd bought for him, unopened on the counter.

"Well, damn it, what did I expect?" Nell grumbled to herself as she fixed Eb's cereal. "His mother disappeared on a regular basis, and now Jake seems to have taken up the habit."

But somehow, while she and the boy were sitting up late at the kitchen table, while they talked over beer and peanuts after Eb went to bed, Nell thought she detected a difference in Jake. He had a kind of seriousness, and a humility, that was forever missing in his mother.

He had definitely grown past the fourteen-year-old she remembered, and she sensed that the maturing had not been easy.

CHAPTER SIX: JUST JAKE

Millicent Farley, the girl at the front counter, noticed him come in—rather, she noticed his shades come in—and her light-blue eyes watched as he walked slowly around the perimeter of the store, looking for something.

The Goodwill was scattered with fifteen or twenty shoppers—grazing the tight aisles beneath the singing blue fluorescents. The slim-hipped, good-looking older guy in a leather jacket and sunglasses wasn't browsing for clothes, however, and now he arrived at her cash register.

"You got a bike anywhere?"

The girl with the short blond hair, just long enough to spike out in platinum highlights in every direction, put down the *People* magazine from last year and tucked her chewing gum in her cheek before she looked up at him, swiping her bangs to the side of her rhinestone-rimmed glasses. "For you?"

He flushed. "Well, yeah—for me. Seem to be temporarily without transportation."

"Oh. Well, sorry. We haven't seen a grown-up bike in here for months. We get good ones though, sometimes—mostly for little kids—but I can put your phone number on a waiting list—if you want."

His mouth pulled back at the corner in a lopsided grin that didn't quite reach his eyes. "Well, if a good bike comes in for somebody my size—would you call my number before anybody else's?"

She feigned demur and her eyes held a giggle. "I spose—specially since you'd be the only one on the list." She chewed her gum. "How much do you want to give for one?"

He shrugged. "Oh, fifty, maybe sixty, for the right bike."

"Hmmm." She eyed him thoughtfully. "You know—I'm pretty sure I saw one behind my cousin's house. Tires may be flat on it though. He never takes care of anything. Want me to see about it?"

"Sure—I'd appreciate it. He don't use it anymore?"

"No. He's in Afghanistan." She shrugged. "And he never rode it much after he got his old Mustang, but I can ask Aunt Margaret—that's his mom. They Skype ever Thursday." She tossed the hair out of her eyes. "My bet is he'll want the money."

"That'd be great." He reached across the counter to feed some receipt tape from the register, tore it off, and jotted down the number of his new disposable cell phone.

She smiled up at him and tilted her head quizzically. "Where you from—Florida?"

This time there was no smile and no answer.

"I mean, where they need sunglasses . . ." Her face turned pink as she turned toward new customers.

He forced a smile and raised his chin. "Let me know about the bike." She nodded and he meandered away from the counter.

Two women had labored up behind him with a pile of baby clothes and a stroller, and her spiky head bent like a field thistle over the cash register.

She watched from the corner of her eye as Jake fished three quarters from his jeans pocket and bought a local newspaper from the blue metal rack by the door. He found the classifieds, spread the paper on one end of the glass countertop where they kept the jewelry, and began to study the Help Wanted ads, taking off his sunglasses.

After the two women left with their baby stuff, another woman stepped up and flopped three purses and a girl's coat on the counter. She was wearing perfume so heavy Jake started breathing through his mouth. The girl was quick and efficient on her cash register, and soon the fragrant customer was wrestling her bags through the door.

"Whew! Enough to gag a maggot," the girl said, and this time when Jake smiled, his dark eyes smiled too. She liked his smile, but now she noticed the bruises and the healing cut on the bridge of his nose.

"I'd like to see the other guy," she joked.

Jake looked at her blankly.

"Looks like he landed a few punches."

"Oh, nah. Just an accident." He touched his nose with his forefinger.

"Looking for a job?" she said, glancing at his paper.

"Yeah. Know anybody hiring?"

She shook her head. "Not really. I gave up a while back. I'm just working part-time in here for my crazy aunt." She sighed, pulling at a strand of hair. "I sure would like a real job though—I'd be a good employee—I like to work."

"Says here Kroger's looking."

"Yeah—well, they're always looking. I worked for them about two weeks, but their night manager creeped me out and I quit." She paused and then added, "Pay and benefits is pretty good if you can stick it though."

"Well, the first thing I need is transportation. Can't expect to borrow my way around a strange town, miss."

"Forget the 'miss'—just Milli." She grabbed the receipt tape with his number on it.

"Okay, let me know what you find out." He put his sunglasses back on and turned for the door.

"Wait," Milli called. "What's your name?"

He turned back. After a short hesitation, he said, "Jake." He looked at her and nodded. "Just Jake."

CHAPTER SEVEN: GROCERIES

Jake knocked on the door and then tried the handle, but it was locked, and he heard Nell's irritable "Hang on, hang *on*! I'm *coming*!" She opened the door with a jerk.

"Well, where have you been?" became "What on earth . . . ?" as he walked past her and swung a couple of grocery bags to the table.

Eb watched him, his mouth open in a big smile as he bounced in his chair, a spoonful of macaroni and cheese forgotten in his hand.

"I thought I'd fix supper tonight," Jake said as he shoved his sunglasses to the top of his head. He pulled out bagged salad, a couple of flank steaks, and a large bag of frozen french fries. Finally with a flourish, he pulled out a half-gallon box of ice cream and wagged it at Eb, who responded with a thumb stuck high in the air. His mac and cheese slid off his spoon and landed on the floor in a yellow slump.

"You know how to cook this stuff?"

"Well, no, but how hard could steak be?"

"Probably harder to put away than it'll be to fix . . ." Nell grumbled, opening the fridge door and shaking her head at the contents. "I guess I need to go through here and throw out all the green fuzzy shit." She began to sort and stack things in the small refrigerator to make room.

From the depths she asked, "What did you do this for, Jake? I already bought food for you. In fact, you missed out on Twinkies by sneaking out this morning."

He looked up. "Twinkies!" He blinked. Twinkies had been his comfort food on bad days. He wondered if she remembered or if it was just a coincidence.

"Where'd you go so early? You were long gone when we got up."

"Aw, I couldn't sleep, so I got out and walked awhile." He sat down on a vinyl kitchen chair and started fooling with the circulars and other junk mail that littered the table, making neat stacks of them.

Finally Nell stood from her reorganizing and closed the refrigerator door. "Want something to eat? There's some more mac and cheese in the pot."

"Yeah, that'd be great. I guess I haven't eaten since last night."

Eb was finding Jake's face more interesting than his television show.

"I called about a job at Kroger's this morning."

"You did? That's good. What did they say?"

"I'm supposed to come in at four and talk to them."

"You sure haven't wasted time!" Nell plopped the cheesy pasta on a plate, added a piece of bread, and put it in the microwave.

"Nell, could you and Uncle Eb run me over there in your car? Shouldn't take very long. I already have a good work history with them, down in Bedford Green."

The timer on the microwave chimed, and Nell pulled the plate out and put it in front of him.

"Yeah. We can do that, no problem, but how are you going to get over there ever day? You know Kroger's hours will be crazy, and I didn't see no vehicle get off that bus with you."

Jake grinned over at Eb. "I got a lead on a good bike. Looks like I'll be driving a bicycle until I can save up for another auto-mo-bile."

Eb nodded happily. "A . . . BI-CYCLE?"

"Through the *winter*?" Nell asked at the same time.

"No." He turned back to Nell with a slight frown. "If the weather turns rotten, and you aren't needing your car, I was hoping maybe I could borrow it."

She looked skeptical, and wary. "Probably. Just depends."

36

CHAPTER EIGHT: THE BIKE

Jake was slouched on the sofa, drowsily watching reruns of *Two and a Half Men* with Nell and Eb. He was longing for sleep after bouncing restlessly around town and putting on a good face for his interview at Kroger, and had begun drifting off, when he was startled awake by the techno-funk ringtone of his cell phone. He fumbled to dig it out from his hip pocket, while the two others watched him curiously from their chairs. He'd never gotten a phone call before. They hadn't heard it ring.

"Hello?" Jake asked.

"Is this 'just Jake'?"

"Huh? . . . Who?" he asked in momentary confusion.

"Jake?" said the voice.

Jake sat up. "Oh yeah! Wait a minute." He got to his feet and made a hasty exit through the trailer door to stand on the stoop, hunched against the cold. "Now I can hear you. It's Milli, right?"

"Well durn. How did you know?"

"Might be because I've only given my new cell number to two people, and the other one's a man."

"Oh. I thought you recognized my lovely little voice." She sounded deflated.

"Well, you got a bike for me?" Jake asked.

"I might. Billy Mac says it's okay to sell it, but I don't know if you want it. It's an old trail bike. Twenty-four gears and everything."

"Where can I see it?"

"It's at my aunt's. If you want to, I could take you over there tomorrow."

"Your cousin . . . What's he want for it?"

"He said he wants seventy-five, but he'd take less. I know him."

"Could work."

"I get off tomorrow at four . . ." Milli said.

"Hang on." Jake stuck his head in the door. "Nell, I found a bike, I think. You need your car tomorrow afternoon around four?"

She hesitated slightly, but then said, "Nah, you can have it—if you bring it back with its fenders still on."

Jake nodded, returning to his phone. "I'll be there."

§

The next afternoon, Jake walked out to Nell's car, shivering in his leather jacket and jeans. It was cold and damp, a typical late November day in Kentucky, and the bare trees in the trailer park stood in clusters of wet, shiny black against leaden clouds. Everything looked dull through his shades. He thought about snow, and the fact that a trail bike with its larger, nubby tires was probably just what he needed. Not at all that he wanted, being used to four wheels on the ground and a heater blowing warm air. *But*, he thought, *there's something just right about not needing my driver's license or paying insurance for a while. Low profile, Jake, low profile. Don't need to be putting a Social Security number out there. I'd just as soon Roger not be able to track me down for a while.*

Would the police think to check the old quarry? Nah. Why would they? Unless somebody saw . . .

He shook himself and realized he was sitting in the parking lot behind the Goodwill and didn't remember driving the mile or so to get there. He wiped his face and opened the car door.

"I'm looking for Milli . . . ?" he asked the large woman in an oversized men's flannel shirt at the front register. She looked him over curiously and nodded before she pointed toward a door in the back wall.

Jake walked to the back, past the Employees Only sign, and saw Milli before she saw him. He stood and watched her for a minute. Today's outfit distracted him from the business at hand. She wore a little orange sweater with brown leggings and a black leotard with a pale-pink, frothy tutu standing out around her hips. Her spiked blond hair swooped to one side. He noticed a tattoo circling her neck that had been covered up when he saw her the first time. When she turned toward him, he saw the rhinestone-edged spectacles and black lipstick—a detail that made her teeth flash whiter than white as she smiled at him. Jake suddenly saw the very vulnerable girl behind the flamboyant getup and brave smile, and he shook off a fleeting interest in her.

"Hey there, Jake! You look cold!" She held up a down jacket. "You can find some good warm deals around here."

He shrugged and said, "I'm fine," then busied himself unwrapping a pack of gum. This friendly girl made him a little nervous. He hoped she wouldn't chatter on and on.

"Well, can you wait a few minutes? We got three loads in this afternoon, and I need to do up this last batch before we go." She hesitated. His eyes were down and she couldn't read his expression. "You could help, make yourself useful."

He shifted the gum in his mouth and looked around. "Whoa. You kidding?" he asked in stupefaction as he stared at the boxes and bags of household odds and ends that were heaped against the wall. She gave him an encouraging smile and proceeded to demonstrate the sorting system that store employees used: electric appliances went on one table, small toys on another, women's clothes on a sizing table, men's coats over there, etc., until he could begin to see the order forming itself out of chaos.

He found the mindless work kind of enjoyable, especially since Milli had gotten quiet as they worked together. He would hold up a mystery item and she would nod to its destination. After a half hour of working together, they had sorted and distributed the small mountain, and Jake had found a hooded canvas jacket he could use when it got cold.

Milli took him out to the cash register. "This here is my crazy Aunt Gert," Milli said. "And this *here* is Jake."

The woman gave Jake a crooked-toothed smile and stuck out her hand. "Pleased to meetcha, Jake."

A small grin answered from beneath his sunglasses as he shook hands.

"Milli tells me that Billy Mac is gonna sell you his bike."

"Yeah, maybe." He kept his head down as he fished a ten-dollar bill out for the coat. Seemed like too many people were interested in his business. He didn't know quite what to make of it.

The transaction was quickly rung up and Gert shooed them off.

Milli grabbed her short down jacket and led Jake out the door to the parking lot. He noticed in a vague and distracted way how her child's tulle ballet skirt fluttered around her butt in the bitter wind.

§

The bike would do. It was a bitter come-down from his black Honda, but he found nothing wrong with it but a little rough usage, so Jake handed over fifty bucks to Milli's aunt Margaret without argument. They chatted a few minutes about Billy Mac's tour in Afghanistan while Jake adjusted the height of the seat, and then Margaret scurried back into the house and out of the cold.

Jake lifted the bike into the trunk of the old car, on top of the old newspapers and other treasures, tied down the trunk lid with a bungee cord, and turned to thank Milli for her help. But she stopped him with a hesitant hand in the air.

"Um, would you want to stop at McDonald's and get coffee with me?"

Jake looked at her with surprise as she stood there. She grinned uncomfortably in the silence before she shrugged. "Oh, that's okay . . ."

But he nodded. "Sure. Okay. Lead the way."

CHAPTER NINE: COFFEE AND COKE

The light was falling out of the day, dimming the large plate glass windows to gray and making the brightly lit interior of McDonald's seem a good, warm place to be. Jake ordered a coffee and Milli a large Coke, and they were heading toward a table when a voice caught them.

"Milli! Hey, Milli!"

Jake kept going to a spot by the window while she stopped to talk to two girls near the door. He laid his leather jacket across the back of a chair, sat down, and set his sunglasses on the table. When she came and joined him, she rolled her eyes.

"Sorry," she said, taking off her jacket and sliding into her chair, without noticing the wary expression in his eyes. "Gail-Betsy had to ask who the hot guy was. We call them Gail-Betsy because they are inseparable nuisances."

Jake leaned to take a drink of his hot coffee. *God, I feel so much older than this girl and her friends. What am I doing here? This is such a waste.*

"Sorry." Milli was watching his dark expression with concern. "I could have pretended not to see them, but it would have made it worse."

Jake shrugged, his mind wandering.

"They're terrible gossips." She hesitated, then tried to fill the silence with words. "Like most of us around here, I guess. Not much else to do."

Jake stared at Milli, letting her voice settle over him, not thinking too much, relaxing slightly under the flow of her talk.

"The trouble is," she went on, looking out the window, "the story always gets crazier as it goes around. I'm sure one of my cousins will hear from Gail-Betsy and get all the family worked up about my new 'boyfriend.'"

Jake frowned, his mouth tight. "You trying to make your real boyfriend jealous?"

"Don't have one, don't want one, thank you very much." Milli's voice was firm.

He shrugged. "Yeah, I bet."

"No, really. I'm off men."

"Good idea."

She watched him turning his cup between his hands. Finally she said softly, "You look like you been beat up pretty good."

Jake lifted his hand to his face and rubbed it across the bruises. He looked up at her. In her pale-blue eyes he saw a well of sympathy—deep waters, calm and quiet—and he suddenly wanted to trust this girl, tell her everything. But he took a breath, and then just shrugged. "Nah. I'm okay."

She shook her head. "You're safe with me, you know. I never gossip." Her pretty mouth tightened, and a dimple flashed. "Most of the time."

Jake's eyes narrowed, and he snorted but couldn't muster an answering grin.

She shifted in her seat. "Found a job yet?"

"Oh yeah—Kroger's. They want me to start tomorrow. Must have gotten a good recommendation from Bedford Green." He halted, embarrassed—surprised to be talking about himself.

"Bedford Green!" Milli repeated in surprise.

Jake felt a sudden alarm go off in his gut, and it flamed in his eyes before he could tamp it down. "You know Bedford Green?"

Milli's eyes widened. "Not really. It's just, my Gran lives on a farm near there." She studied his face, and he shifted uneasily beneath her gaze.

"Ah." He buried his flushed face behind a drink of coffee and Milli stirred the ice in her Coke.

"So you worked at a Kroger's before?" she persisted gently.

"Yeah."

"It's a real pretty town. I love it over there. I wish I lived there."

Jake could feel himself pulling way, way back from this conversation. He was trying to think of an exit line when she asked, "What's the deal with Bedford Green?" He could feel her watching him. "I bet there's an angry husband out looking for Jake McGee!"

"What?" Jake looked up and frowned, distracted, unable to follow her mood shift.

"Oh, I make up stories and names for my friends," she said. "McGee goes to only my best men-friends." Her eyes sparkled as she smiled.

Jake grinned in spite of himself. He had wished for a different identity, and dang if she hadn't given him one. "Where'd you get McGee from?"

"You know, from the song—'Me and Bobbie McGee.'"

"Ah. Janis Joplin. Good song." He was a beat behind her, not used to her kind of joking.

"Okay. So tell me about your life back in Bedford Green," she urged. "I'm thinking maybe you've got a little history back there."

"Nope. Nada." Jake leaned back in his chair, caution rising like bile in his throat. "I just lived in the area for a while and, you know . . ." He shrugged and shut himself up.

She played with the straw stuck in the lid of her cup. "I'm sorry. I didn't mean to wander into territory with a fence around it."

Jake looked at Milli. Her apology was real. There was openness in her eyes—kindness in the depths behind the black eyeliner and rhinestone-crusted glasses. He relaxed slightly and said, "Yeah, well, I bet you're the one with a story to tell."

"Nope. Wish I did. I'd love to have a secret life I could tell you about."

She turned her head to look out of the window at the cars passing. Her face had taken on a wistful longing that reached through Jake's defenses and tugged. He watched her and drank his coffee, momentarily distracted.

She took a slow draw on her Coke before she said, "However, Mr. Mc-

Gee, if there's a Mrs. McGee in your life, lurking around the edges, ready to pounce, I'd like to know about her."

Jake shook his head. "No missus. No girlfriend anywhere, and right now I'm definitely not looking for one. I'm just trying to get my feet under me. Make a new life for myself somewhere."

"Oh." Milli nodded. "Right. Did you have to go away from your old life in order to do that?"

"Well, yeah, I guess I did."

"I ask because I keep trying to start over and make me a new life right here. But it ain't working out exactly."

Jake considered her serious eyes. "Why?"

"Oh, well . . ." She sighed. "Let's just say—I'm a Farley. That means I'm one of a great big, rowdy family here in Union Gate, and I love them to death—well, most of them—but it's like . . . How do I say it? It's like they think this town's supposed to be enough for anybody." Milli paused before adding thoughtfully, "None of 'em has any dreams. Nobody thinks about, oh say, going to college. Doesn't that word sound good, college?" She rolled the word around in her mouth wistfully, smiling at him.

He just shrugged. Survival was his concern now, and his hands drew up into fists under the table.

"You look like somebody that's serious about things, like about going places," she added, leaning forward, shoulders drawn up, arms folded on the table.

"I thought I was going places once." Jake spoke reluctantly, voicing thoughts pulled like cold molasses from a jar. "I finished two and a half semesters at Western. But now I'm here. This is as far as I got."

Her eyebrows rose above the silly glasses. "See? I thought so. Western University. I thought you looked real smart. But oh well, why'd you quit?"

"Oh, you know, usual crap—flunking English Comp, ran out of money."

"Bummer. Flunking *English*? Wow. I coulda helped you with that. English was always easy . . ." She put her elbow on the table and propped her chin in her hand. He watched as she gazed past him at her own impossible future.

After a moment, she changed gears. Suddenly the gloom disappeared. She straightened and her face was pure sunshine as she said, "Now, wait, there is one thing the Farleys are good at! Making babies. They're mighty good at that!"

Jake smiled a little. "And how many do you have?"

"Not *me*!" she laughed. "The rest of them. The Farleys plus spouses have produced five new ones in the last year!"

Jake mused, "Milli Farley. Well. I didn't know your last name."

"Yep. Milli Farley: fashionista and karaoke star." She laughed, and a flash of her fingers threw marquee lights around her name.

"You're a singer?"

"No, not really . . ." She grinned at him. "You'll fall for anything, Jake. But what's your last name? I guess it ain't McGee."

"No. My name's just Jake. Jake Wrong." He kept his face casual as he pulled out an old grade school joke he used to play on the unsuspecting.

She dropped her head, her mouth gaping in surprise. "Jake Wrong? With a *W*?"

"No." He grinned in spite of himself. "It's Jake Wright with a *W*—you just heard wrong!"

"OH NO. No! Not funny! Gag!" She stood up and dragged her puffy coat from the back of her chair. "I'm leaving. You can absolutely not be my friend, making dumb jokes like that." Her eyes danced but she kept a straight face.

Jake stood and slid into his jacket. "Well, thanks anyway, Milli, for finding the bike for me."

"No big deal. Just don't fall over and do more damage to your face."

Jake smirked as he covered his wounds with his shades.

As they left the restaurant, a fleeting and unfamiliar gratitude filled him, and he found himself saying, "You want to do this again sometime—if I keep the corny jokes to a minimum?"

She grinned at him, head atilt. "I might."

CHAPTER TEN: SUNDAY MORNING

December brought mostly gray days. The lowered sky seemed to sit on the brown earth as though an aluminum lid had been clapped on the world. The air itself was thick with a fine silver mist—cold, but not enough to snow.

In less than a week after his arrival, Jake had added a paper route to his job at Kroger, after Nell agreed to let him use her car on bad weather days—if he would put gas in the tank. The extra money was nice, but the real benefit was that he was too exhausted for nightmares.

On his first Sunday at the trailer, the paper was extra heavy with Christmas advertising, and when he was finished—at 6:00 a.m.—Jake returned to the trailer and fell, fully dressed, facedown on the lumpy couch. Sleep immediately rolled him into its depths, where he stayed, oblivious to the small stirs, the coughing, the bathroom door clicking shut—all the indications of a waking day.

Later, rising through the fragments and shades of consciousness, Jake became aware of a deep male voice, the lift and fall of talking without reply—a lecture. The lilting sound paired well with his drowsing until he began to notice a smell that was delicious and familiar. *Smells like . . . Ah, roast beef! Mmm.*

He turned his head on his folded arms. Through squinting eyes he saw Uncle Eb in his big chair at the end of the couch, wearing a tie.

A necktie? What the hell?

His eyes focused. Sure enough, atop a faded striped shirt that strained over his belly, Uncle Eb had on a blue tie, which was looped once under his triple chin, the two ends hanging straight and tidy down his front. Jake's eyes moved to find Aunt Nell sitting in the rocker without rocking, her attention caught and held fast by the man on the TV. Then Jake realized the man was preaching and suddenly the words came to him like the thundering voice of God Himself:

"And I will bring the blind by a way that they knew not: I will lead them in paths that they have not known: I will make darkness light before them, and crooked things straight. These things will I do unto them, and not forsake them."

Halfway between sleep and wakefulness, Jake's mind drifted among the words, taking them in, like important cargo to carry with him, and then he slept again.

Later he heard—as if from miles away—another speaker saying, "God forbid that I should sin against the Lord in ceasing to pray for you . . ." And then there was music, the lyrical voice of a soprano who sang without accompaniment.

Jake sat up and rubbed his face. *"I'll be praying for you."*

Nell smiled at him, at his matted hair and puffy eyes. *"Good* morning."

"Yeah. I guess. What smells so good?"

"A nice rump roast. We've got one more service to listen to, and then I'll get dinner on the table."

He rubbed his face and squinted at the television. "Is this a regular Sunday thing?" he asked. But Nell only vaguely nodded and shushed him when a gospel quartet began to sing "Rock of Ages."

Jake got up and went to take a shower.

§

Dinner was as satisfying to Jake's heart as it was to his stomach. Nell had remembered his favorite dishes from when he was a boy. Tonight's was a four-pound roast with mashed potatoes and gravy, creamy corn pudding, flat green beans shining with bacon fat, hot rolls, and a red Jell-O salad with pineapple and pecans in it. Every bite was comfort food, and the atmosphere at the table was almost as good as Jake remembered. But at the end—after ice cream, and after Ebenezer had gone back to his recliner in front of a football game—Nell got quiet and Jake got nervous.

He had managed to work long shifts and sleep too much to allow for a lot of questioning, but he could feel Nell coming now. He realized he should tell her *something*. Obviously, she needed some kind of explanation for her uninvited guest. But he couldn't think of one—a big enough reason for him to be sleeping on her couch—so he got to his feet and cleared the table, hoping for a reprieve. He filled the little sink with hot, soapy water and asked for a dishrag, but sure enough, with the first pause in the clatter, Nell asked, "How'd you get around in Bedford Green?"

Surprised, he looked down, staring at the meringue of bubbles in the water.

"Jake?"

"Yeah, well . . . I had a car. Roger gave it to me." He tried to sound casual as he glanced up through the window above the sink.

"*Roger* gave it to you?"

"Yeah. My father." His mouth twisted slightly on the word.

"*What?* You have to be kidding!" Nell's pale eyes behind her crooked glasses were wide with shock.

"Yeah. Mother called him. I thought he was dead—that's what she always said—but no, she knew where he was all the time, and she somehow made him take me while she went to prison." The information was doled out in a voice as flat and empty of expression as a desert wind.

Nell stared at the back of his head as it bent above the soapy dishes. "*Lord*, help us! I forgot all about him."

Jake shrugged.

"What was it like—living with him, I mean?"

Jake looked out at the gray day, and his hands stopped moving. After a long pause, he said, "I forget," and lifted a small stack of dishes into the water.

A silence descended until Nell's voice came, graveled by years of smoke, but soft with sympathy, "That bad, huh?"

"Well, I guess you could say he mostly resembled that tree stump out there. Never said a word he didn't have to. He treated me okay most of the time, only knocked me around if I got in his way while he was drunk—so I stayed clear of him most nights."

His father's only effort at real speech had come on the first night. After he showed Jake where to throw his backpack and stuff, he led the way back to the kitchen and pointed to a chair at the table. "Sit down, Jake."

A short, brown-skinned Hispanic woman stood beside the stove, where a pot of beans simmered. Jake's mouth watered. Roger tossed a thumb in her direction and said, "This is Teresa. She cooks." She nodded and smiled, sending a shy dimple in Jake's direction. Jake frowned, looking at Roger again. It dawned on him that in his father's brown skin and wiry stature there must be a measure of Mexican blood, and that when he looked at himself in the mirror, he saw more of his father than his mother. There was no trace of the heritage in Roger's speech, but it was noticeable in his face, and Jake felt a part of the puzzle fall into place.

The man had gone to a strip of cup hooks on the wall, chosen a set of keys, and tossed them on the table. He backed up to lean against the cabinets and said, "You got your driver's license, KatieLyn said."

Jake nodded.

"Well, the Civic in the side yard is yours to use. You'll need to get yourself to school and find yourself a job. I'll give you a couple hundred to start off on, and I'll pay your car insurance and food, but from there, your cash is up to you to find. Kroger's is hiring sixteen-year-olds." The man's hard eyes looked at him with a degree of sympathy. "I'd say you've already been taking care of yourself for quite a while."

Jake looked away, nodded once in the direction of the floor.

"Yeah, well, KatieLyn's a piece of work," Roger said, "but you seem okay—a survivor, like me. So. Here's the deal. I really don't like anybody messin' around in my business, just so you know. People come and go out there in the garage and none of it needs your time or attention, you got it? Don't let me catch your ass out there. I can kick it for you pretty damned hard." Jake nodded and Roger poured himself a cup of coffee. He raised the carafe toward Jake, but Jake shook his head.

"You'll see Pepe around. He's Teresa's brother, lives over the garage. He makes deliveries, but now you're here, you'll be taking over that little job, once a month—and again, no questions.

"Vehicles are dropped off, they get fixed, and picked up at all hours. I work mostly at night, so for God's sake, keep it quiet in the morning so I can sleep. Get yourself fed and off to school and Teresa will have food fixed when you get back. Just don't bother me, don't ask questions, and I won't bother you." He paused until Jake looked at him. "How's that sound so far?"

Jake shrugged and made no objection, his eyes on the floor.

"It's too late, and I'm too old to play dad. You wreck the Civic, you pay to fix it same as anybody else. You get in any kind of trouble, and you have to figure it out yourself. So keep your nose clean, and we'll get along fine."

Jake didn't feel like telling all that to Nell. He sure as hell wasn't going to tell her what Teresa had said. He had wandered into the kitchen one night after he heard Roger leave, and found a red-eyed Teresa sitting at the kitchen table with a bottle of tequila, her hand wrapped around the neck.

She looked at him and raised the bottle. "You?"

He considered, and then went for a jelly glass in the cupboard. After she poured an inch or two in the bottom of the glass, she pushed it toward Jake, tossed her head back and took a gulp from the bottle. Jake sniffed at the jelly glass and set himself down at the table. She watched him until he tasted it and when his lip curled in disgust she laughed and nodded in agreement. "Gotta be loco to like this stuff."

They sat listening to the salsa music she had on the radio. Occasionally, Teresa sniffed and rubbed at her eyes and once he caught a tear sliding down her smooth round cheek.

Outside, Jake heard the shrill shriek of a power saw start up, and he looked out the window at the lights in the shop. A welder arced inside, and blue flame lit up the door window.

"What're they doing out there?" Jake asked.

She looked at him and shook her head. "You don' know? I no telling—but it sure as hell ain't legal."

Jake stared at her flushed face. "Is it what I think? They choppin' cars?"

She shrugged, inscrutable. "Maybe so, maybe no, but it ain' legal is what. You stay out." She took another drink, offered him one, then laughed at his full glass. "You de serious boy. Serious shit boy, no? You study a lot de books. I see you sometime."

He smiled with the side of his mouth and shrugged. "Just keepin' my nose clean, Teresa. That's all."

She looked at him and slid a little down in the chair, took another sip. She shook her head lazily. "Pepe ain't legal, Teresa ain't legal, ain't nothin' round here a little bit legal. But you don' know. Okay? You no know dis I tell you."

"Okay, Teresa, I no know it. Thanks for telling me."

He sat and turned the glass between his fingers, shaking his head. "He could get sent to prison, then I'd have a matched set . . . both parents convicted felons. Cool, huh? I'd have street cred then, for damn sure."

"No, no, no. He no go to prison. No worries der. No prison to Roger."

"What do you mean?"

Teresa took the long comb out of her topknot and let her hair fall down her back, shook it vigorously, and then took another swallow. She looked at him from eyes half closed with drink and sadness. "Nada . . ." She twisted her hair back up and pinned it with practiced ease. She laughed lazily and her mouth turned down at the corners as she nodded with certainty. "Ah, shit, he know de man. He know many mans. He no go to jail."

"Oh. Great. Thanks, Teresa."

She frowned at him. "Guarda silencio." She put her finger to her mouth, her eyes suddenly wide and darkening with anxiety. "Silencio, okay?"

He stood and pushed his glass over to her. "Sí, sí, señorita. For sure, I won't say a thing." And he went back to his room.

Jake shook himself from the memory to find he'd finished washing the dishes and started drying when Nell asked, "Does he know where you are now?"

Jake shrugged. "Nah. He won't miss me. He found somebody else to deliver for him soon as I started college."

"Deliver what?"

He exhaled quickly and bit his lip. He turned and saw the concern in her wrinkled face, and his throat swelled with affection.

He swallowed and shook his head. "Oh, just some stuff to a friend of his. I never asked."

"He married?"

"Nah. His Mexican girlfriend cooks for him—and me. She was a good cook."

"Why aren't you calling to tell him where you are?"

Jake turned around, a small pan in his hand. His eyes were on the tea towel as he circled it around and around the inside. "Him and me never got friendly. When I moved my stuff to the dorm at Western, he never said a thing. Just looked me over like I was a zoo animal and walked off. Both of us are better off not knowing each other."

Nell waited. He leaned over to put the pan away. When he stood up, he leaned back against the cabinet and began to fidget with the towel, folding it into smaller and smaller squares, shaking it out, starting over, folding, folding.

He looked at her and she was still waiting, so he said, "He had a garage where he worked at night. Way back off the highway, and he seemed to have lots of business. He didn't want me hanging around there, so I mainly worked and went to school. That was pretty much it, for him and me." He turned away and picked a spatula out of the drainer, began to dry it.

"So you're not running away from him?" Nell said with the breath she

53

had been holding.

"No, no, he was okay. I got no complaints." Jake paused and looked at her. "The day he picked me up at Mom's apartment? We drove the two hours to Bedford Green and never spoke." He shook out the towel, kept drying the utensil, turning it over and over. He shrugged. "I got no complaints about somebody not talking to me."

After a silence, Nell asked, "What happened to the car? Why are you on a bike?"

Jake hesitated a fraction before he answered. "I wrecked it." He rubbed the new knot on the bridge of his nose. "When I broke my nose, remember? Totaled it."

There was a long silence and the sound of halftime from Eb's game filled the trailer. Nell took off her glasses and wiped her face with a napkin, stood up, and took the tea towel away from Jake. "Here," she said. "You're going to rub another damn hole in that spatula."

Jake stepped to the side and leaned his butt against the counter with his arms folded across his chest. He stared at his feet, struggling with the temptation to vomit out the truth to this sympathetic listener, now that he had started. But he couldn't do it to Nell. He shook off the urge.

"I was always afraid of that guy," Nell said, moving around Jake, putting utensils in the drawers. "He had those mean little eyes. What KatieLyn ever saw in Roger was way beyond me."

"Well, I gave up trying to understand my mother a long time ago," Jake said.

"Yeah, me too." Nell reached to put dishes in the cabinet, and Jake saw a tear slide down her cheek.

"Hey, it's okay. You never need to worry about me. I can take care of myself."

"Yeah, but something's wrong, Jake. Something's bothering you, and I hate it that you can't get past . . . whatever it is that's eatin' you."

"Yeah, well, maybe one day." Jake looked out the kitchen window at the heavy, sheet-metal sky, the back of a neighboring sheet-metal mobile home, and the littered yard in between.

After she put the last of the flatware in the drawer and shoved it closed, Nell turned to him with narrowed eyes and a last question. "Does your mother know anything about Roger? Or did she just send you to a perfect stranger?"

"All she thought she knew was that he owned a garage and sent my support money every month." He looked at the living room wall. After a pause he said, "Maybe I'll paint us another mustang while I'm here."

CHAPTER ELEVEN: CHEERIOS

Jake stopped breathing. Standing in the brightly lit grocery aisle, four bright yellow boxes between his hands, he was stunned by the clarity and detail of the memory that had rushed upon him.

In the moment to which he was suddenly transported, he was awake but didn't want to open his eyes until he knew it was safe. He sucked on his curled forefinger and listened. Faint noises came to him from other apartments and from the hallway. Someone was walking around overhead. The sound stopped and he heard an angry word from the ceiling he didn't understand. His eyes slowly blinked open and roamed the empty apartment, but his ears had already told him that he was alone.

He sat up and slid from the edge of the couch to the floor, stood with his back pressed against the nubby sofa and his faded gray blanket pulled tight against him, and looked around. The late-afternoon sun lit the window blind in mustard yellow, and the smell of food cooking drifted in under the crack of the door, beyond the wall, down the hall. The green glass ashtray on the table in front of him was full of cigarette butts and he was glad for the stink of them. It was a familiar smell, not nice like his mother's spaghetti, but familiar. He sniffed and stared at the door, wishing she would come home.

He needed to pee and walked, stiff legged with sleep, to the bathroom. Only partly awake, he raised the seat and pushed his pants down with one hand. Holding his blanket in a wad under one arm, he leaned up to dangle his pee-pee over the side and let go, watched the splashing, dancing stream until it stopped. Pants back in place, the loose corner of the blanket tucked back under his arm, he made his way to the commode handle and flushed. He watched the yellow water swirl round and down, then made his slow way back to the other room.

His eyes found the large photo of himself as a laughing baby lying on a furry rug. It hung crooked on the wall in a big frame. He looked at the picture for a long time.

The smells coming in under the door made him hungry. The hollow feeling in his stomach came and went, but finally the emptiness came to stay, and he walked into the kitchen side of the room, dragging his pale blanket with one hand. He looked at the refrigerator. He knew he couldn't open it. When he had tried, the scary thing inside sucked hard and held the door shut. He pulled his cheeks in between his teeth and gazed at the refrigerator. His mother had told him about the sucking Thing.

He looked at the cupboards over the counter and finally dropped his blanket. Getting behind a metal chair, he pulled it away from the table and pushed it, shrieking, across the floor. It bumped into the cabinet and he climbed onto the seat. Then he pushed his knee up onto the counter and leaned over until he was lying in the middle of some plates and other stuff from last night and the night before. He shoved the greasy skillet over to make room and sat up, then wriggled around to kneel and get his footing on the chipped Formica, holding on to the cupboard door handle.

When he pulled at it, the latch held for a moment and then let go suddenly. The rush of it nearly threw him to the floor, but he caught himself, fingers clamped on the edge of a shelf. He looked up at the yellow box in the top of the cupboard and knew he could reach it, but just barely. He rose on tiptoe and his fingers snatched at the slick cardboard corner, trying again and again. Slowly he was able to shift the tall box slightly outward, outward until it toppled, turning over and over to bounce on the counter, where it burst open, a fountain of o's showering the kitchen floor.

Jake curled his forefinger into his mouth and sucked on his knuckle as he stared at the small mountain of cereal. Then he knelt down carefully, got himself one bare foot at a time onto the chair, and then lowered himself to the floor, where he sat and began to eat.

At first he picked them up one by one between two fingers, but then he grabbed them by handfuls, stuffing them into his mouth until they were gone.

He got to his feet and gathered the faded blanket under one arm again and stood still, fingering the smooth binding between thumb and forefinger, looking out the dark window, until the key turned in the lock.

His heart jumped in his chest with a thump, and his eyes grew very big.

"There you are, my big boy. What are you doing over there in the dark?" Her voice was cheerful. She came into the room and switched on a lamp, kicked off her pointed heels and tossed her purse onto the couch, hurrying. "Now come here, Jakey, you have to be a big boy a little bit longer. Mommy's got company coming."

"Come on, now." She pulled him into the main room and held both of his shoulders, leaning down to stare into his eyes. Hers were lined with black eyeliner, and narrowed by annoyance. "Now, Jakey," she said, giving him a small shake, "be good for Mommy. Don't you cry. It won't take long. Do you want to watch Winnie the Pooh or the Wind-up Mouse?" She drew him by the arm toward the closet.

He stood looking at the familiar setup: the red Spider-Man beanbag chair on the closet floor among the shoes, and the small television set with the VCR almost hidden under the coats. He watched as she hurriedly untangled the power cord, pulled it under the door and stretched it to a wall socket in the living room. The screen lit up and she grabbed a DVD, shoved it in the slot, and adjusted the volume with efficient movements.

"See? Aren't you lucky? Not many little kids have their very own playhouse with a television set. You be a quiet little mouse in there, and when I'm finished, I'll make us some nice spaghetti for dinner, okay? Don't you dare come out now. Don't forget. Have you peed? Okay.

"Here. I'll get you some crackers right now . . . Aw no! Jakey, what in hell is this mess all over the floor?"

The doorbell rang.

"Never mind, never mind . . ." She turned on the tape player with her pounding music and shut the closet door.

Jake turned slightly, shaking off the vision of himself eating cereal off the floor. The bright lights, the tinny Christmas music, the metallic and familiar sounds of the grocery store filtered through the moment, and he went back to work.

A voice came from behind him. "Can you tell me where to find the Cheerios?" the girl asked in an exaggerated drawl, expanding every vowel.

When Jake slowly turned, the wasteland of suffering in his expression was not what Milli expected. She took a step back and her grin faded.

They looked at each other a moment, before he found a break in his thoughts into which he could insert the girl who stood uncertainly looking at him. An embarrassed half smile pushed lines into one cheek and he said, "Hi, Milli. Sorry."

Her eyes were full of the empathy that he found so surprising the first time they met. She spoke tentatively. "I'm sorry . . . Is something wrong?"

"No, no, I just got lost a minute." He reached up, his fingers spread, to put three of the boxes on the shelf before he turned and gave her the last one.

She blushed and gave it back. "I was kidding."

His embarrassment dissipated, sluiced away by her discomfort, and when he spoke, his voice was gentle. "What are you doing here, if you're not in the market for Cheerios?"

"Well, I'm supposed to be picking up milk, but I guess I was really looking for you to see if we are going to . . . maybe . . . get coffee again?"

He gave her a blank look, disarmed by her honest answer. "*Oh*, oh yeah . . . right. I haven't been—I mean—I've been working extra."

"Oh, that's okay." Her eyes were large and lustrous in her pale face. He saw a shade of hurt in them before she backed away a step and started to turn, but he caught her wrist.

"Wait. I get off tonight at ten. Is that too late?"

§

They sat across from each other at a table outside the brightly lit windows of the Starbucks. It was a warm evening for December and perfect for sitting outside.

"Are things going okay for you?" Milli asked him, without preamble, a sincere interest in her soft blue eyes.

He sat hunched and tired, head bent over his coffee. "Yeah. Okay, I guess. Got a second job. Saving money. Existing."

"Wow. Okaaay . . ." She blew on her mocha and waited.

He sat up straighter and took a drink, scalding his tongue. After some noiseless, awkward articulations of his mouth, he asked, "What about you? You haven't left town yet?"

"No!" she snorted. "I spose this life and this place are gonna have to do for right now."

His shoulders slumped. "Yeah. Me too."

Two cars swung into the parking lot and joined the line at the carryout window. Jake's eyes followed them. "Don't they have anything better to do than wait for fifteen minutes in line to get a cup of coffee? Why don't they park and go in?"

She looked over at the cars. "They probably don't have any pants on."

He laughed out loud—a surprised guffaw—while she looked at him with a deadpan expression and the raised brows of pretended innocence.

He sputtered, "What the hell? What gave you that idea?"

"Oh, I was pantless in the pickup line not too long ago." Her eyes were twinkling now.

"What are you saying? How'd you lose your pants?"

"Well, I took my nephew, Tommy, to the creek to throw rocks, and of course Thomas the Terrible would go and slip off a boulder into the water. He was okay, but he was bawling so hard I had to wade in to get him. The car seats were cloth, so we had to shed our wet clothes."

Jake stared at her. "Okay . . . Go on . . ."

She cocked her head as he continued to grin. "Well, I calmed Tommy down by promising him ice cream, so here we were at the Frostee Freeze drive-thru window. Course, I just happened to have an old sweatshirt handy—so what's-his-name at the window didn't know the difference—but still . . ."

He looked over at the line again, shaking his head. "So you're saying that's probably a bunch of thirsty folks in those cars with no pants on?"

"Probably." They laughed together and the night was a more peaceful place.

After a few minutes, though, Milli asked, "What were you thinking about when I interrupted you at the store earlier? You looked so sad."

He looked away, off at the view of the littered parking lot under the cold streetlight, and shook his head. "Oh, nothing." He took another sip of his coffee.

Milli lifted her cup also, but her eyes above the rim were large with questions.

"Yeah, nothing." He straightened and tried to smile. "How about you tell me more about Terrible Tommy? I like your kids' stories."

She tried once more to see into him, but gave it up and said, "Oh, we call him Tommy Toothless now, after he swallowed one . . ."

And the conversation went on from there, mostly one-sided as Milli shared stories of babysitting adventures with her cousins.

"How old are you?" he interrupted, surprising her.

"Uh, I'm twenty. Am I boring you?"

"No, no. I'm just curious." He swallowed the temptation to talk to her about his mother, who must have been about that age when he was four. "Sorry . . . You were saying something about a kid named Colby?"

She looked at him, still frowning with confusion, still sure she had been stupid and uninteresting.

But Jake looked at her directly as he explained, "I'm sorry, Milli, I got a shitload of things on my mind right now." He turned the corner of his mouth into a smile and shook his head. "But I really like to hear you talk about your family. It's different . . . I mean, it's good."

She smiled and shrugged diffidently. "I'd really rather hear about you. What was your family like?"

Jake pulled back slightly. "Nah, nah. Not tonight. Maybe some time, but for now . . . You want a refill?"

"No thanks, I should head back to Gert's. I have a sitting job early."

"Gert's?" He asked.

"Yeah, she's my dad's sister and the one I seem to roost with the most. I've lived around with all of them, but Gert and I get along the best. She's crazy, but it's okay there. She pretty much leaves me alone." Milli paused. "I do the laundry." She gave her empty cup a shake. "She cooks some . . ." Her voice waned.

Jake's cup was empty too, and they sat for a few minutes longer. Jake sensed the unspoken realities that lay beneath Milli's bright, reflective surface, happy to sit in silence with the questions unasked.

She was maybe the only person able to pull him through his dark moods into shallower, happier water—for a little while—and he smiled slowly as he watched her face. She smiled back and they stood up together.

Jake started to move toward the trash container, crumpling his cup in his hand, but she stopped him, reaching out, but not touching his arm.

"Listen, Jake." She bit her lip as he turned toward her and waited. "If you ever want a friend to talk to . . . I'm right here. So call me sometime, okay?"

He looked into her eyes for a long moment, searching for guile, for hidden motives, before breaking eye contact. He still hesitated, frowning slightly, and Milli said, "I have my own set of troubles, but when I talk to you, I don't feel by myself so much, and I'd like to be just regular, easy friends. No sex—nothing heavy—just friends over coffee. Would that work for you?"

He looked down at the cup in his hand and suppressed a smile. When he finally looked at her, he said, "I guess it would work for me. I've never known a woman that way. But you make me laugh, so I think I'll try the friendship gig. It's good to have someone to, um . . . sit with. Just don't crowd me, okay?"

"Good enough." She grinned. "No crowding, and we'll just sit together sometimes."

He nodded and raised two fingers in a farewell salute.

CHAPTER TWELVE: CHRISTMAS PAST

Christmas decorations were everywhere at Kroger. He hated Christmas. His mother was arrested on Christmas Eve the year he was seven, so he spent that particular holiday in a foster home, watching piles of presents being passed out to everyone but him. The family tried, but their children were older, and all they could produce for Jake on short notice was three pairs of white socks, a set of plastic racecars, and a candy cane from the drugstore.

It hadn't helped that Jake knew his mother had a gift for him in the closet. It seemed to him that the closet, the apartment, and his mother might be gone. He thought he'd never see them again. He was cold in the warm foster house for three days, shivering by the window. That was perhaps the worst, but no other Christmas was much better.

He remembered the night of the arrest with precise, exhaustive detail. He and his mother had been watching *Rudolph the Red-Nosed Reindeer* on her little seventeen-inch television, and he was squinting at the jolly Santa through a haze of blue cigarette smoke when a loud knock on the door startled them both. Jake's eyes flew to his mother and she looked back at him. When he saw her suck in her lip and tears fill her eyes, his heart began to race. She stubbed out the brown cigarette and fanned the air furiously while she shoved the ashtray under the ragged couch.

The door bounced against its frame with the pounding, and an impatient man's voice called her name. She finally got up and went to the door.

When she took the chain down and opened it, he saw two hulking policemen in the hall, and he sat very still.

She argued with them, but they showed her a paper and she seemed to shrink up and get quiet. She came and sat beside him, but the frightened look on her face made him whimper, and he knew the worst fear of his life. He slid down to the floor, with his hands closed tight over his ears, but his eyes followed the policemen.

The big men were banging around in the kitchen and the bathroom, and when one of them opened a drawer, it crashed onto the floor with all her forks clattering everywhere.

He sat very still, staring out from behind his knees. "Why are they mad, Mama?"

"Shut up, Jakey."

He started to cry, and she came down to the floor beside him, gathering him into her lap, but he could feel her shaking.

The policeman with red hair said, "What's this?" and the other one came to watch as he pulled a paper bag out of the freezer. They opened it up and poured something out on the counter. His mother said, from the floor, "That's not mine. I never saw that stuff before." But her voice was strange and Jake could see they didn't believe her. He turned his face against her shirt and squeezed his eyes shut.

"Come on, ma'am, we're going downtown. You got family he can stay with?"

"No, no, no. I'm not going anywhere! For God's sake—it's Christmas! What's the matter with you people? Leave us alone. I didn't do anything!" His mama's voice rose to a scream, while Jake looked up at the men, trying his best to make them to go away, his begging eyes full of tears.

One of the men spoke into the radio on his shoulder, while the other squatted down beside them and talked to Jake in a low, calm voice. Jake heard "foster family," and then he began to fight back with all the strength of a hysterical seven-year-old. He remembered the firm grip of the policeman holding him in check as he cried out, and the sight of his mother

65

eventually pulling the little yellow suitcase out of the closet and packing it with his clothes.

The appearance of that suitcase in his mind's eye brought with it other vivid memories, and he cringed, drawing his shoulders up as he paused stocking a shelf of canned beans. KatieLyn's boyfriend Jackson was bad—loud and mean—but at least Jake knew who he was. It was much scarier when she brought strange men back to the apartment. He tried resisting once, but she smacked him, and he'd learned the drill: shut up, go into the closet, and turn the volume up so he wouldn't hear anything. He had to sit on a pile of dirty, smelly clothes and lean against a yellow Barbie suitcase. He looked at Barbie and Ken smiling across the front of the tattered luggage and thought about how happy they seemed—happy and rich. It had been his mother's, she told him, when she was a child. It still had a frazzled Barbie in it. She had one sparkly high-heeled shoe on. At first, he had tried to listen to the TV, but soon he taught himself to go straight to sleep. He could make himself go to sleep inside five minutes. It was the best skill he learned in kindergarten. He used it often, even now at twenty-two.

But since the night of November 14, going to sleep hadn't made anything go away. Over a month had passed, and still the nightmares were worse than staying awake.

The Christmas tree lights all over town failed to lift his spirits, and the inflatable Santas in the yards either tilted like drunks or flopped dead on the ground. He couldn't understand the passion for Christmas stuff. The people in Union Gate loved their decorations, and he just felt more and more outside of it all.

Nell had wanted to string lights around the door but he had groaned, and after she looked at his face, she put the box away.

The endless Christmas carols looping over the store's speakers only served to highlight the phoniness of it all. *Who was the little drummer boy?* he thought. *What the hell was THAT about?* The bored bell ringers outside the sliding doors kept that jangle going until Jake thought his headache would split his forehead open. The closer it got to December 25, the harder it was to find a smile around the store. Kids fussed and whined and mothers seemed to shop with their teeth gritted.

A few mothers did bring their love into the store with them. They patted their children and spoke kindly while they pointed out the sleighs hung over the frozen meat counters. But they made him feel even worse, almost numb in his isolation.

Jake thought he couldn't get much lower than he was the day after November 14, but his life seemed to be caught in a death spiral, and he had no hope that anything would ever change. That night in November he had done unimaginable damage to himself and unknown others. His hope of a good life was as vaporous as if it had never existed. He couldn't find the energy to call Milli, and as he pictured her busy with her family at this time of year, he felt like he was heading deeper and deeper into darkness with no brakes for the ride he was on.

But the afternoon of the nineteenth, Milli called him, and he answered.

§

When he got to the McDonald's, Milli was already waiting for him at a corner table. With a grin, she hopped up to join him in line at the counter.

"Hey!" he greeted her with one eyebrow raised over his crooked smile. He was amused again by her outfit. This time she wore black tights and combat boots under a short ivory dress that looked like a child's lacy Easter outfit, with a blue satin ribbon tied over her almost-flat chest. The black tattoo that encircled her throat was visible above a silvery metal chain that draped her prominent collarbones. Her hair was shaggy all over, like she had styled it with a hand mixer, and dyed bright UK blue.

"What, does Kentucky have a game tonight?" Jake asked.

She flinched. "No. I *like* this color!" She looked away, her hand going to her hair, smoothing it a little, her face going pink. Then she turned toward him and said, "You're so dang serious all the time. Can't you lighten up a little?"

He frowned slightly. "Sorry, Milli. You look great."

While they stood in line, she looked at him sideways. "You look a little ragged around the edges."

"Well, I've been up since two thirty and going hard all day. I reckon I got a right to look ragged."

Milli looked nonplussed. "Why on earth?"

"Ah—the paper route. I pick up the papers at three a.m."

"Whoa." Milli's eyes ballooned. "Why work so hard? You make welfare checks look pretty decent." She was watching him as they moved up to the counter.

"Well . . ." He shrugged. "I can't discuss that question on an empty stomach. You know what you want?"

§

Between bites of his hamburger, Jake asked about her tattoo.

"Celtic knots," she said. "I just liked the design. No special meaning."

"Cool." Jake was suddenly self-conscious and tugged at his shirt sleeve.

Milli caught the movement. "Oh, come on, let me see it."

"Nah," Jake said. "I had it done in a former lifetime, but I don't like it now."

"Are you serious? What is it?" she asked, interested. "A girl's name? No. I bet it says *MOM*!"

Jake threw his head up with a bitter laugh. "No! Never!"

Milli eyed him. She dipped a cluster of fries into her ketchup and put them in her mouth.

Jake shifted against their jackets piled on the seat beside him.

Her patience broke. "Well? You've got me really curious."

He shrugged and pulled up his sleeve to show her his rattlesnake. It seemed alive as it twined its diamondback shape down his forearm to his wrist, where the wicked head was raised in the act of striking, fangs bared and dripping.

The thing was a relic of the early days of working for his father. He was making the first money of his life, and at the same time acutely aware of his status as a skinny nobody in a new school. At the time, the vicious snake said "Don't mess with me." Or he hoped it did. It was around that time also that he had perfected the stance that had completely succeeded in keeping others off balance and respectful: head held back, half smile, narrowed eyes.

Milli was still staring. "Wow. That's a real piece of art, I guess. It's amazing! Every scale is perfect."

He shook his sleeve back in place. "Thanks."

Jake stared at his hands as they rested on the edge of the table and turned his cup around and around. He couldn't think of anything to say. He hadn't had enough sleep for days, and his eyes were bleary with exhaustion. The pause grew awkward before Milli asked, "Where are you living? Did you find an apartment?"

He looked up into eyes that were kind and genuinely interested. He said, "Nah. No deposit money." One side of his mouth smiled a little. "Right now, I'm staying with my aunt Nell and Uncle Ebenezer in a trailer."

"Oh. One of those double-wides?"

"Nope, just a single—two bedrooms. Nell found me a bed at the Goodwill that makes a kind of couch in the daytime, so I sleep in the front room. Her old couch was ready for the curb anyway."

"Sounds like tight quarters."

"Yeah, it is a little, but I don't plan to stay there long. It's just a place to crash for a while."

"While you get your feet under you," she said.

"Yeah." Jake let the answer float to the table while they finished up their meal. He asked if she wanted a refill, but she said no and shook some ice into her mouth to crunch on.

After a few moments, Milli asked another question. "Where do your mom and dad live?"

"My mom lives in Louisville." After a hesitation, Jake added, "She has a new baby."

"Oh, good." Milli smiled. "A new little person!"

Jake raised his eyes. "Maybe good . . . maybe not."

Milli returned his level gaze with raised eyebrows, inviting, but not insisting on further explanation. She sucked on the ice and Jake finally dropped hard words into the empty moment. "My mom's a piece of work."

"Oh."

"Yeah." Jake glanced up at her but quickly hooded his eyes again. "Ah, I guess I don't know her really." Jake looked away and wondered how much to say. Finally he opened it up. "Lots of drugs, lots of men, lots of booze. Like I say, I can't figure out why she's like she is."

"Oh. Wow." Milli's voice faltered, and she waited. Jake didn't volunteer any more, so she asked, "What about your dad?"

"He's the one lives down near Bedford Green. That's who I lived with while I went to high school. While she was in prison." He kept his eyes on the crumpled hamburger foil on his tray, waiting for a horrified gasp, or some other sign of disgust.

When he finally looked up at her, he was surprised by the sadness in her eyes, and a lump came into his throat.

"Ohhh," was all she said, the word skittering across the table, gentle and cold like snow falling.

There was a long pause and Jake watched a group of basketball players come in with their jackets and their confident swaggers.

Milli glanced at them and saw a way to change the subject. "Did you play sports?"

"Nah. I slept a lot. Worked. Went to school. Ran errands for Roger—my dad. I was a real standout in high school." He grinned his one-sided smile, but no light reached his narrowed eyes.

"Sounds like it was, uh . . . relaxing?"

Jake shrugged. "Well, not really."

"Did you like living with your dad?"

This time Jake's smile was wider. "Well, the food was great. His live-in girlfriend was a super Tex-Mex cook. You like Mexican food?"

She chuckled, "Sure, I love tacos! I'll make some for you sometime. They come in a nice blue box from Kroger's. All you need is ground beef and shredded cheese."

His eyes crinkled as he shook his head. "Nah, not that stuff. Teresa made hot fajitas and I'd give a hundred bucks to have some right now . . ." He grimaced, catching himself. "*If* I had a hundred bucks to spare."

He turned his eyes up to hers. "What about you? Did you grow up around here?"

"Yeah, right here. My dad's address is on my driver's license, but . . . It's not like I have a nice little house where I've always lived, where I can say, 'That's my house.' I get shuffled around between the aunts—Dad's three sisters. Most of the family lives within several blocks of each other on the south side of town." She looked down and paused before adding, "My mom died of cancer when I was three, and Dad is gone a lot. He works all the time, so my aunts took me over and just kind of handed me around for a while . . ." Her voice tapered off. "I think he paid them something to feed me . . ."

"I thought you said before that your family was all on welfare."

She looked at him with surprise. "Oops, I did say that. Well, I exaggerated. Most of them work at something, they just don't make much money. Dad does okay—he's a cop. He says the county's understaffed, so he works long hours. The rest of the time he stays with Rita."

"Rita?" Jake fidgeted in his seat at the word *cop*.

"His girlfriend."

"I guess he doesn't know what to do with a daughter."

"Never did." She shrugged. "It was weird when I was little. I stayed with Gran while my mother was sick, and then after she died, I *wanted* to stay there. I remember that part." She looked up at him. "And she really wanted to keep me with her and Gramps, but Dad blew up, yelled at her and made her

71

cry, stomped out of the house and hauled me off back here. I cried the whole way. I was only three, almost four, but I remember it plain."

She looked away out the window. "He says Gran never thought he was good enough for Momma. Too 'low class,' but who knows, I never heard her say anything like that. It was a bad time for everybody. Dad's pride would never admit it, but bringing me here never really worked out too good. His sisters had their own families and didn't need an extra kid to raise." Milli watched her fingers fold her straw up into a small accordion, which popped open when she let go of it. "So they just took turns passing me around like a package—a few weeks here, a month there. Pack up and move on. I got real . . ." She hesitated. "Sad, I guess you'd say, and the school people stepped into the situation. So then the family had me stay a year at each house. After several years, I finally came to roost mainly at Gert's. She's the oldest and didn't have any kids. I only see my dad at family parties."

She paused, then brightened slightly as she said, "I sure look forward to my summer months with Gran. I get a lot of lovin' over there and try to haul it back with me . . ."

Jake was watching the light come and go from her face while she talked, and didn't know how to respond, so he sat without speaking for a few minutes before she added, "They left me at the fair when I was eight." She gave a short laugh that wasn't a laugh, trying to negate the pain.

"You're kidding!" Jake watched as she slipped down further in the seat, her arms outstretched on the table, her eyes lowered to watch her hands ceaselessly twisting her straw.

"Yeah. Nothing happened, really. Nothing bad, I mean. It just scared me." She worked the straw some more. "Made me mad. I think about it sometimes."

"What happened?"

"Well, all of the family but Dad went over to the Bluegrass Fair at Lexington. About dark, I started watching some people trying to hit a target so this big guy would fall in a tank of ice water."

Milli checked his face with raised eyebrows and Jake nodded.

"Well," she said, frowning, "I thought Sue Ann was right behind me, but she was gone and I couldn't see nobody. I got scared and went to look for the cars and the parking places were empty. It was a big lot, but I knew for sure we left both of the cars under the big *D*, and they weren't there."

"God, Milli, what'd you do?"

"Well, by now, it was really dark, and I didn't know what to do, so I just stood there by this lighted-up sign trying not to cry, and finally this nice man in one of those Lions Club vests came over on a golf cart. He took me to the office and they called my dad." She paused, remembering. "He came for me in the police cruiser. He was really mad at Gert and them. But everybody thought I was in somebody else's car, and little Jenny had fallen and skinned herself up, so the aunts were all worried about her. It wasn't really anybody's fault."

Jake watched her face, her long eyelashes blinking back tears, listening to the loneliness beneath her words.

"But it felt like they didn't care. Always has felt that way."

After a breath, Jake said, "You seem to have survived pretty well."

She smiled at the table and shrugged. "You think?"

"Well, you sure are different from most girls I've met, and it's not just the way you dress and dye your hair."

"Okay, explain. What's so different?"

He studied her, eyes narrowed and head cocked to the side. "I don't know. I'm still trying to figure it out." She waited while he tried to find the word. "You seem . . . peaceful, most of the time."

She laughed. "Oh yeah! What you mean is 'really boring.'"

"No. You don't get it." He was earnest. "I'd give anything for one easy-feeling, peaceful day."

Milli appraised him, nodding slowly. "You know, I saw that, the day you came into the Goodwill." She paused and then went on. "And more than most people, you keep your thoughts hidden way down."

"Yeah, well, you don't want to know my story, Milli Farley."

"So all this hard-working, nice-guy stuff is just an act you're putting on?"

"That stuff doesn't change anything." Jake looked at her for a long moment. "Truth is, I've done some things I wish I could undo."

She held his gaze until he lowered his eyes to his hands.

After a long pause, she said, "Maybe we all have."

He shrugged, his face a mask. "I doubt it. Not like me."

"Maybe you could pray about it," Milli ventured cautiously.

He looked up at her in surprise. "*Pray* about it?"

"*I'll be praying for you.*" The trucker's voice sounded in his ears again.

"I try to pray, and sometimes it helps." She shuttered her eyes.

There was a long silence. "What do you say when you pray?" Jake asked.

She shrugged, not looking at him.

"I mean—I really don't know anything about prayer," Jake said. "There was a guy said he would pray for me once. I've wondered ever since, what exactly a person means by that." He shivered involuntarily.

Milli looked at him with a quizzical expression. "I sort of thought everybody talks to God when they feel bad."

"To God? Well, no." He laughed then stared at her. "What do you say to God?"

She smiled a little at herself and rolled her eyes as she said, "Oh, mostly I say, 'HELP!'"

A guy in a McDonald's shirt was wiping down the table next to them, and Jake watched until he had moved off. Somehow he didn't want to be having this discussion in front of anyone. He felt naked, talking about God, but something in him didn't want to stop either.

"You don't believe in God?" she asked.

Jake sighed and leaned forward with one hand rubbing his forehead. "I don't know, Milli. I don't know much of anything, and I guess—probably the truth is—I really wish there was a great force in the universe that I could go to, like asking the genie to change things."

"How do you know there's *not* such a . . . being?"

He looked at her and suddenly his eyes were soft and amused. "Listen to this, this is weird: the last semester of Astronomy we learned about dark energy, a puzzle that's tripping up minds way bigger than mine. It turns out that everything ever observed with all of our instruments, all measurable matter, adds up to less than five percent of the mass-energy of the universe."

Jake paused and looked at her. He hadn't lost her. She was still with him, her chin propped on her fist, looking at him with interest.

"That means that more than ninety-five percent of the mass and energy in the universe is made of things scientists can't yet define. It holds the universe together, kind of, but we don't know what it is. Maybe that's God. I don't know. I wonder about it."

"Wow. That's *amazing*."

Jake tapped his cup. "The trouble is I just have a hard time imagining a God I can talk to, I guess."

"Yeah, I know prayer comes more natural to some than others."

"Are you a Christian?"

"Well . . . I don't know what you'd call me. When I'm with my Gran, I'm one person—and I honestly believe in the God of the Bible, Jesus, and all of it. I pray and everything . . . and sometimes . . ." She looked at him, wondering how he might react. "Sometimes when I pray there . . . I swear I know He's there, listening. But when I come back here . . ." She frowned, looking out the window. "After a while, it seems like I drift away. No one in the family believes anything or goes to church anyway, and pretty soon I'm just thinking and talking like everybody else." She looked at him with pain in her eyes. "I'm not baptized or anything, so no, I guess I'm not officially a Christian, but I go when I'm at Gran's house."

"Go?"

"Oh, I mean go to church with her when I'm in Bedford Green."

"Oh." Jake nodded.

"I think you'd like my Granny." Milli cocked her head and smiled out the window. "She's amazing. She's a piano teacher, and her students love her.

She's the one that believes in God, and she is absolutely certain He hears prayer—and answers. I've learned a lot from her. She makes me think about . . . things."

Jake nodded, still in neutral, listening.

Milli leaned forward on her elbows and sighed. "Maybe I just wish for the Bible to be true."

Jake leaned back in his chair and sat looking at the space between them.

Milli dropped her head. After a breath caught and held, she said, "Well, I sure know I need for there to be something bigger than myself, or my dad, or my Gran. I need *big* help, and I need it pretty damn soon."

Jake stared at her, and a comfortable silence stretched between them. "You want to talk about it?" he asked.

Milli gave him a long, frowning look, before lowering her eyes and shaking her head. "No, not right now."

He slowly shook his head. "I cannot believe I'm sitting here talking to a girl about God. This is way the hell away from my former life."

"Sorry, Jake. I like to make you laugh—I like to hear it—but I haven't done a good job this time."

"Hey, wait! It's not your job to make me laugh, Milli. Truth is, I don't even feel like laughing most of the time." He paused and looked at her. "But real talk is harder to come by than joking." His narrow hand spread long fingers and rubbed at his forehead again, then pushed through the thick dark hair, shoving it back from his face. He raised a thoughtful gaze to her and said, "I think a lot about . . . stuff, and it seems to me like there has to be some meaning somewhere that makes life worth living—some kind of cosmic justice that can take care of 'adults' that hurt kids, for instance . . ." The way he sneered the word *adults* made Milli look up at him, frowning, but he quickly added, "You know, like those dictators in Africa, or child abusers." A deep flush had spread over his face and he shut his mouth. "How's a god just going to let that happen?"

Milli looked at him with thoughtful concern.

"Sorry. Sorry to go all heavy on you, and hell, if I'm asking for a cosmic judge, He'd probably come for me first with His bolt of lightning, so I'll shut up." He forced a grin.

She smiled at him, and the color in her cheeks deepened, her pale blue eyes embracing him. "Thanks, Jake, for talking like this. Gran is the only who will talk to me, and she lives on the other side of the world it seems like."

They stood and he handed her jacket to her before sliding into his own.

"I hate to end this," she said.

"Can we do it again sometime?"

"Absolutely." Milli's eyes lit up as she nodded.

They walked outside, and as they separated, Milli stopped and turned back. "Hey, Jake. Have a good Christmas!"

"Yeah. You too, Milli." He watched her walk away before he went to unlock his bike. A fragmented Christmas carol drifted out the restaurant door, and as he pulled gloves out of his pocket and slowly drew them over his cold hands, he looked again in her direction.

CHAPTER THIRTEEN: NIGHTMARE

He was in a dark tunnel with fragments of light flying past. Uncontrolled speed, nausea, a bone-white object flying at his face, a pair of staring eyes . . . then a shoe. Jake became a writhing, groaning, thrashing thing that woke with a strangled cry.

It was the night after Christmas. He had been sleeping better on the real mattress of the daybed, even if it had a slight smell of age and use. But he had found little relief from his haunting conscience.

When he awakened, he was standing shivering and sweating with the blanket gripped in his fists. Nell had arrived beside him, her face pale with alarm and still puffy with sleep. "JAKE! Jake, what on earth?"

Ebenezer stumbled into the front room, drunk with the sudden interruption of a deep sleep.

They stood there, a small triangle of pain and baffled sympathy in the dark.

Eb began to moan and Nell led him back to his room, murmuring nonsense to comfort him, while Jake folded his shivering body into a clutch of half-awake dread on the edge of his bed.

Before long, Nell came back into the room, filled the teapot at the sink, and turned the flame on under it before she came to sit in her rocking chair.

Jake sat, hunkered over, a cold stone sucking the warmth out of the room. The space between them was crowded with hard words to speak, and Nell sat, arms wrapped around herself, waiting as the silent minutes ticked by.

The teakettle muttered, but before it could shriek, Nell pushed herself up and went about the business of making two mugs of instant hot chocolate. When she brought one to Jake, his outstretched hand was trembling too much to accept it, and she set it down on the coffee table in front of him.

"What in holy hell is it, Jake?" Nell's question hung in the shadowy room, spreading out until it occupied all the corners. When he shook his head, she suddenly came at him with razors in her voice. "Okay, I am fed up with all this mystery! You act like you're running from the cops—that's all I can figure out—and if you're about to make us accessories to a crime we don't even know about—by damn, Jake, you owe it to me and to poor old Eb to spit it out. Your mother brought me awful close to jail before, and I ain't going to no prison for you."

Jake was startled by the outburst and turned to look at her with a frown. "No. No, Aunt Nell, it's not like that." He leaned over with his elbows on his knees, his hands gripped tight together, and said quietly, "I promise you I've been clean for a long time, over two years now. Drugs are not the issue here. But, but, you don't deserve . . . I just can't load this on you. It's my problem, and I'll either get over it or solve it on my own."

After a moment he offered, "I could move to the Salvation Army, though, if you want."

Nell melted, softened by the sight of the dark head drooping from the rack of bony shoulders, his raggedy hair in need of a cut. She said, "No. No, forget it, Jacob." She sagged back in her chair and rocked a slow creak. "I just worry about you a lot. I think whatever you're holding on to so tight is wearing you out." She studied him over the rim of her cup and shook her head. "You look just terrible, so much older than you are!" She reached out and touched him gently on the arm. "You were my little boy for a while, and I felt like you were an amazing gift from God sent to a woman who wasn't ever gonna make a baby of her own." Tears welled in Nell's eyes, and she hushed up. Then she added, "I just can't help worrying about you, that's all."

He gently patted her hand on his arm, releasing her to shed his tears for him.

CHAPTER FOURTEEN: THE FARLEY PARTY

"McGee, can I ask a favor?" Milli's voice was uncharacteristically serious.

"Uh, I guess it depends." They were sitting in the yogurt shop next to Kroger, and outside the day was cold and dismal. The Christmas snow had melted into dirty puddles on the parking lot, and now the clouds seemed to be holding their heavy burden close to the treetops, leaving the ground damp, expectant.

"Do you think you could come with me to a family party on New Year's Day?" Milli seemed nervous and there was a note of pleading in her voice.

Jake frowned and slowly shook his head. "Sorry, Milli. No parties right now. Don't feel like being in a bunch of strangers. Or drinking." She looked so disappointed that he added, "But I'm off at four that day. Let's just go to a movie or something."

"I wish I could, but I have to go to Margaret's. I can't go to a movie."

"What's up?" he asked. "I thought you liked hanging with your family."

She just stared down at the yogurt, stirring the pattern of cookie crumbles around, but Jake continued to probe. "Really. What's changed?"

Milli put down the clear plastic cup and began to fiddle with her yellow-green Pop-it bead necklace, snapping it open and back together until he reached out and slipped it from between her fingers. She grimaced. "Sorry."

"Billy Mac came home on leave," she finally said.

"So?"

"Yeah, well, I'd just feel better if you were there. We could shoot pool. Margaret has a good, big table in the basement."

Jake stared at her. "What's your problem with Billy Mac?"

"Umm, I guess we sort of have a . . . history." She picked up her cup again and scooped out a cold mouthful, her eyes on the treat in her hand, but she returned the spoonful to her cup without tasting it.

"Oh." Jake stared at her, trying to understand the thing not said. "You and your cousin. Have a history?"

She raised her eyes to his. "Can we maybe drop it? I'd just like you to come to a party with me."

Jake thought about it and persisted, "Why, exactly?"

Again her small face dipped downward and she didn't look at him. "I just need you to come. Please?"

He looked at the black hair hiding her eyes, and at how small she looked in the booth. His shoulders sagged but his mouth turned to a half-hearted smile.

"Okay, okay."

She looked up and her eyes shone with such gratitude that he caught his breath. She grabbed his arm, "Thanks so much, Jake! Four o'clock Saturday, Aunt Margaret's."

§

Jake rode his bike up the car-lined street and into the yard. A lot of students at Western rode bikes—considered cool, green transportation—but at times like this, he felt self-conscious and embarrassed not to be driving a car. Did people think he was too young to drive, or too poor?

Noise and laughter and a stir of people going through the door announced clearly where the party was. He parked the bike at the end of the porch and attached the heavy chain lock to the rail, and when he turned and started to go in, he saw it. He stopped and stood still in the chilly gray afternoon, not thinking to slip his hands in the warm pockets of his canvas jacket. In the driveway, one of the cars was a black Honda Civic. The sight of it hit him like a fist in his belly.

Oh my God! I can't believe it!

The sounds of life going on around him—the party music, the laughter, the bushes rustling in the winter wind—disappeared in sudden blindness and deafness, as memory cracked Jake open. It was the same make and model that Roger had given him, the same as the car that rested in the mud, eighty feet under the black water of the rock quarry where he had pushed it.

He stood, head down, and finally turned back to the bike.

Milli came out onto the porch, sporting a strapless red satin prom dress, an angora bolero jacket, and high-top basketball shoes, her pixie haircut bleached white blond.

He took off his sunglasses and looked up at her. "Sorry, Milli." He shook his head. "Not feeling good."

She came down the steps and peered into his face. "Whoa, you don't look too good—and I don't feel so hot myself." She took his arm and pulled him toward the porch. "Come on. I'll find us a quiet corner and some Pepto-Bismol, okay?"

When he looked into her eyes, he could see the urgent "Please?" bottled up behind them. He released his grip on the bike and walked with her.

Inside, people were shouting to hear each other. The country and western station had been cranked high, and in the living room several women were line dancing, cheered on by relatives. Groups of people parted to admit Jake and Milli, and the necessary introductions were brief, before the pair passed on to the edge of the room.

Jake assured Milli that Pepto-Bismol would make him sicker, so they grabbed Coke cans from a tub of ice and found a place to perch on the ledge along the basement stairs, from which vantage point they could watch both the pool game in progress below them and the constant stream of people to and from the bar in the kitchen above. Someone on the way to the basement handed a baby to Milli and she took him with a smile. The boy reached for her and giggled as she brought him close and bumped his nose with hers.

Jake was glad he had stayed. It was better than going back to the trailer and facing himself.

Milli was a gracious hostess who introduced the passersby to Jake and then entertained him with good-natured tales of each relative's foibles and exploits.

Suddenly, however, he felt her stiffen. Following her eyes, he saw a blond guy with a crew cut and broad shoulders come carrying two twelve-packs through the kitchen door with a swagger that proclaimed him the walking definition of *cool*. His bloodshot eyes also revealed an early start on the liquor cabinet—or a late New Year's Eve. Milli glanced at Jake, and he didn't need a nametag to know it was Billy Mac.

She buried her face in the baby's hair, murmuring nursery rhymes and tickling him, but Billy Mac saw her. Jake watched a ring of admiring men coalesce around the guy. He chatted casually, all-American handsome and a smooth operator as he left the circle to get a beer from the ice chest and return in their direction.

Jake leaned toward her and said softly, "Here comes the conquering hero."

Milli stood abruptly, turned her back to Billy Mac and started down the stairs, saying, "Let's go watch the pool game." Jake stood to follow her, escaping just as one of the men yelled from the kitchen, "Hey, Billy Mac, c'mere! Wanna ask ya somethin'."

The two of them plus baby disappeared into the lower-level recreation room. There, Milli found a free cousin with empty arms and unloaded the little guy. She grabbed Jake's hand and headed toward the door to the backyard.

She paused by a gangly redheaded kid who was sprawled over the edge of the pool table, lining up a shot. "I get the winner," she said.

He glanced up at her and grinned. "You got it, Milli. That'll be me."

"Cool." With one eyebrow lifted, she said, "I can beat you with just one hand."

The boys around the table hooted and she pranced a little as she led Jake toward the door. "Let's get out of here for a minute," she said, and Jake was glad to follow her out into the quiet cold of the darkening afternoon.

"Milli, you're not going to be able to avoid him all night."

"I know, but I need to calm down."

Jake could see she was trembling, and he shed his jacket, wrapping it around her shoulders. She led him to the gazebo in the back of the yard where they were sheltered from the north wind. They sat down in a corner and Jake waited for her to say something.

After chewing on her lower lip a while, she said, "This is the first time I've seen him in two years." She hesitated. "I thought I'd gotten past it . . ." She put her thumbnail to her mouth, biting at the quick.

Jake watched her.

Finally Milli stood and began to pace. "The truth is, I had a terrible crush on him. Everybody did." She glanced at Jake. "He was seventeen, the family's golden boy—you know, one of those straight-As, all-state football quarterbacks. I was only fourteen and he was really nice to me." She lowered her head and her voice was almost a whisper. "I was so thrilled when he paid attention to me. I was a nobody—just a scrawny little kid—and he was not only grown up, but a town hero. He used to take Robbie and me fishing."

"Who's Robbie?"

"Billy Mac's little brother. He's the tall, skinny redheaded guy playing pool."

Milli stopped pacing, her arms folded around herself under Jake's jacket. She stared at nothing, and when she began again, the cadence of her speech had slowed. "It was the day after eighth grade let out. He, uh, he came to pick me up to go fishing. Robbie wasn't with him. It was a really hot day." Milli shook her head a little. Parts of this story she couldn't tell. "He said that his brother had a virus and that we'd just go by ourselves." Her face tightened and when she spoke, it sounded like a plea for understanding. "I was . . . honored—kind of . . . flattered—so I said, 'Sure.'"

She walked over to the arched doorway and leaned against the weath-

ered jamb, looked out into the winter-bare yard and watched the trees toss-
ing the last of their leaf burden to the ground. Jake couldn't see her expression from his corner seat as she raised her face to the sky. He leaned forward
with his elbows on his knees and waited.

When she turned toward him, her bitter voice shocked him. "He said he
wanted to play a *game* . . . I was so stupid! I should have known . . ."

She looked past Jake. "He said . . . it was my fault! That I was asking for
it. And that if I told anybody, he'd say I was lying." Her cheeks shone with
tears, but her eyes flashed furiously. "And he didn't have to tell me that. I
knew the family would believe him over me any day. Everybody worshiped
him. Still do. You've seen them."

Her voice was husky with pain; Jake felt sympathy pass through his gut
like a knife.

"I thought he was so nice." She sagged onto the bench.

Jake's voice was hard when he said, "Milli, you were fourteen years old,
for God's sake—and way littler than him. You don't weigh more than a hundred pounds right now. The guy was worse than a bastard to even touch you."

Milli leaned forward and cried into her hands, her shoulders shaking,
and Jake started to put his arm around her, but she flinched away from him
and stood up. Facing away from the house, she began to search the jacket
pockets for a tissue, laughing an apology. She found one and tried to make
herself presentable again.

She took some deep breaths and smiled through a skim of tears at Jake.
He nodded at the improvement and said, "That son of a bitch has just earned
himself a permanent place on my shit list. But it's you who's gonna have to face
him down one day. Might as well be today, while he has to deal with me too."

She looked at him and nodded. He watched as her anger straightened
her back and took over again. When she said, "Come on, Jake. Let's go play
pool!" the grit in her voice made him wonder if he should be sorry for the
marine.

§

They returned to the recreation room, but a new game had begun and they took seats on bar stools against the back wall. When Jake glanced at Milli, he saw that her mouth was still tight with determination.

It wasn't long before she had her opportunity. Billy Mac came down the stairs with the straight back and tucked-in chin of a man who believes he is master of all that he surveys, and as his gaze swept the room with his self-satisfied half smile in place, Jake thought, *I'd like to hurt Mr. Cool—hurt him bad.*

He could feel Milli tense up next to him and he stood up, faced her, and blocked her view. "You're fine," he reminded her under his breath, and she nodded at him, sat up taller.

"You want another Coke?" he asked.

But she shook her head and whispered, "Don't leave!" as the tall marine advanced on them.

"Millipede!" the voice was deep and mocking. "Haven't seen you in a coon's age."

She stayed seated, erect on the stool, and stared at Billy Mac without speaking. Jake turned to face the guy who had at least four inches and maybe fifty pounds over him, and following Milli's lead, Jake looked at him without expression.

Billy Mac seemed to notice Milli's companion for the first time and grinned slowly. "Hey. You the guy that bought my bike?"

"That's me," Jake said, stone faced, letting a chill frost his voice.

Billy Mac recognized the shift in the terrain, and he was almost visibly thrown. His confusion showed in his eyes and he took a half step back.

The others in the room detected the hostile change in the atmosphere too, and eyes watched furtively from the corners of the pool table. The loud clacking of ball against ball stopped, and the stillness in the room was thick.

Billy Mac's eyes slid to Milli, and he turned slightly away from Jake, grinning again—but the bravado was gone from his jawline. "Cool hairdo," he remarked.

Her smile did not reach her eyes as she said, with a small, sharp edge, "I'm not so impressed by yours, Private."

He stepped back again and pointed to the new bar-and-crossed-arms insignia of a lance corporal on his sleeve. "Hey, hey."

"What do those mean—semi-private?" she asked, enunciating the sarcasm clearly. Somebody at the pool table snickered.

Billy Mac's face flushed. He said, "Well, who stepped in your breakfast, Milli!"

By now the room was holding its collective breath.

But when she spoke, it was low and clear, intended just for him. "You might could say that I just don't have much time for you, Billy Mac. I learned a few years ago that it was best to avoid you, something like, oh, the plague."

His eyes narrowed and he stepped back from her, lifting his shoulders in a shrug for the benefit of their audience. "You crazy, girl? We used to have a lot of fun!"

She stared up at him, her eyes hard, and cocked her head. She kept her voice low as she said, "You might have had fun, but that's not what I called it."

He glanced at Jake and back to Milli, his eyes sparking with anger. "You've lost your mind, sure enough! I guess I'll just see you later—when you're not showing off for your friend here."

As he turned and took the steps three at a time, Jake watched him go, puzzled by something unsaid. He had seen the shock in Billy Mac's face, and true bafflement as he had glared at Milli. Jake turned to look at the mysterious girl beside him, but Milli's head was down and he caught the glint of a tear caught in her lashes. *What the hell is going on here?* Jake mused. *That guy was either a great actor or he actually had no clue why Milli was mad at him.*

The sounds of the room returned to normal with the clack of the balls on the pool table and shouts of laughter or dismay echoing around them. Jake watched her and waited. In spite of his questions, he found he wanted to put his arm around her. All he knew for sure was that she was hurting, and it occurred to him that he had been feeling sorry for himself for way too long. It was a relief to lose himself in someone else's trouble, to want to comfort someone.

But he resisted the thought and folded his arms.

After a quiet few minutes of watching the pool game, she sighed deeply and puffed out her cheeks. "Thank you, Jake. It helped a lot for you to be here."

"You want something to drink?" he asked.

When she looked at him then, her eyes were dry and she had recovered herself enough to grin at him. "Yeah. Bourbon and water. How about you?"

But while they waited at the bar along the back wall for their turn at the table, her eyes were restless as she watched the stairs.

CHAPTER FIFTEEN: JANUARY JOY

Milli was still staring at the first page when she sensed he was there and looked up. Jake had walked through the glass doors of the library's café and as he stood there looking around for her, Milli realized the gladness springing up in her was new, and deeper than before. His serious listening, his unhesitating belief in her, and his staunch support had flipped a switch in Milli, and she regarded him with fresh eyes.

That honeyed, dark skin, those high cheekbones that stretched the planes of his face down to an angular jaw, the oddly crooked structure of his face—*Broken nose, maybe?*—yet somehow it was all handsome. He was built as lean as a distance runner, with narrow hips, and his dark hair was pulled back from his face in a ponytail. He pulled off the black knit cap he wore on these cold winter days. Milli noticed the lack of sunglasses.

The sardonic half smile that habitually pulled at his mouth softened into a real smile as he finally spotted her. As he walked toward her, lightly, hips swiveling among the tables, the grin widened further.

Milli returned his smile. "Thanks for coming, Jake. You are my new hero after last night."

"What, just because I could beat you at pool?"

"NO!" she laughed. "But I would have appreciated a heads-up that you were a pro with a cue stick! Where the heck did that come from? The whole family's talking about you this morning!"

"Well, you're not so bad yourself, you know. You left me a few shots I had to think about . . ."

They laughed.

"Want a cup of something?" he asked, gesturing at the coffee shop counter across the lobby.

She asked for chai and then watched him thoughtfully as he headed for the counter.

When he returned with the hot drinks in cardboard collars, he sat looking at her over his steaming cup. "You sure set him down last night, Milli."

Milli just shook her head. "Thanks for believing me, Jake. I can't tell you what it meant to have you on my side."

He shook his head slowly back and forth. "Semi-private! That was amazing."

She smiled at him. "I felt strong for a little bit there, but I didn't sleep much last night." The smile faded quickly as Milli dropped her eyes to her hands where she turned a cheap ring around and around on her finger.

Jake's eyes narrowed beneath his heavy brows. "He hurt you real bad, didn't he?"

"Yeah, real bad."

They sat quietly, avoiding each other's eyes. Milli continued to toy with the ring and sucked in her lower lip, holding it between her teeth.

Finally Jake asked, "When did you say it happened?"

"The first day of summer vacation, after eighth grade. So almost seven years ago."

"What happened afterwards? What did you do?"

She shifted in her chair uneasily. "Well, I couldn't tell anybody. I knew nobody would believe anything bad about Billy Mac, so I just kept to myself—told them I felt sick. I was leaving for Gran's the next day anyway." She sat looking down, turning the ring round and round.

Jake sat still. He knew how it felt to have nobody to tell. It was the way he grew up also, and he shrugged in half-hearted resignation.

Milli slid further down in her chair, her arms folded across her chest. She went on, "Ever since Mother died, I have loved to spend summers with Gran after school let out. But this time she knew something was wrong and kept asking until I told her what happened. She's the only one I've ever told—except for you."

"What did she say?" Jake's gaze flicked to her. "Didn't she want you to go to the police or something?"

"Yes, of course. She wanted me to tell my dad. But I didn't think even Daddy would believe me over Billy Mac. I'm telling you, I'm just half a member of that family. I refused—didn't want to talk about it to anybody, but she really helped me through it anyway. She kept me all summer that year, and she helped me feel better."

"How?"

"Well, she kept telling me over and over that no matter what people do to the outside of you, they can't touch the soul inside—unless you let them." Milli rolled her eyes. "Oh man, I'm saying this all wrong. I can't put it into words like Gran does."

He studied her. "Why don't you go to your Gran's place, now—until he leaves?"

"I've thought about it, but no. Billy Mac will be gone soon, and sooner or later I have to, um, get over it," Milli said, avoiding his eyes.

"Yeah, well, I'll keep my phone on. Call me anytime—day or night."

"Thanks, Jake." She smiled sideways at him. "You're an awful nice guy."

They watched the library patrons coming and going for a few minutes before he said, "This isn't the first time in my life to wish for a gun."

Milli stared at him open mouthed. "What? NO way!" But then she flushed and laughed, meeting his eyes.

CHAPTER SIXTEEN: EBENEZER LISTENS

Jake woke up in the dark, his clothes twisted around him and a fuzzy feel in his mouth. When he stood up, he realized he had fallen asleep in front of *The Little Mermaid* and had failed to wake up when Nell and Ebenezer went to bed.

His watch read 1:54.

He went to the tiny bathroom and scrubbed his teeth, trying to keep quiet, but flushing the commode made a sound like Cumberland Falls. As he headed back to bed, grimacing with fear of waking the others, he pulled off his sweatshirt. As he stepped out of his jeans, Ebenezer appeared in the doorway, a darker shadow in the room lit only by a streetlight outside the little window, his knuckles rubbing the sleep from his eyes.

Jake smiled a welcome and gestured for him to sit down.

Eb lumbered over to his chair, turned and carefully backed up to it, then lowered his bulk onto the plump La-Z-Boy cushions dimpled with the memory of long hours with him.

Jake stacked his pillows against the wrought iron arm of the bed and propped himself up, knowing he wouldn't sleep anymore until time for his paper delivery.

They sat there for a long time without speaking, Jake staring at nothing in the shabby room, just glad for Eb's unflappable company. The old man began his habitual rocking, his body moving slowly in the chair, tongue resting on his lower lip, rubbing the hem of his flannel pajama shirt between his chubby fingers. Jake could barely make out his face in the dark, but Eb always seemed to inhabit such a place of serenity, like a large and friendly Buddha sitting there, waiting for the world to turn another degree on its axis.

"You warm enough?" he asked.

Ebenezer nodded and kept nodding awhile.

Finally, Jake got up and got a pack of Nell's Marlboros out of the kitchen cabinet. He found her Bic and came back to sit in her old rocker. He held up the pack and said softly to Eb, "Remind me to pay her for these, okay?"

Ebenezer said, "Yeah," pronouncing it broadly, always agreeable without needing to understand the question, and they smiled at each other.

Jake shook a cigarette out of the pack and lit it, the saber of blue flame brilliant in the dark room. He took a drag, coughing a little. He pulled his legs up, rested his arms on his knees, and stared in front of him, watching his fingers turn the cigarette over and under, back and forth. He inhaled again, the tobacco crackling, and blew a stream of pale smoke at the ceiling. He rarely smoked—he was one of the few he knew who never became addicted to nicotine—but when he "borrowed" one, he enjoyed fooling with the rituals of smoking more than the smoke itself.

Then he spoke into the dark, "I don't know myself anymore, Uncle Eb." He paused until memories turned into words. "Drugs. I used to experiment with ever damn thing I could get hold of. Started dealing my sophomore year, gracias to Roger Wright—who was also the hero that introduced me to Kentucky bourbon." His eyes lost focus as he thought back.

"Made a whole lot of money for a kid. Nobody at school knew a thing. I was just the kid with the rattlesnake tattoo. Roger didn't want me sellin' to anybody I knew. I suppose people probably suspected something." He took a long drag and stared into the darkness, considered the way the smoke clouded, darkness into darkness. "But then I became the math whiz, and that became who I was in school," he chuckled to himself, to Eb. "Weird life. Daytime math nerd, Roger's delivery boy at night, a semi-criminal if there is such a thing."

94

The dark room and his Uncle Ebenezer encouraged him to remember, and to speak. The gentle giant in the lounger never reacted to words that held no meaning for him. He just listened.

"I tried out for the football team." Jake smiled a big, dumb grin at Eb. "That was a dumbass thing to do! Didn't make it of course. Anyway I started dealing shit and partying hard every weekend. Lots of sex." He paused to allow a few memories to linger. He smiled. "And it was good, if I do say so myself. You can ask any of a hundred girls back there." He looked over at Eb. "I might have exaggerated the number there . . . But still . . ." He frowned. "What's with this righteous case of celibacy I've got going on now?"

He shook his head. "I pretty much quit the drug trade when I won the scholarship to Western. Kept my nose clean. Made Roger mad, but I didn't care. I was gonna *be* somebody, ya know?"

He finished the smoke and stubbed it out in the ashtray stand by the rocker. Leaning back, he locked his hands behind his head and stared up at the ceiling. "I don't know what happened to that person. The old Jake."

He started Nell's chair rocking. *Creak-creak. Creak-creak.* The sound eased him a little.

"Weird. It really screwed with my head, you know?" Jake's voice was so low the words fell to the floor unheard by the big man in the recliner.

The moon came from behind a cloud and threw a shaft of pale light into the room, across the old carpet and up Eb's pant legs, over his belly, and across his face. Jake saw that Ebenezer wasn't looking at him, was just sitting, a man-mountain in his recliner, but somehow alert, and his benign presence acted as a gentle balm to Jake's spirit.

Jake stopped rocking, lit another cigarette, took a puff—and realized he didn't want it. He stubbed it out and just sat there, flicking the Bic on and off. The moon disappeared again before he spoke into the darkened room, "One day, you're just walking around—on track toward a real future in aerospace or something—everything's cool, and then BOOM. A terrible gap, a fraction of a second gone wrong." He rocked on without putting words to the jumble of protests and frustrated pain that careened around in his mind.

After a few minutes, he shook his head and said, "Another totally weird thing, Uncle Eb. I met this weird girl! She is outrageous." He paused before adding, "Well, messed up, some, like me. But she's interesting. A good person to talk to." He stared out at the darkness, thinking. "It is so strange to have a friend that's a girl. That you think about, without always and only thinking about sex . . ."

He leaned his head back against the carved top rail of Nell's rocking chair. *Creak-creak. Creak-creak.*

Finally, Jake checked his watch. "Look out, old buddy. It's time for Jake to go deliver a bunch of newspapers. Let's get you to bed." He helped the older man up and put his arm around the sloping shoulders as he escorted Ebenezer back to bed.

"We'll try to go out for a walk again as soon as it warms up, okay?"

CHAPTER SEVENTEEN: SLEEP

Across town, Milli turned onto her side and adjusted the covers, pulling them up over her bare shoulder. She stared out at the stars glittering through the sheer curtains.

She rolled back onto her other side and checked the digital alarm clock. 1:54! "Go to sleep!" she ordered herself.

She jerked with surprise when the cell phone on her bedside table began to vibrate, loud in the stillness. She snatched at it with her heart pounding. Checking the number only confirmed what she had guessed, with her heart suddenly leaping.

"Don't answer!" she hissed to herself, but in spite of the shock and the warning, the old hunger uncoiling in her belly wouldn't be denied. When the phone buzzed again in her hand, she pushed Talk.

"Millipede." His voice was almost a whisper—slow and low.

She held her breath, chewing on her bottom lip.

"Millicent Farley . . ." A singsong tease. "I want you . . ."

She hit the disconnect button with a trembling finger, smacked the phone back on the table and flung herself onto her stomach in the bed. The phone danced again. She pulled the pillow over her head, but she could still feel the vibration of the phone at her side. It stopped, then started again, and finally she turned over and picked it up, her heart in her throat and her body buzzing.

"Hey, girl." He waited. "What's going on with you? I know we have to keep our little secrets, but don't you think your act at Mother's last night was kind of over the top?"

"I'm done, Billy Mac," she said in a small voice. "I'm really done this time."

"I know. You've said that before." She could hear the smile in his words. "But I know you, Millipede. You love it as much as I do, and we won't ever be completely done, baby cousin. I'm coming to pick you up. Go get ready. I'll give you five minutes to get down here."

"No, Billy. No."

"Yes, Milli, yes. Come on down now. Just one more time." And the phone beeped off.

She turned onto her back, and as she stared up at the ceiling, hot tears began to run into her ears.

§

She had come to think of him as a snake. He would simply stare at her with narrowed eyes and she was paralyzed, unable to resist him.

Billy Mac started up with her when she was thirteen.

The night everything changed for her, she was an eighth grader and he was a junior—a popular, broad-shouldered football player. He moved like the athlete he was, handsome and confident as he made his way through the crowd of kids milling around outside the stadium after the game.

Uncle Dart was driving and Aunt Margaret sat beside him in the front seat. Milli sat in the back with Billy Mac's little brother and another child-cousin. She was living with Gert at the time, but Margaret had brought her along because she knew Milli loved to watch Billy Mac play. The game had been close, and everyone was still jumpy with excitement.

Billy Mac had showered, and he smelled wet and clean when he slid into the back seat and pulled her into his lap. The children beside them were still chanting cheers, hyper with the thrill of the win. It was very dark, and since Billy Mac often roughhoused with them, sitting on his lap was not an unusual occurrence, but as Milli giggled and jostled around, pretending to dry his hair with her sweater, she suddenly realized he was touching her body in a new way. He was laughing and joking with the others, but his hidden hands were exploring her newly sensitive body beneath the bulky sweater.

There was a very small voice in her head saying, "No. No. This is wrong. Stop." But the words never rose to her mouth. Besides, new feelings rose in her, making her breathless with pleasure.

As if through a haze, she heard Uncle Dart describing the short lateral on the fifteen-yard line that Billy Mac had caught and run in for a touchdown. His voice seemed far away from the roaring in her ears. The conversation and laughter racketed around the car, while Milli felt her bones melting. She made a faint effort to stop him, but his hands were insistent and slowly made their way over all of the sweet flesh he could reach.

He was her hero. She loved her big cousin, and he had singled her out from the others. She was awash with surprise and warm sensations. His breathing had quickened, hot against her ear. She could feel his hands begin to tremble, his intense pleasure in her body.

When they got back to Gert's house to drop Milli off, his hands had withdrawn, and he put one finger up to touch her lips, a shushing warning, and she understood. She gave a slight nod and he opened the door. As she climbed out, her knees felt too weak to hold her up, but she stumbled and straightened, looking back at him with wide eyes.

His window purred down and he said, "Hey, Milli, did you say you're having trouble with Spanish?"

She was stunned. She had indeed said that and it was true. She nodded.

"Well, if I can find time," he said, his grinning face slightly flushed, "I'll come over one night next week and give you some coaching."

Her cheeks burned in the dark as she stared at him. "Okay. Thanks."

And so it had begun: a secret both of them kept so well that none of Billy Mac's string of girlfriends, nor his self-preoccupied family, ever suspected.

The "Spanish coaching" was of course a cover for Billy Mac's sexual "games" that grew ever more intense over six months. It never occurred to anyone in the family that their golden boy could even be remotely interested in his wiry little cousin—so much younger and so ordinary in comparison to the fabulous blonde cheerleaders and dark-eyed club presidents he dated publicly. They thought his helping with her homework was one more piece of evidence that proved what a great kid he was. In fact, his mother made him mention his "tutoring" on his college applications.

She smiled to herself in study hall. It felt so good to know he could have anybody, but he wanted her, and her alone.

Then he raped her. The rape that Milli had described to Jake was real. It occurred the spring after the autumn night of the football game. The day he forced her, Billy Mac had smoked a joint, and when his brother withdrew from their planned fishing expedition, Billy Mac was excited to have Milli to himself out by the lake. He knew exactly what he wanted to do. No more games. It was going to be real today, and no amount of protests, or cute little "No, Billy Mac" could stop him. She had permitted every liberty, and enjoyed fooling around. Why would she seriously want him to stop now?

But she had really fought hard, adding fire to his lust, and afterward as she lay sobbing, curled in on herself, Billy Mac sobered up and stared at her with fear in his eyes. There had been more blood than he expected, and as he clumsily tried to help her clean up, he mumbled profuse apologies. She stayed silent, and the hurt of betrayal flashed from her eyes as he helped her stand.

She moaned briefly as she sat down gingerly in the truck, and didn't speak to him all the way back to town. As they pulled up at Gert's house, he said, "Milli, I'm real, real sorry I hurt you. I kind of lost my head for a while. Please don't tell anyone, and I'll make it up to you, I promise."

She jerked on the truck's door handle, but it was locked, and before she could release it, he said in his low, clear baritone, "Milli? They won't believe you."

Her chin was quivering and her eyes filled again with fresh tears as she reached behind the seat for her jacket. She glared at him fiercely as she backed away and slammed the door with a jarring crash. Without another glance, she spun on her heel and marched to the house.

The next day her dad wondered at her silence as he drove her over to Bedford Green to spend her vacation with Gran, but he had no idea how to talk to her, or what questions to ask.

Over that summer, she was cherished and loved back to health by her grandmother, whose blissful ignorance was made possible by Milli's proud and determined secret-keeping. She simply couldn't bring herself to tell the truth. She was afraid she would blurt out all the "games" they had played that led to it, and Gran would see her part in it. Gran could sense that something in Milli had changed, but after a few gentle questions, she left her alone, trusting in her good cooking, all-encompassing love, and prayers to heal whatever wound Milli had brought to the farm with her.

And that summer Milli joined Gran's church. She went down the aisle and asked to be baptized, praying that the Lord would forgive her for her behavior with Billy Mac and help her never do that again until she was married to the man she wanted to have a family with.

Gran was thrilled.

§

Twenty minutes after his call, his Jeep was sitting on the corner. The corner was as dark as always—the streetlight was still out—and Milli stood trembling in the deep shadows beneath the trees, watching him smoke.

Pulled irresistibly by her old attraction to him, and fighting every step of the way, she moved forward, opened the door, and slid in without shutting it, leaving one foot on the ground. He grinned at her, his teeth gleaming in the dark, and flicked his cigarette out the window.

Her hands were shaking and she wrapped her arms around herself, a barrier against him. "I came to say stop. You've got to leave me alone, Billy Mac. I mean it."

"Okay." He kept grinning.

"No. I'm serious, Billy. It is really, really wrong, and I'm not doing it anymore. I think Gert is suspicious again, for one thing."

He pulled his head back, his face lit by the vehicle's overhead light. He reached up and switched it off, and the darkness fell around them. "What makes you think so?"

"Well, she looked at me funny when she told me you were coming in for your leave."

"She looked at you funny. Well, wooo! Don't be so jumpy. She don't know squat about us. Nobody does."

As her eyes adjusted to the dim lights on the dashboard, he pulled a packed condom out of his jeans pocket and held it up between two fingers, twirling it back and forth across his knuckles.

"Put that away, Billy. You won't need it tonight or any other night with me. I'm done sneaking around."

"Yeah, okay. This can be the very last time. You can be done tomorrow." He flipped the condom to his left hand and turned the key in the ignition. "Let's go." The motor started, but Milli jumped out before he could get in gear.

She could barely see his handsome, all-American face as he leaned his head down to look out the window at her. She shook her head. He kept smiling his lazy smile and beckoned slowly with the devil's own finger. Desire rose in her to choke off her breath.

"Just one more time, Millipede . . . Come on."

CHAPTER EIGHTEEN: NEW MORNING

The next day was Sunday, and Milli's alarm dragged her from the bed at 8:00 a.m. She staggered as she made her way down the hall to the bathroom. Aunt Gert was still snoring in her room, and Milli was glad not to have to face her this morning.

She waited until the water was hot and then stepped into the shower, pulled the curtain closed behind her, and began to cry. She scrubbed herself all over with vicious swipes of the washcloth, and as she shampooed her hair, tears ran with the suds into the drain.

While she blew her hair dry, she avoided looking at herself in the mirror. She hurried to dress, feeling like the jeans from last night were not hers, like last night's T-shirt and sweater had been worn on the body of some slut she didn't know. She slammed them to the bottom of her closet with other dirty clothes and pulled on a sweatshirt over torn gray sweatpants, socks, and running shoes, then grabbed her coat and left the house.

She jogged through the crisp, clear morning with her teeth gritted until she got to Mary Beth's, where she opened the door and prepared to lie to her cousin.

Two-year-old Bobby came flying through the house yelling, "Milli! Milli!" and flung himself against her, attaching himself to her leg. She walked him into the kitchen on her foot, where Mary Beth was bouncing Molly on one arm, trying to settle the wailing baby as she walked back and forth in the kitchen while packing a cooler with beer. When she looked at Milli, she did a double take and said, "Well, good Lord, Milli! What the hell have you been doing? You look a total mess."

"Thanks, coz! Why don't you say, 'Thanks for getting over here so damned early on a Sunday morning when you could have slept in?'" She shook off Bobby, took Molly, and cooed and danced with her until the baby's wails quieted, and Mary Beth finished packing sandwiches and energy bars for the hiking trip into Red River Gorge.

"Where's Rod?" Milli asked.

"He went to get gas in the car." Mary Beth looked at her again. "Are you okay? Your eyes are swollen."

"Sorry, but this is the way I look with no makeup and not much sleep last night." She swung Molly into the air and nuzzled her fat little tummy. "Molly doesn't mind how I look. Do you, sweetie?"

Mary Beth watched with a skeptical look on her face. "You have a big date last night?"

"No, of course not. The whole daggone family would be on high alert if I had a date—you know that." Milli sat down with the baby, and Bobby rummaged through her coat pockets, looking for any toys she might have tucked away. He pulled out a little drugstore Terminator figure and crouched on the floor to play.

Milli could still feel Mary Beth's eyes puzzling over her blotchy face, so she volunteered false information. "I got sucked into *Breakfast at Tiffany's*. It started at midnight and I couldn't quit watching those clothes!"

"Yeah, that's such a great movie. I can watch Audrey Hepburn all day." Mary Beth's tone was conciliatory. "Listen, Milli, thanks so much for this. Really. I'm going to owe you *so* much babysitting, if you ever get a move on and find you a guy!"

Milli made a face at the baby and tickled her until she gave out the delicious baby laugh that always made all adults within hearing laugh with her.

"I can*not* believe you aren't dating anybody, Milli! You are so cute when you dress up."

"Thanks again, Mary Beth! Why don't you all get on out of here so I can have these babies all to myself?!" Rod came in the back door, and Milli was grateful that, for now, the questions were over.

§

Milli had gotten both little ones down for naps when the blues came back, and she sat in a living room recliner and sank into the disappointment.

She twisted a strand of hair around and around, pulling it out straight, and then twisting it up again, misery a dark clot in her stomach. Finally she went to her coat and got her cell. She pulled up the number and punched it, checking her watch, and when she heard the dear voice, her heart twisted in her chest.

"Gran!" Milli's voice cracked as she bit down on an urge to cry again. "I'm so glad to hear your voice!"

"Milli, sweetheart! How are you?"

"Oh, I'm fine," she lied. "But I'm calling to see how you're getting along. Were you able to go to church today?"

"Oh yes, honey, I was able to go back just a week or two after the funeral, and finally I've started packing. But what I want to know is how *you* are doing. You don't sound too good. What's going on?"

"No, no, I'm fine." Milli cleared her throat. "Just a frog in there. I'm okay."

"Well, it's lovely to hear from you. I think I'm over the worst of it for now and almost looking forward to the move. Time moves along and being busy helps a lot. It's a big relief to know Hank will keep the house."

"I know it must be hard. Don't you want me to come on over to help you?"

"Well, of course, I'd love to have you, but don't you have a job and babies to tend to?"

"You just say the word and I'll be there."

Milli's voice must have carried something of her longing over the distance between them because her grandmother replied, "All right, I'm saying the word: *Help!* Come on over if you can. I could sure put you to work. I have years of boxes and drawers to go through, and I'd love the help."

"I'll be there as soon as I can get a ride."

CHAPTER NINETEEN: MISSING MILLI

Jake sat on a couch in the library lobby waiting for Milli, the coffee cooling beside him while he watched the double glass doors. He hadn't heard from her in the week since their last visit in this comfortable corner, and as the dull January days passed in long repetitive work hours, the only bright spots were thoughts of Milli—her genuine laughter at the pool table, her courageous stand against the smug Billy Mac, and her eyes as she looked at him across the coffee and soda cups of their conversations.

But he frowned as the minutes ticked by. This was the arrangement they had made last week: next Thursday, same time. "Just friends over coffee" was their agreement.

Ten minutes, then fifteen, passed. He had tried calling her last night to double-check, but when she didn't answer, he decided to just show up. By the twist growing in his gut, he knew that somehow their "friendship" had veered a little off course—at least for him—but he was pretty sure she felt the same way. He had caught her looking at him with a certain gleam in her eye last time. And as they played pool at the party, she had teased him and flirted outrageously—hip-bumping him aside to take her shot, and touching him more than was necessary. He smiled to himself. He had enjoyed that party. But he had stayed cool and not let on he was getting interested.

He fished out his cell phone and punched in her number. No answer. He didn't leave a message.

Thoughts of Milli had been keeping his tiger at bay. That feline stalker—the guilt that lay around every corner waiting to pounce and drag him down—was silenced while he was thinking about her. He replayed their conversations in his head or pictured her in the red satin dress she wore for the party.

He tapped the speed dial for Milli's number again. This time he left a message. "Milli? You coming? Call me if you're not."

He glared at his cold coffee, took it to the trash, and went outside to pace up and down in front of the tall library windows.

He smoked a cigarette—*The last one, definitely*—eventually flicking the butt into the bushes lining the walk.

He went back inside with gritted teeth.

He found a free computer, logged onto the Internet, and looked up the *Bedford Green Messenger* for the week of November 14. He found it easily. It was front-page news. He fought the nausea until he got to the men's room.

§

As he came through the doors of the Goodwill, he saw a stranger behind the cash register and swore under his breath. With any luck, Milli's aunt Gert would have been at the front counter, but no, of course she wasn't.

The pudgy, mustached guy raised his eyes from a magazine and looked at Jake without expression. "Can I help you?"

"I'm looking for Milli Farley."

"Yeah? Well, that makes several of us, buddy. She was supposed to work today *and* yesterday, but we ain't seen hide nor hair of her all week. I'm supposed to be stocking, but I'm the lucky guy gets to cover the register for her."

Jake frowned. Now he was seriously uneasy—*God, what if Billy Mac* . . . But he kept it casual and asked, "Really? Know where she's staying? I'd like to check and see she's okay."

"No idea."

"What about her aunt, um, Gert?"

"Ain't seen her either."

Jake let his anger seep into his hard stare until the guy said, "Gertie works Thursdays and Fridays."

Jake turned to leave, but when he heard, "Maybe Milli ran off to join the circus," he wheeled around with a scowl. This time the man straightened and put his hands up. "I'm just sayin' . . ."

Jake shoved the door hard.

§

He had worked late and then delivered the paper, so it was almost noon the next day when he woke up in the trailer. Sharp winter sun etched a rectangle of white on the window curtains, and when Jake drowsily pulled the sheers aside, he was surprised to see snow. It had melted on the asphalt but still lay bright on Nell's concrete table, and a partial blanket draped over the tangle of toys and broken yard furniture in the yard across the way.

That's what I need—a nice layer of snow covering my life, making it clean.

He went to the bathroom and when he came back, he sat on the end of the daybed next to Ebenezer, who was watching the Cooking Channel from his recliner.

Jake's concern for Milli's safety had grown overnight, so he grabbed his cell phone and dialed her number again.

She answered on the first ring and his heart jumped with gladness.

"Oh, hi, Jake! Sorry. I should have called you. I decided to take your suggestion. I got Aunt Gert to bring me over to Granny's for a while."

"Oh." Jake felt flattened by her casual tone.

"Don't be mad. I just felt like I needed to get away and had to make plans kind of quick, you know?"

Jake answered tonelessly, "I went by the Goodwill when you didn't show at the library, and some guy was mad about having to cover for you."

"Oh durn! I forgot I was on the schedule for yesterday. I bet I get fired."

Jake sat without speaking, and she sounded embarrassed when she added, "I'm sorry. I should have called to say what was going on. The days kind of blurred together."

Jake frowned. There was something about this conversation that smelled. Her voice sounded . . . too casual. Silence stretched and finally Milli said, "Jake? You know why I had to leave."

After another pause, Jake said, "Okay. Fine. See you around, Milli," anger dulling his voice.

"Wait! Wait, Jake."

He sat, stewing on the sour gall of her disregard.

"So will it be okay to call you when I get back to town, Mr. McGee?" The effort to sound cheerful cost her, he could tell.

"Yeah, okay. See ya." He ended the call. Then he threw the phone hard against a pillow at the other arm of the daybed. "Fuck it!"

Ebenezer's watchful gaze was anxious above a tremulous half smile, but when Jake noticed Eb's discomfort, he relaxed his shoulders and rolled his eyes. "Women!" he muttered, shaking his head, and Eb's smile grew. His eyebrows lifted with his effort to mirror Jake's eye roll, and they both laughed.

But as Eb turned back to the television, Jake sank slowly back into himself.

When Nell came back from the grocery, she stopped inside the door with her bags and looked quizzically at the two men, but Jake kept his feelings tucked behind a mask, and Eb just looked up with his innocent smile.

CHAPTER TWENTY: A TRAIN

Jake sat at the table outside the trailer in the February darkness and stared at nothing. Sometimes his thoughts wandered, but no distraction lasted more than a few moments. Over the past weeks he had been thinking of suicide. He even called the suicide prevention hotline once but hung up before anyone answered.

He felt sure that if he never said the words out loud—never brought the burden of guilt out of the black hole in his gut—he would fly to pieces. The knowledge of that night, the images caught in his brain, all of it was swelling inside him again like an infection, like some rotting thing.

Work was a drag, and he dreaded the empty future. Nothing would change. He'd be stuck in this trailer park, working for minimum wage, forever. No way to go back to school now. No way to even lift his head up, to respect himself. No way forward.

I can't keep going like this. With a sudden sure sense of inevitability, he made the decision. He went to the shed and got his bike. His watch read 2:00 a.m. He didn't need to pick up his papers for a couple of hours, but today? Today they just would not get picked up. The world wouldn't end if 264 people didn't get to read the newspaper with their morning coffee today . . .

This would hurt Nell and Ebenezer. *Should I leave a note for her?*

No. What could I say?

He rode through the deserted streets, between the dark houses, without seeing a soul. He didn't feel the thirty-degree cold. He didn't hear the dog barking.

When he came to the railroad crossing on West Main, he dismounted and began to push the bicycle over the rough gravel and hard-packed earth along the track and far back into a stand of woods where it wouldn't be seen by a passing car. He dropped the bike in the underbrush and groped his way back through the copse until he could see the gleam of the rails stretching out under the starlight, curving into the town to his left and off into the distance to his right. The shining pathway of goods, of coal and the raw materials of industry, stretched away from him, accompanied by a rock ledge bordering the woods. He mounted the embankment to the track bed, his footfalls crunching in the loose gravel, and he walked along the track away from the lights of town for a mile or so and into an area where thick woods stood sentinel on both sides. Facing into the shadows between the trees, he sat down on the frigid steel rail and folded his elbows across his raised knees.

He knew the train came at 3:00 a.m. He had heard it every day as he picked up his papers. He sat for an hour or more. His heavy canvas jacket did not resist the cold, but he endured it, accepted it; his body's misery was just another aspect of his suffering. Time had no meaning to him. He wasn't anxious. He wasn't checking his watch. He simply sat and stared at nothing, barely noting the gray clouds he exhaled into the night. He thought back over his twenty-two years, occasionally shaking his head, sometimes snorting with bitter laughter.

Then he heard it, the mournful wail of the train whistle, so far distant that he couldn't hear the sound of the wheels clicking along the track, but soon he felt the rail begin to vibrate beneath him. It came on slowly at first, and he sat huddled, listening to the growing sound, and another dissonant triad of trumpet wail came to him. He stared down the silver converging ribbons until he saw the tiny headlight in the distance.

Now the sound was growing into something malevolent, and as it began to rage closer and closer, the sound of five thousand tons of freight train rushing toward him acquired a screaming, maniacal quality, high pitched and rising higher. He stood up as the ground began to tremble and the gravel jittered at his feet. Death came on, the headlight got brighter and brighter, and a sudden, horrendous blast of horn reverberated in his bones. Against Jake's will, his body recoiled from the danger, and he stumbled backward, lost his balance, and tumbled down the embankment. Overwhelmed with the force of sound, he whipped his head toward the train and struggled to push up on his elbows. He glimpsed, then it passed, the fury crashing into a low register, and grit flew into his face, cutting him like razors. As he clamped his eyes shut, the engineer's startled stare registered in Jake's consciousness and hung there.

Amid the rumble and the rush of wind, Jake stood up, his coat snapping around him, tears streaming. The engineer's face, the eyes flared wide at the sudden sight of the man below on the gravel slope, so close to the train . . . The driver hadn't seen the shadow of him in time to apply the brakes. Wouldn't have done any good.

Grit burned his eyes, and he could barely breathe in the sucking draft of the train tearing a hole in the night. He stood there until all of the boxcars had flown past—CSX, CSX, CSX in mind-numbing repetition. Finally he watched the lights disappear around the curve, his cheeks wet and dusty.

"Fucking coward!" he shouted to himself, then gritted his teeth.

He stumbled to the rock ledge that followed the track and his legs gave way. He bent into a huddled mass, still feeling the passing shock waves of violent death. The wind and the smell of it kept rattling through him, stunning his thoughts to silence.

Night closed in around the raw opening the train had left, and the depth of the cold began to slide down his back and into his spine. A rigid numbness gripped his brain and his body, and as the wind subsided, he became part of the rock.

§

A sound penetrated: the slow, gritty shuffle of footsteps approaching, a stop, a sigh. Silence again.

Jake didn't raise his head. Uncaring, incurious. Numb.

Then the night settled into endless silence.

Finally, as the first birds stirred in the woods behind him, he moved. He lifted his head and began to rub at his painful neck. When he opened his eyes, he recoiled from the dark hulk sitting several feet away on the ledge.

"God!" He sprang to his feet.

The figure stood also, bear-like, but the voice was a calm rumble. "No, sorry. It's just me."

"What the hell?" Jake flashed, anger following the fright.

"Didn't mean to scare you." The man resumed his seat and Jake continued to stare, trying to bring into focus an even blacker mass of shadow than all the other shadows in the pitch darkness.

"You want something?" Jake asked.

"Nah, nothin'." Jake thought the voice had the tone and cadence of a black man's. "Just doing my night thinking."

Jake continued to stare, gradually coming down from the adrenaline.

"Track's at the back of my neighborhood," the voice said. "Good place to walk on a nice night."

Jake sagged back onto the ledge. "You're shittin' me, right? It's fuckin' cold, mister!"

There was no reply, and after a while in the silence, Jake felt a kind of warmth coming from the man ten feet away. Unthreatening. Patient. And in the presence of the man, there was a sharing of the burden. Jake was barely aware of his despair lightening a shade, making life bearable. Almost.

At last Jake stood again, finding that his legs seemed stronger, steadier. He turned to study the man and could make out the heavy features and the glint of eyes looking up at him from behind glasses. He was wearing a black track suit with neon stripes, and sneakers. Jake felt a flash of something like recognition, a profound knowing held in common, but he couldn't name it, and he let it pass. He gave a brief nod and turned to go. As he walked away, the bass voice followed him as if the earth had spoken from beneath his feet. "Take it easy now."

PART TWO
CHAPTER TWENTY-ONE: ALTERATIONS

Milli looked at herself in the hall mirror and saw Jake's face instead—his eyes, darkened by sympathy, his faith in her, and his laughing admiration. She hung her head. Her heart wrinkled in pain and she shook herself back to the present.

Gran's Maine coon cat rose from her doze in the cushioned window well and did her stretch before circling Milli, coolly appraising her. "What do you think, Mozie? Like it?" Milli gave a little pose in her outfit.

Mozart the cat had been part of the farm, helping Gran teach her piano students and raise her garden, for years. But he was Milli's cat. And he knew it. Milli remembered with a smile the day she had found him in the mailbox, a tiny kitten abandoned to the kindness of strangers, and nothing could part Milli from him except her firm father's no at the summer's end. So Mozie stayed with Gran to be Milli's favorite buddy every summer.

She adjusted the folds of the starched lace ruff around her face and tried to form her scarlet lips into a smile in the tall, cracked mirror. The late afternoon sunlight from the tall window fell across her bare shoulders and lit her strapless dress with slanting stripes. The deep ruffles of the collar scratched her chin, but she loved the halo effect behind her spiky, newly dyed black hair, and she was able to grin at herself, putting her worries away for now, concentrating on her latest design.

The dress beneath the fabulous collar was a simple, sparkling knit sheath that fell smoothly from the six-inch fold across her breasts to the floor. Still unhemmed, the fabric lay bunched up on top of her combat boots, and as she turned around, she realized she hadn't removed enough stitches from the back seam to allow her to take more than baby steps.

But baby steps she took, so thrilled with her new creation that she had to get downstairs to show Gran.

She slid her feet from the boots and descended the staircase barefoot, lifting the long dress with one hand. Mozart following soundlessly. Her grandmother had been playing "Clair de lune" as she waited for her first piano student to arrive, and the romantic melody filled the front hall. When Milli came around the turn of the staircase, she paused on the landing, adjusted the long skirt, and waited while the cat streamed around her and silently descended to the first floor. He took a seat and wrapped his paws, waiting for Milli.

Gran bowed her head, listening to the final chord, and when she lifted her hands, the eyes behind her glasses found the slim girl on the stairs. Her smile broadened as Milli turned slowly around. The narrow strapless sheath was like a blade of silver, banding Milli's small breasts and narrow hips into a simple vertical column, and her black hair stood in dramatic spikes above the rich folds of the ornate lace collar.

Gran took in a breath and held it until she laughed aloud and began to applaud. "Milli! That is amazing! Is that my old tablecloth you have around your neck?"

Milli nodded, giggling, and lifted her chin—posing, raising one shoulder, pursing her scarlet lips and peering down her nose.

"Come down. Come down," Gran ordered, and began to play the grand march from *Aida*. Milli padded down the last three steps into the front hall, where she raised herself on her toes, picking the skirt up with one hand, and began a model's strut along the room, moving regally with the slow, striding chords, turning on the ball of one foot and sweeping the tail of the dress behind her for the return trip. As she faced her grandmother, she sucked in on her cheeks and held her chin even higher, trying mightily not to giggle as she pranced back along the wide-planked floor.

Her grandmother struck a final chord, and they laughed together as she stood up to admire Milli's creation. Gran held the bony shoulders and turned her to finger the ivory velvet ribbon which tied the ruff behind Milli's neck and the seam down the back of the glittering dress, tracing a perfect vertical line. With an experienced eye she pulled the top fold away from Milli's spine to see the raw selvedge and then patted it back in place as Milli said, "Nope, I haven't done the finishing yet. I was in such a hurry to show off."

"Well, you certainly have mastered my old Singer! I am so impressed!"

"Thanks, Gran. I'm really tickled it turned out so good. Of course, I can hardly move in it, and the starch in the collar is scratchy as all get out, but durn—I feel like it looks great! Don't you?"

"I do, I do! And is there a grand affair to which Queen Millicent will wear this spectacular outfit?"

Milli felt her shoulders droop a little in the chill of reality until Gran wrapped her in a big hug and said, "Well, when the engraved invitation arrives, girl, you are going to be ready!"

Milli smiled and shook her head as she turned toward the staircase. "I wish I had the courage to submit my ideas to *Project Runway*."

"Well, why don't you? What have you got to lose?"

Milli turned back to give her grandmother a long, thoughtful look and a wistful smile.

The doorbell chimed, the cat disappeared, and Milli hauled the dress up with both hands and took the stairs two at a time before Gran opened the door to her student.

§

The slender girl stood by the tall window in the workroom at the end of the hall, looking out at the light snow falling through the silvery afternoon.

The sounds of scales, played by hesitant fingers, echoed from the first floor.

The ruffled collar rested around the neck of an old dressmaker's dummy, where it seemed to glow in the unlit room. She had slipped quickly out of the glittering dress and folded it on top of the sewing machine, shivering a little as she slid into her jeans and black T-shirt. She had intended to finish the hem immediately, but melancholy slowed her movements and pulled her to the window, where she folded her arms across her chest and leaned against the window frame.

Feathers of snow rode the gusts and swirls of wind past the house and veiled the barn and silo in white wreaths like smoke. Her eyes followed the plank fence back into the field until it disappeared in the pale dusk.

When Gran had asked her where she would wear the dress, her mind's eye flashed on the other strapless dress—the red satin one she had worn New Year's Day at Aunt Margaret's—and memories formed, slowly blinding her to the snowfall.

Jake had been her salvation that night.

Warmth coursed through her, pinking her cheeks as she remembered the sudden attraction that had surprised her, as though Jake's simple understanding and acceptance opened a door inside her that she had thought locked.

But she hadn't told him the truth. She had left out the secret part, the part of herself she couldn't seem to overcome—the part of herself she didn't want Jake to know.

A tear escaped and she swiped at it roughly with the back of her hand.

She walked over to the dress and picked it up, switched on the floor lamp, and sat down next to the sewing box with a heavy sigh.

CHAPTER TWENTY-TWO: BACK ON THE BIKE

Snow fell on February 5, and during the ten-day cold spell that followed, Jake needed to borrow Nell's car to deliver his papers. But lately there had been a thaw, and this Sunday morning he skipped the car and was back on his bike, huddled in his coat, icy slush splashing up on his pant legs.

He found himself thinking of the man beside the track—his strange appearance from nowhere, the kindly ease of the man—and had about decided he had imagined him.

As he rode the bike over the curb and into the trailer court, his cell phone rang: a customer saying he hadn't gotten his *Herald Leader*.

That's the blue house—all the way at the end of the friggin' route! I know I hit his porch. He sighed and got back on the bike.

§

It was a little after ten by the time he was heading back toward home, after handing the paper to the irritated customer himself and stopping for a doughnut at the BP station.

He hadn't slept very much, and since the papers were extra heavy on Sundays, he was exhausted. As he turned a corner, the chain rattled off the sprockets of the derailleur, and he had to hop off and carry the bike over to some nearby concrete steps where he could sit and work on it.

It was a quiet morning and the empty trees formed a web of black lace against the pewter sky. No dogs barked, no cars moved, no breeze shifted the branches overhead, so the surprising sound in the air was clear and bell-like. Music. The harmonies of a vaguely familiar tune drifted from above the steps, and it dawned on him that the building was a church. Though he passed it every day, he hadn't paid any attention to it.

The white clapboard structure squatted on the corner without a steeple and rose above the sidewalk on a stone foundation, with five concrete steps leading to a small stoop in front of the entry. A rusty, wrought iron railing bordered the stoop and descended beside the steps. No one was around, and the music was so nice that Jake sat down with a sigh on the steps and just listened. He couldn't make out the words, but the hymn was in a minor key and the mournful sound made him feel . . . not so alone in the gloom that haunted him.

Suddenly the door swung open and an extra-large guy in jeans and an open windbreaker hustled down the steps past Jake. "Excuse me," he said in a rumbling bass voice.

Jake watched as he rummaged in a car at the curb and then stood up with a diaper bag. He was as stout as the old linden trees that lined the street, and his broad shoulders strained at the seams of his jacket. His white button-down dress shirt was crisp, contrasting with the black skin of his powerful neck, below which a red tie hung loosely around his unbuttoned collar. He pulled a bottle from a pouch on the side of the bag and began to shake it vigorously as he headed back toward Jake with a grin and eyes shining behind glasses with thick plastic frames.

He lifted the bag's strap onto a massive shoulder and said, "I can't believe we left *this* in the car!" His voice held a chuckle beneath the words. Then he stopped to stare down at Jake, and Jake blinked.

Jake stared back, his mouth open. *That's him.*

"Don't you want to come inside?" the man said. "Sounds better in there."

"No, I'm okay." Jake looked away, acutely uncomfortable, starting to fidget and reach to dig out a tool. He glanced back at the man, who looked as though he wanted to say more, and blurted, "You having choir practice?" to stop any reference to the other night.

"Oh, no. We don't have any choir. It's just the congregation singing. A cappella. No kidding, man, come on inside. We like company." His teeth flashed in a warm smile.

"Nah, thanks. I've got to get on home." But Jake continued to sit rooted to the step, tired to the bone.

The man hesitated, looking thoughtfully at Jake as he kept shaking the baby bottle. Then he said, "Okay, cool. You take it easy now," and he took the steps two at a time. He turned at the top and said, "Hey, I'm Pete, and that's my number on the sign." He tilted the bottle toward a glass-fronted box mounted on the wall. Then he opened the door as a new hymn began. The sound swept over Jake like a sudden, sweet rain, before the heavy door muffled it.

Jake read the marquee letters over his shoulder:

NEW HOPE CHURCH
Sunday Services 10 am and 6 pm
Pastor: Peter Andrews
Phone: 555-460-4288
"He shall lead the blind in a way they know not."
Psa. 94:22

CHAPTER TWENTY-THREE: PETE ANDREWS

555-460-4288. The number had grown roots into Jake's head and kept appearing behind his eyes as he went about his work.

Maybe those numbers are coordinates on a map—a way out.

The urge to confess was stronger and more painful every day. He could not bring himself to tell Nell what had happened. He could often feel her loving him from across the room in her rocker. She was happy having him with her. He didn't want her to know what he had done. But how could he trust anyone with the truth?

The last thing I need is a holier-than-thou, I-can-save-your-soul kind of lecture. Still, isn't there some kind of rule about confessions? Something about things said in a confessional? Is that just for Catholics?

He went out in the alley behind the huge grocery store and entered the number in his phone's keypad. He began pacing back and forth, took a deep breath, and touched the green Talk button.

Three rings, then the recorded message said, "Hey, this is Pete. Leave me a message."

Jake stopped pacing and cursed under his breath.

He punched the red disconnect button hard, sat down on the narrow curb, and leaned back against the brick wall. A cold green light washed over the loading ramp and the big dumpsters. He shut his eyes against the burning frustration.

The phone rang in his hand. He looked at the number: 4288. He let it ring twice, then touched Talk. He put it to his ear.

"Hey. This is Pete Andrews. Did you call?"

Jake hesitated, unable to make up his mind.

"Hello?" The rumbling voice managed to sound patient.

Compelled by some instinct, Jake finally said, "Yeah, uh, hello. Sorry to call so late . . ."

"No problem. I get late calls all the time. Anything I can do?"

"I don't know. Probably not. I, um . . ." He heard a baby cry and a woman's voice start to sing.

"Were you sitting on the church steps a few days ago?" asked Pete.

"Yeah. That's me." The singing continued in the background, but the baby had hushed. "It sounds like you're busy," said Jake.

"Oh, not really, we've got a colicky baby here, but she'll settle down soon. Can I do something for you?" A pause, and then, "I thought maybe you needed somebody to talk to when I saw you that morning."

"Yeah, I guess I do." He hunkered over and picked at his thumbnail.

"I have office hours tomorrow." Pete seemed to sense Jake's hesitance and added, "Or do you want to meet tonight?"

"Well . . . I work until midnight tonight. That's probably too late." He bit the skin by the nail and it started to bleed.

"Nope—not too late for me. How about the Pancake House on West Main? You know, by the truck stop?"

"Yeah. Okay, good. Thanks."

Off and on through the rest of his shift, Jake felt his stomach clench with nerves. As he left work that night, he thought about just changing his mind and going back to Nell's trailer, but as though without volition, he steered the bike toward West Main. The night was silent except for the occasional passing car, tires sighing on the street. Jake rode in and out of the pools of light from the streetlamps and began to count them automatically, a trick he had taught himself long ago to keep himself from thinking.

§

He was locking his bike at the rack beside the door when Pete Andrews walked up, dark skin shining and glasses glinting in the light pouring through the windows of the Pancake House. "Man, that's a cool mountain bike! You race it?"

"No. Just bought it a few weeks ago for transportation." Jake was so nervous he felt sick, but he smiled weakly and said, "Thanks for coming."

Pete looked at him, and into him, for a moment before nodding. "Sure thing." He was almost a foot taller than Jake, and a kind smile shone down. "I'm glad you called. You looked pretty done in the other day and I've been wondering about you. By the way, you got a name?"

"Jake." He was still so nervous he could barely pronounce the single syllable.

"Okay, Jake." The handshake was firm and quick.

They entered and were given a booth next to a front window, and a waitress took their orders for coffee.

"The baby was crying," Jake said, suddenly aware that Pete had left a family at home.

"Oh, she's fine. Settled right down, and my wife was heading for bed when I left. She's our first and we're just getting used to her."

"Ah." Jake searched for conversation. Anything to delay. "Have you been pastor of that church for long?"

Their coffee arrived and Pete added sugar to his, stirring as he answered, "Just over a year now." He looked up at Jake and gave a half grin. "My first church."

"Ah. I don't know much about your . . . um, line of work."

Pete chuckled. "That makes two of us. I reckon I have to say I'm pretty much winging it." His grin was so easy that Jake felt the muscles across his back begin to relax. "Small churches like New Hope are hard to fill up these days. We don't have much in the way of entertainment to draw people. They gotta be looking for us pretty hard."

125

The small all-night diner was almost deserted. A young couple sat further down, completely absorbed in their pancakes.

Pete tested the hot coffee, then set it down, pushed it aside, and leaned forward on his folded arms. "So, Jake, are you new in the area?"

Jake nodded. "Moved in with my aunt about two months ago." He avoided the eyes across the table.

"You working?"

"Yessir. Kroger's." Jake hesitated a beat. "And I carry a paper route." He looked up at Pete. "Gotta pick them up in a couple of hours."

"Gee whiz, man, when do you sleep?"

"Don't sleep much. Too many nightmares."

The two men sat quietly beneath the buzz of overhead lights. When Jake glanced at Pete, he saw him nod.

Jake felt a slow ease coming over him. It was as though the large man across the table was radiating warmth into the space around them.

Jake started to say something and stopped. He shook his head slowly. "I'm not sure you can help me. I don't really know why I called you. I'm not a Christian, and what I have to tell is a hell of a thing to lay on anybody. But I think if I don't talk about it, I might . . ."

Pete nodded. "When I saw you sitting on the church step, I recognized you from the train track, and it was pretty easy to see you're trying to carry something too heavy for you."

Jake felt the unfamiliar sting of tears behind his eyes. The kindness of this stranger almost overwhelmed him, and he bit his lip to keep control of himself. When he was able, he asked, "What if a person tells you about a crime? What do you do?" He looked into eyes that did not flinch.

"It depends, I guess. I haven't faced that particular problem before, but I've learned over the years to talk to God whenever I'm confronted by the unfamiliar territory He sometimes leads me into." Pete tilted his head quizzically. "Are we talking about a police matter here, Jake?"

Jake could feel sweat threatening to bead on his forehead. He swallowed hard. "Well, yessir." He took a deep breath. "I killed someone. There was an accident. I was drinking—and I killed a man."

"Ahhh." Pete's deep voice had sorrow in it, and when Jake looked at his eyes, the sympathy there was too much. He bit hard on his lip to stop the tears and reached blindly for his napkin.

There was a long silence while Jake fought for control, and suddenly in the kitchen someone dropped a tray of cutlery with a huge crash, startling them both into embarrassed laughter. The surprise helped restore order, and Jake blew his nose and wiped his face on the napkin, and then sat in the quiet space, looking down at the table, waiting for Pete to speak.

The words came. "Jake, God hears you. He knows you and He knows the man you killed. You were not alone that night."

Jake's face swung up to look at him, and Pete went on, careful to make himself clear. "I know you say you are not a believer, and that's fine; you don't have to believe in Him for God to take hold of you. God is an absolute, powerful reality, and I promise you He is the one that has you on your knees with grief right now. Your conscience is a gift from Him, and He is in your suffering."

Jake stared for long moments, not seeing Pete, but seeing Pete's words in the air between them.

Jake pushed his coffee cup away and gripped the edge of the table. He watched his knuckles, bone showing close beneath the skin. He thought of the Ferris wheel at the county fair when he was six—being at the top, gripping the bar in front of him as the car creaked over the 150-foot apex and began to drop through the dark sky. He didn't remember who was with him then, if anybody.

His head was down and he spoke in a low voice, but his words were distinct. "It was a Friday. November fourteenth." He shook his head and sighed. "Fall semester, sophomore year. I was doing good—had just gotten an A+ on an astronomy exam, so I was celebrating." He snorted a short bitter laugh. "I was thinking that finally I was getting my life onto the rails. Maybe old Jake could be a winner after all." He stared off past Pete, who had leaned forward with his elbows on the table, listening.

"Okay, so there was this bar outside of Bedford Green, just over the county line. Country music and stiff drinks. Mostly farm workers and local labor—you know, people that didn't expect a lot of talk. My date stood me up.

"I had two, I think, maybe three, shots of bourbon with beer chasers—enough for a nice little buzz.

"I remember writing my cell number on a napkin and tucking it under my last beer bottle for Suzy. Suzette was cute. Sexy. I'd seen her in there before. We'd been flirting some, while she waited tables, so I thought she'd probably call."

He looked out the window at nothing. "Funny, the details that stick in your memory . . . I can still see that Bob's Bar sign outlined in bright green neon. It had a tilted martini glass in yellow that flashed on and off, and when I came out, there were puddles standing in the parking lot, so everywhere you looked you saw the sign twice."

He stopped, and Pete nodded. "Yeah, I see it."

"I remember driving. I was kind of jacked up, wondering if I ought to turn around and go back, put the make on Suzy, you know. I guess I was feeling jittery with the possibility of an easy lay. How stupid—a quick few minutes of sex, meaning nothing—and I killed a man for the prospect of it."

Jake's voice had fallen into an automatic, dull monotone. Pete sat across the table with his head down, listening.

"Then, my cell phone rang. I had put it on the seat next to me. It sounded like a whole circus merry-go-round all of a sudden, out of the dark. Made me jump.

"And that was it." Jake's eyes burned with the image. "One look down at the phone—to check the number calling. I thought it was Suzy, and I reached for it.

"When I looked up, I had topped a hill and the guy was right there in front of me. Just this shape in the headlights. I saw his eyes . . . He was out in the road, I think . . . but . . ." Jake squinted at nothing but memory and he licked his lips. "I couldn't react. My foot wouldn't move to the brake."

Pete waited through silence before Jake went on.

"You wouldn't think a body would be a hard thing to slam into, but it is. I hit him so hard my face slammed the steering wheel. And the body . . . it, he, smashed against the front and there was a drag, like, down under, and then, oh God . . . I could feel the wheels go over . . ."

Jake dropped his face into his hands and sat shuddering, but when he straightened, his eyes were dry. He looked to the side, where his gaze lingered on the tile floor. So neat and clean, those squares. Pure geometry. He shook his head.

"I pulled over. The windshield was all busted up. There was a weird noise going on and on. It was my teeth chattering, making a god-awful noise. Finally when I looked . . .

"It was there in the rearview mirror—a piled-up heap at the edge. I tried to think maybe it was a deer. So I put the car in reverse and backed along the shoulder until I saw the shoe. There was this empty shoe standing in the road." Jake's eyes sought Pete's face and found his own horror reflected back at him with a level of understanding that shocked him—almost as though Pete had been with him, riding in the car.

"Nobody can imagine how terrible that shoe was. Just that leftover bit of a person, standing on the asphalt, just one pitiful old shoe. I couldn't look at the body over in the gravel for more than a second, but that was long enough. His head . . ."

He stopped again, rubbing at his mouth, and looked down at the plastic tabletop—staring without blinking, not noticing the tears making channels down his cheeks.

Pete asked, low and steady, "Did you get out of the car?"

Jake slowly shook his head. "I couldn't think . . . No, I didn't. And that's the worst. I can't forgive myself for not getting out and . . . But it was like, if I could just get going—just drive—that somehow it wouldn't have happened.

You know?" His eyes pled with Pete. "I got the car back on the road, but in the rearview mirror I could still see that shoe standing on the road. Oh God . . ."

His anguish had spilled into every syllable, and Pete echoed the expletive as a prayer. "Yes. Oh, God."

Jake's confession bound the two men in undistracted silence for a while. When Jake finally gathered the courage to look up at Pete, he was surprised by sympathy in his dark eyes. "You were sure he was dead?" Pete asked.

"Yeah. The body was all broken up . . . His head . . . It looked like his neck was broken."

"Do you have any idea who it was?" came the gentle question.

"Yeah. It was a guy named Roebling. I looked it up on the Internet." He paused. "I guess he was . . . somebody a lot of people knew. It was a front-page story."

Rain began pelting the windows. Pete asked, "What did you do next?"

"I completely lost it. I sure didn't want any cop asking me to walk straight. It was like the end of the world—for me. I only thought about me, at first. All I could think about was getting out of there, or I was going to prison. No more college for Jake. Everything ruined for me. All I could think about. Selfish bastard." Jake stared down at the table, into the black coffee. "Car was a total bloody mess, so I drove it to a rock quarry I knew about and pushed it into deep water—real deep water." He stopped and looked around the room, disoriented by the memories rocking him. He frowned for a moment and then went on. "I walked maybe ten miles to the interstate and hitched a ride with a trucker going to Louisville. Stupid. Like a little kid: run to Momma. Can't believe I did that."

"Your mother lives in Louisville?"

"Yeah."

"Was there nothing for the police to find? What about your phone?"

"Oh, I did call 911 sometime before . . . It was a temporary phone though, and it's at the bottom of the quarry too."

Jake's eyes narrowed and his mouth twisted as he judged himself. "Oh,

I know how to get my ass out of trouble. A drug dealer knows how to get out of . . ."

He saw Pete flinch for the first time and Jake shook his head, staring at the darkness under the table, until he said, "My whole life has been one mess after another." He curled his lip in disgust. "The other night—on the railroad track? I wanted that train to take me out of here. Didn't want to face myself one more day—but I couldn't do it. Man, I really wanted to. Still do, I guess— if I knew an easy way." Jake wouldn't raise his eyes.

Pete waited, listening.

The waitress reappeared with a pot of fresh coffee. Pete said, "No thanks," and Jake shook his head. She looked at the almost-full cup in front of him, and at his face, before she moved away, and a silence fell over them.

Jake's eyes followed as an eighteen-wheeler pulled into the nearby parking lot, its headlights flashing on the rain-slithered windows. When the driver of the big rig came in, shaking rain off his ball cap, he nodded at them, and Pete acknowledged him politely in return. Jake didn't turn to glance at him.

The driver settled on a stool at the counter and began to chat with the waitress. Pete sipped his coffee and Jake fiddled with his spoon, turning it in circles on the table. "The driver of the truck that picked me up, after it happened? I told him I wrecked my car. When he let me out, he said, 'I'll be praying for you.'" Jake shook his head and fell silent.

He finally looked up at Pete and blew out his breath. "Okay, what do you think I should do?"

Pete raised his eyebrows. "You tell me. What do you think you should do?"

"Well, since death by train didn't work, I guess I'm out of answers." His words fell to the table in in broken pieces.

Pete shook his head slowly. "That is one sure thing: the train is no answer."

Jake looked at him with exhaustion etched into every line of his face. "*Is* there an answer?"

Pete hesitated and then said, "Yes. But not an easy one, Jake. Confessing to me won't ease the burden for you, I'm afraid. In my own nightmare of guilt, the right answer came with prayer, and I will pray for you, of course. But for you to see the way ahead, I believe *you* need to do the praying."

"Don't I have to believe in God before I try to pray?"

"Not in my experience. The only requirement for prayer is to recognize that you don't have any answers yourself."

Jake stared at him and chewed on his lower lip, frowning. "I guess I need some time to work up to prayer."

"Sure . . . You're right. Wouldn't do a bit of good to force yourself. A man's got to want to get down on his knees. A guy like you—and like me—we got to come to the absolute end of ourselves before we really go looking for God, and for divine help."

"Was that how it was for you?"

Pete shrugged his powerful shoulders. "That's about the size of it. I'm real familiar with your kind of desperation. Maybe God set me down in your path—on the railroad tracks even. You might want to think about that."

Silence.

"You think I have to go back and turn myself in, don't you?" Jake heard the blood pounding in his ears.

Pete sat quietly. "Well, this is what I think, since you've asked. It seems to me you got some facing up ahead of you before you can get free of this and put it behind you. First of all, once a man's conscience gets hold of him—strong enough so he thinks about suicide—it doesn't let go. And the conscience is actually God, whether you believe in Him or not. He's in there. So there's facing Him—and what we church people call repentance—that's basically what you're doing now, the real disgusted-with-yourself turning away. That's a soul-deep thing, not a cheap promise that blows away after a bad night's sleep, but a thing that turns a switch inside, and makes you into somebody different."

Jake nodded slowly. He knew he was already a different man than he was two months ago. So maybe that part was mostly done.

Pete went on, sharing his thoughts plainly. "And then there's your obligation to face the laws of the land. Obeying the law is required of Christians just like everyone else. I think it's called vehicular manslaughter—something on that order—and the consequences are serious, as I'm sure you know."

Jake felt simple, cold dread seize his gut.

But Pete went on. "Then there is the offence to the victim's family. They were your victims, just as he was. That is perhaps harder than anything to face, and the most important in God's eyes. Every family in a wrongful death case wants to know what happened, and sometimes they find out in the courtroom. But trust me, what they really want to know is that you hate what you did, and would undo it if you could. Then, perhaps, you will have given them a real possibility for finding forgiveness and resolution. For what it's worth, I think you owe it to them."

He looked at the pale, tight-lipped face in front of him. "You asked me, Jake, so that's what this Christian thinks you should do if you want to move on with your life. And it sounds to me like you were going to college, headed someplace good."

Jake nodded without looking up. Then he seemed to square his shoulders, to become more resolute, and to lift himself up from the invisible bindings around him. He raised his gaze to Pete's. "What you're saying rings true to me. It's pretty much what I was afraid you would say, but . . ." He grimaced with gritted teeth and couldn't finish.

Pete reached out to rest his hand on Jake's arm for a moment, and the touch felt startlingly warm to Jake. A shiver of courage and health seemed to pass through to him.

Pete withdrew his hand and they sat still for a while before Pete said, "You have made a brave start toward wholeness tonight, Jake. When you're ready, we can talk again."

Jake's expression was bleak, but he nodded.

"You know," Pete added, "the conscience that is troubling you so deeply right now never exists apart from the ability to love. And love, both earthly and heavenly, given and received, is our greatest gift from God. To my way of thinking, you belong to Him, and He will help you through this."

For a brief moment, Jake was convinced. Frowning, he nodded.

The waitress showed up again with her pot and Jake looked at his watch. "No thanks, ma'am, I've got to go," and he fished in his hip pocket for his billfold.

Pete held up a hand. "This is mine." He looked at the woman and nodded, and she put the bill on the table.

As they stood, Pete put his hand out to shake Jake's cold one.

"Come by my office anytime, Jake. I believe you are a good man, about to become a better one, and I'll be keeping you in my prayers." Pete opened his wallet and held out a business card. "Here's that phone number. I'm there most every afternoon."

"Thank you, Pete. I'll think about everything you've said. Believe me."

CHAPTER TWENTY-FOUR: AMONG THE STARS

For the remainder of the week, Jake pulled double shifts at the store and still carried the paper. Through the repetitive physical work, he was able to step out of his nightmare and find a resting place.

Deep in his mind, Pete's words turned over and over.

One night about a week after talking with Pete, he was looking over the unsold, out-of-date magazines as he pulled them off the shelf for restocking. He came to the last month's issue of *National Geographic*. Something about the nebula blazing away on the cover caught Jake and held him still. It was 1:00 a.m. and the store was almost empty, so no one noticed when he folded himself down onto the floor by the magazine rack and lost himself in outer space.

He stared at the photographs from the Hubble telescope—brilliant stars and planets—and the thoughts that rippled through his mind were of his astronomy course, of Dr. Greathammer and the order he described in the universe, class after class. Jake remembered the names of many constellations, the physics of star rotation, the mathematical precision of the orbiting planets, the spectacular images of the moons of Jupiter. Awe filled him up again.

He tucked the magazine under his arm, finished his shift, and paid for it as he left.

Later, he lay on his bed studying it until time to deliver papers.

His mind struggled to find words for his thoughts, and without realizing that a small door was opening inside him, he thought of Pete's urging toward prayer. The question rose into his mind as he frowned at the photo of Venus:

Are you here, God? Pete says that I belong to You. Is that true?

Jake waited in rapt silence, barely breathing.

The small, shabby front room of the trailer gradually seemed to fill with . . . nothing he could name, yet *something* almost . . . visible—as if a sentient being was just at the edge of vision. Time passed and Jake's every sense was singing with unfamiliar, exhilarating, vibrating energy. He was not aware of breath or heartbeat, only of the immensity of Presence near him.

Finally his wristwatch alarm reminded him of the newspaper route, and he came back shakily into his reality. He started to get dressed and found himself trembling with a peculiar, intense joy that seemed to fill his chest, and he became aware of his pounding heart. He stopped, stood still, and stared as a subtle light seemed to expand the room, pushing at the walls before it vanished.

Jake put out his hand, pale in the darkness that was not quite as dark as before, and he breathed a question. "What was that? *Who's there?*"

§

After the last paper was bagged against the light drizzle and thrown onto the porch of the last house with a satisfying thunk, Jake pedaled homeward through the dark streets. At the corner where New Hope Church stood, a light-gray bulk against the darkness, Jake dismounted and laid his bike on its side against the front steps.

Up on the stoop, he tried the front doors, but they were locked, and he wasn't surprised. His wish for a sheltered seat where he could just think awhile seemed silly and unfamiliar to him.

The threshold was elevated from the stoop and deep, and he sat down on it, his back against the maroon wooden doors, waiting while his heart and breathing slowed. He stared out at the glimmering streetlight on the far corner and listened to the whispering leaves above him in the dark. A car passed, its headlights pulling it along over drizzle-slick streets. Jake pulled his jacket hood up over his head and folded his arms across his body.

He had laid aside Pete's invitation to talk again, but something strange was moving in him and he couldn't make sense of his experience. He could still see the Hubble photos of the varied and profoundly mysterious sights of outer space. He had found his heart wrenched tight, only to explode with joy. The experience was vivid and still with him. What would Pete make of his sudden, intense desire to look mystery in the face? He dropped his head back against the doors and closed his eyes, listening to Pete again. *Your conscience is a gift. Get on your knees and hunt for God.*

He brought his head up and looked at his hands folded in front of him, elbows on his knees.

No. He didn't know how to start. He couldn't speak out loud to an invisible—what—being? A consciousness beyond human experience?

He started to get up, but it was so quiet and peaceful in this sheltered spot. Was there any chance at all of getting past this? Would Dr. Greathammer help him get his scholarship again, allow him back on the track into astronomy, once he served his sentence? *Nah. Felons probably don't get to be astronomers.*

He stood and stretched and walked down the steps to pick up his bike, but he hesitated a moment, looking above the treetops where the clouds were catching the newborn light along their edges, and a roseate future seemed faintly possible. The world around him seemed to shift a little, and just maybe, there was more to all this than he had thought.

CHAPTER TWENTY-FIVE: REASONS

Jake sat, his arms folded, looking off through the old trees. It was un-seasonably warm and sunny, and Pete had suggested meeting in the park, so after walking through some small talk, they had sat down on the same side of a picnic table near the swings. Jake leaned forward, trying to find words for his tumbling thoughts. The sky beyond the trees seemed to quiver like the surface of water beneath a wind, and Jake blinked, focused his eyes again on nothing, and sought a way to start.

He opened his mouth and a few words came. "I just . . . Something really strange happened. It was like . . ." He shook his head. "Sorry, Pete, now that we're here, in the light of day . . . Let me start over. Um, the thing is, after we talked, I've thought a lot about your take on this mess I'm in." He stopped. "I guess I keep circling around the question . . . whether there's a God or not."

He turned to look at Pete, who was resting his back and elbows on the edge of the table and had stretched his legs out long in front of him. His head was bowed as he listened, and he nodded.

Jake went on, "Somehow it seems important to figure out what's going on. I know something is different in me. That sinking, sick-gut feeling—you know? I've never had that before, and it just won't go away, and I don't know any way to understand it, except, like you say, it's my God-given conscience, eating on me."

Pete nodded again, his chin resting on his chest.

"I don't think it's the law part of this that bothers me so much. I sure as hell don't want to go to prison, but I kind of got used to breaking the law in the old days. Living outside the law and getting away with it was kind of a game, in a way—and I can live with that part of it, no problem. But getting away with dealing drugs and getting away with killing somebody have proved to be two different kinds of big deals. So I guess it's the God part that seems like it's killing me." He turned haunted eyes to Pete.

Pete smiled and commented in a low rumble, "They don't call Him the Hound of Heaven for nothing," he said, and Jake looked puzzled. "God—the Hound of Heaven. A poem by a guy named Francis Thompson."

"Oh."

Jake frowned intently into the space between them, and said, almost angrily, "It's almost like, if I didn't have to deal with the conscience thing, then I don't see that I would have to go back to Bedford Green and turn myself in. See what I'm saying? So basically, I don't want this stuff you're all about. There's no proof that there's a God and I don't want to believe in Him."

Pete pushed his lower lip out and nodded, his face grave.

Jake continued, "Listen, before I came here . . ." He turned his head toward the swing set with a frown. "I never met anybody that believed in God, I've never even heard much of anything besides the Christmas story, and all that about lambs and angels just seemed to me like fairy-tale stuff. In my other world, life was all about gettin' money, gettin' laid, gettin' more money without gettin' caught, etcetera. Then I got to college and saw maybe it was also about learning enough stuff to impress people, and making enough money to get to do what you want, and—well, anybody doing anything religious was sort of kooky, you know?" He glanced over at Pete. "Those people in the yellow robes on campus sure didn't seem to have a lot going for 'em, you know?"

Pete nodded. "Maybe under those yellow robes were extra-large hearts for God. They can be pretty impressive, if you talk to them."

Again Jake looked at him blankly, before continuing doggedly, "So,

Pete, what's the difference between religion and superstition? Where's your proof? Why don't I just, I don't know, cross my fingers and forget the whole hit-and-run thing, hope it all goes away? Seems like, if I stay busy, keep my nose clean, I can probably get past it."

Pete's eyes turned to meet Jake's. His eyebrows lifted. "Think you can? Can you do that? Seems like we wouldn't be here if you were having any success with the 'forgetting it' idea." Pete sat forward and swung a leg over the bench seat, turning to face Jake. His face was serious. "It's a fearful thing to fall into the hands of the living God, Jake. That's Bible. And I have been right where you sit now. Sorry, man. You have my fullest sympathy. But could we back up just a minute—to whatever it was that made you call me. You started to try to tell what happened and couldn't. Could you try again? I would really like to hear it, however you can tell it."

Jake sat, hesitating, but to his core—and for no reason he could name—he trusted Pete. Finally, he said, "Well, it was late—couple nights ago." He took a breath and looked up at the sky. "I *needed* to know so bad. I asked. It sounds so stupid in daylight, but I asked out loud if He was real. I just asked."

"And?"

Jake's mouth opened slightly, then he frowned. He felt something like a wind move through him, and he felt inexplicably like crying. He shook his head. "I can't . . ." He shaped a word and then another before he shook his head again. "I can't describe it."

Pete was still, waiting, watching.

Jake spoke carefully. "It was like my chest filled completely up and broke open, and light . . . came through and around the room. And I was not . . . me. This . . . whatever it was . . . was completely other, outside of me. I was happy, somehow, and . . . warm. And it lasted a long time—not the light—the light went away, but I was not me for a long time, even outside on my paper route. I was happy and . . . It was like I weighed nothing. I hadn't been happy—like, ever. I didn't know what to do. I just grinned a lot." His head slowly dropped. "But it's gone now, that feeling, and I'm sure it wasn't real."

There was a long silence between them, and when Jake glanced sideways at Pete, he saw closed eyes and folded hands and a nod before Pete looked at him.

"So. You've met. You have met both His law in your conscience and His love in your heart. What an amazing grace, Jake."

"But . . ." Jake shook his hanging head. "It just lasted a minute maybe. I can't repeat the experience. I wish I could because the scientist inside me is laughing his head off. I may not ever feel that way again."

"Will you ever forget that experience?"

A breeze moved the branches overhead and the sibilance sounded like a long breath above them.

"No."

"That experience will change your life, unless I'm much mistaken. There are all kinds of different experiences according to the human need, but God has made Himself known to you, and that changes everything, doesn't it?"

Jake thought for a while, and then, shivering, he stood up and began to pace back and forth. "It's so strange. I do know there's been a shift, like a little of the heaviness in my gut has gotten lighter." He looked at Pete and sat down hard on the bench again. "I really don't trust that what happened was real, and I get afraid again. But I also want that feeling back. It was the highest high ever, and without any drugs at all!"

"I know." Pete grinned broadly and took a small leather Bible from the inside pocket of his jacket and handed it to Jake. "You might want to try to read this. These guys are doing the best they can to talk about the truth as they saw it too. And with the help of the breath of God, they do a good job. You can trust it."

CHAPTER TWENTY-SIX: NELL'S STORY

Jake thumbed open the Bible, stared absently at the front matter and fine print, sifting through to wherever it really started.

"In the beginning God created the heaven and the earth," he read quietly to himself, his belly pressed flat against the daybed, the blankets rumpled uncomfortably beneath him.

He read on, the words coming easily, through a bit about a garden and some people sewing fig leaves. But the words wouldn't stick in his brain. The more he read, the more his mind wandered back to thoughts of prison.

Prison. He could see himself sitting there at the dinner table one evening as his father returned from the phone, his face pale like barren storm clouds.

Teresa asked, "¿Qué te pasa?"

Roger shook his head. "Juan. Remember Juan?"

She nodded, her dark eyes large with questions.

Roger spoke the rest to Jake in his characteristic shorthand. "Good little worker. Eight to ten for armed robbery. Got himself beaten to death up at the big house."

Marguerita gasped and began to cry.

Roger went on, "About your size, Jake. Small guys shouldn't go to prison with the animals they got in there. You better start with the weights, kid. Learn some ugly self-defense—just in case."

Seeing Jake's expression, he laughed. "Ah, kid, don't worry. Just keep on being careful. They ain't gonna catch ya."

§

The evening was mild and the earth warmed toward spring. The creeping phlox, flush with purple bloom, sprawled near the concrete steps, and a few jonquils were nodding their pale heads beside the walk. Nell was sitting alone, smoking, at the concrete table in front of her trailer. Jake rode past to stow his bike on his way home from work, but he didn't see her sitting there in the dark, so he didn't speak.

The tip of her cigarette rose and fell, glowing hot and dimming, drifts of blue smoke rising into the dark.

The moon, almost full, dodged in and out of quicksilver clouds. The timid puffs sweeping along made the moon seem to be moving, made it seem playful.

In a few minutes Jake came from Charlie's shed, the bike safely locked inside. He was carrying the groceries she had asked for, and his head was down until she said hi out of the dark.

He jumped and they laughed. He set one of the bags on the bench across from her. "What happened? Did Uncle Eb throw you out?"

She grinned and took another drag before she said, "He's deep into *Aladdin* for about the fortieth time. He didn't even look up when I left."

"Oh boy. We just watched that last week. I think I'll fix a sandwich and bring it out, unless you want to smoke by yourself."

"No, I'd like the company. Come on out. Nice night."

Jake nodded and hauled the groceries inside. When he returned, carrying a bologna sandwich on a plate, a can of Coke in the other hand, and a large bag of potato chips under his arm, he set himself down across from her.

"I thought I was fixing plenty of spaghetti, but your uncle Ebenezer ate up your share. He can sure put away the food. I need to start fixing you a plate and put it in the microwave before he ever sees it."

143

"Aw, that's okay. I'm fine with this." He gestured with the sandwich. "You don't need to worry about me, you know. I been fixing for myself for a long time now."

They sat quietly while Jake ate and the moon poked in and out of the clouds above them.

"You know," Jake said hesitantly, "Eb seems to be getting some strength in his legs. I walked him almost out to the main street Tuesday night, and when we got back, he got up the steps pretty well."

"That's great, Jake. You're good with him. He fell with me one time and I quit trying to walk him anymore."

Nell reached over and got a handful of chips out of the bag. Jake asked, "Want some tea or a beer?"

"Yeah. A Bud would taste real nice right about now."

After Jake fetched the pack and sat down again, she took a swallow, set down the can, and lit another Marlboro. As a stream of pale smoke drifted toward the treetops, she said, "You know, it's real nice having you here. You're a lot like your grandmother."

Jake chewed in silence, then said, "I guess that's good. I never knew her."

Nell peered at him, her brow bunched over her crooked glasses. "What's your first memory—from when you were little?"

Jake was silent so long she thought he'd forgotten or hadn't heard the question. But then he said, "I remember a fire."

"*You do?* You remember the fire?" When he nodded, she said, "You were awful little. Maybe eighteen, twenty months old is all."

He spoke slowly, "I remember somebody screaming . . . and a big, bright fire, but that's all."

The night seemed to close in. No cars passed and the birds were still, listening.

Nell spoke slowly. "You were staying with me. I ran over there with you in my arms, but I was too late."

"Were you screaming?"

144

"Several of us were, but you probably heard your mother."

The silence between them became part of the night.

"What happened?" Jake asked.

Nell took another drag and blew smoke slowly into the dusk. "Well, your mother's mother was my sister, Nancy Ann." Nell took several swallows of beer and went on. "You call me 'aunt,' and I forget sometimes. I'm your great-aunt. Anyway, she was real pretty, and she loved our little baby brother as much as I did. He was 'different,' of course, but that made him more lovable in our eyes. He was just going to be our baby always."

Nell looked at him. "Sorry, Jake, you don't want all this old history."

"Yes, I do. I've never heard it."

Nell chuckled to herself. "Bless his sweet heart. I begged for baby Ebbie so hard. Both of us did. I think we wanted a live doll to play with. I was eleven and Nancy Ann was ten years old then, and God knows we didn't have much to play with. I know Mama didn't want no baby, but Daddy did. He wanted a son and what Daddy wanted he usually got. He was killed on a tractor without ever seeing Ebenezer. Never knew he was afflicted. Probably just as well.

"Mama grieved heavy for Daddy, so she just gave Ebbie over to Nancy and me. I think Mama started toward death the day Daddy was killed. Took her seven years to do it, but she died when I was eighteen. Nancy Ann was seventeen and Ebenezer was, um, seven, and the three of us stayed on in Mommy's house."

Nell seemed to be shrinking as she talked. Jake sat silently and waited.

She took a puff and started coughing. When she could, she went on. "Anyway, Nancy Ann was real pretty and she married a pretty boy. Sam was his name, Samuel Miller Jr., son of the big road contractor, Sam Sr., and even if I shouldn't speak ill of the dead, Sammy Jr. was nothing but Nancy Ann's big mistake.

"He was the son of a drinker, and pretty soon a drunk himself—and worse, a wife beater. He made her life a living hell. But still, pretty soon she had KatieLyn, your mother, and the two of us sisters worshiped the ground that child stood on. So now, Nan had little KatieLyn and I had Eb, and the four of us were together ever single day. That was a happy time—while they were small. We had lots of fun. You should have seen them two babies dressed up in some of the costumes we put on 'em!"

She paused and turned her eyes to Jake. "You can love a child too much, you know. Remember that when you have kids. Don't know which was worse in the long run—the neglect you got, or the spoiling she got." She took a deep last draw on her cigarette and stubbed it out on the lid of her empty beer can, then pulled another beer out of the pack.

Finally she continued in monotone, "Thanks be to God, Sam didn't stick around long. Died of his drunk driving—missed the turn and launched that little sports car right off Carpenter's Cliff. The Millers, his parents, considered themselves good people though, and they finished off the payments on the big house that pretty-boy Sam had bought, so Nancy Ann and her baby daughter had a nice place to live, just three blocks from here.

"When your mama was little, with her bouncy white-blond curls and her cute little ways—well, the whole of Harlan was in love with her from the time she was able to totter around."

By now, Jake was hardly breathing, yet he lost his breath when Nell said flatly, "She aborted the first baby she was pregnant with. KatieLyn did, I mean. She was just thirteen damn years old, thinking she's grown up. How she found somebody to do the abortion—and survived it—I'll never know. We didn't know nothing about it till it was too damn late. Nan just about died when she found out. Had to go to bed, she was crying so hard. Stayed in bed for a week, and KatieLyn just swanned around everywhere, laughing and fooling, showing how it meant less than nothin' to her.

"By then I had pretty much figured out where your mother was headed. She flat couldn't get enough of boys, couldn't keep her knickers on, and nobody could talk any sense into her . . . so I wasn't too surprised when she ran off after that last beauty pageant. Nancy Ann and me still entered her in those, still hoping for fame and fortune in her life—hoping if she won, she'd get some self-respect, I guess. But she ran off. When she showed up again, she said she'd married some guy named Roger we didn't know. He had dumped her after a month or two, and now she's pregnant again.

"This time we managed to keep her out of the damned abortion clinic—and it was you. I thought you were the best, most beautiful baby boy in the world. We—both your grandmother and me—we had great foolish hopes that KatieLyn would be changed by having a baby. We thought you might fix her somehow, settle her down, but . . ."

Nell stopped suddenly. Her voice had droned dully word after word like rocks dropping in sand, as though she had no feelings at all about the sad saga she was weaving, but suddenly she seemed to remember her audience. "Aw shit, Jake. I shouldn't be telling you all this about your mother."

Jake laughed without humor. "No, it helps me figure out some things. I always wondered if it was my fault—her being so unhappy, all the time looking, trying to find something or somebody to make her happy. Something—or somebody—that wasn't me."

Jake stopped talking and stared off at nothing until his voice came again, cold. "I hated her so much and loved her at the same time. How can a person hold both those feelings so close together?"

"I know. Feels like a train wreck inside, don't it? I felt the very same way toward her before the fire. Afterwards I just plain hated her, and some of all that bad feeling got put off on you. I hate to admit it, but it's true. When she took you and moved away, seemed like I just shut down all that loving part and shriveled up into the ugly old lady I am now."

Jake waited for her to continue, patiently listening to the night. After it seemed she had stopped for good, Jake prompted, "What about the fire, Aunt Nell?"

"Yeah. This is the hard part." Nell finished her second beer, and when it was gone, so was her energy for telling. She sat slumped at the table and let the night sounds fold in around them. She shook her head slowly and looked up at Jake. "Sorry, kid. I just hate this story, and it may not help you with your momma none." She looked over the trees at the sky. "But maybe it's a clue to her. Maybe it might show us both what she's been lookin' for all these years—the thing that ain't anything you could give her. I never thought about it like that."

She sat still and sighed. "I better go check on Eb. I'll be back . . . if you're sure you want to know the worst."

When he nodded, she sighed again and leaned forward to push herself up on hands that spread out on the table like knotted roots. Her eyes never left the ground as she walked, and the wrinkles in her face seemed to have grown deeper while she spoke.

CHAPTER TWENTY-SEVEN: THE FIRE

Nell came back out of the trailer, down the steps, one at a time, and made her way over to set a cold drink the table. "Think I'll sit in this old thing, with a back," she said, flipping an aluminum folding chair around to face the table. She tested the loose plastic webbing of the seat, decided it would hold her, and sat down with a sigh.

Jake snatched some trash he had seen blowing around the narrow yard and put it in the garbage can, then came over and sat down on top of the table, facing her, his feet propped on the bench. He bent forward and rested his elbows on his knees. "You okay?" he asked.

She glanced at him, pulled her cigarettes out of her pants pocket, lit one, and said, "I been wondering whether I ought to be telling this—and whether you need to be knowing it. I think maybe Jesus would tell me to hold my tongue and let you think as good of your mother as you can."

Jake snorted wearily through his nose. "Well, I try not to think about her at all, Nell. She's never thought much about me."

A breeze lifted the dry, gray hair from Nell's neck. She took a sip of her icy drink and then rested her forearms resolutely on the arms of the chair. "Yeah, okay. Where was I?"

Squinting into the past through the rising smoke, she said, "Well, the next thing was your grandmother had a stroke—soon after you were born. Rare at such a young age, but it happens. This was a bad one, and then she had several more over a year's time—and she ended up not able to walk. Some strokes you can't fix. A person just has to learn to live with it. But she was just thirty-eight years old—skin and bones—and my beautiful Nancy Ann spent her days in a wheelchair by the front window, always looking for you and your mom to come back home."

Nell flicked her cigarette ash onto the ground and dragged on it a couple of times, unaware of anything but her story.

"KatieLyn was always going. She left you with Eb and me mostly—or some other friend of hers. She never left you alone with her mother. She had more sense than that, anyway.

"She had a job. I'll give her that. She had got on with the dollar store, but never put together enough hours to add up to much. Mainly she lived on her mother's money." She took a pull and blew pale smoke toward the sky. "Not that Nan minded. Not a bit. She wanted you all there every minute and she gladly paid the bills, but it was like your mother couldn't stand being cooped up in that house any more than a tiger likes a cage."

She shook her head and smiled nostalgically. "You were the cutest little guy, and real sweet tempered! Eb and I loved to see you coming. Eb would carry you around all day long. I was afraid you'd never learn to walk, 'cause he wouldn't ever put you down long enough.

"Lots of times if KatieLyn asked me to babysit while she was working, or playing around, you and me and Ebenezer would go spend the day with Nancy Ann. You learned to walk in that house, with the three of us cheerin' for you."

Nell looked over at Jake. "You ever see a stroke victim?"

When Jake shook his head, she said, "Well, she couldn't talk very well because only one side of her face worked, and she couldn't move the left side of her body. Poor thing. Just hated being waited on. Some days were worse than others. She got real skinny because food didn't taste good."

Nell absently took a last drag and blew a smoke ring into the dark, then leaned over and dropped the glowing butt into a beer can on the table.

"Nan needed a bunch of help getting around, and I wanted them to hire a nurse, but KatieLyn kept saying no, she wanted to take care of her mother, and God forgive me, I let the nurse idea drop.

"One night, KatieLyn came to my door, with you on her hip. 'Aunt Nellie,' she called me, in this fakey sweet voice, like she thought the old charm would work on me. She'd say, 'Aunt Nellie, will you watch Jakey while I go to the grocery store?'—and the pitiful little-girl voice did *not* work on me, but you did. Just one look at your sweet face, and I took you. Even though I didn't approve of all these nighttime trips to the 'store,' I didn't say nothing, and she left. I knew she wasn't going to no grocery store—not the way she was dressed—skirt up to her whatsits and a sweater that dipped around every curve, and bright, bright lipstick. Didn't look like no A&P visit to me, but I didn't say nothing.

"Well, time went on. I rocked you to sleep and finally put you down on my bed. I knew that store closed at nine and it was getting on toward eleven, then past, and going on toward twelve. She didn't often stay out that late, and I got worried and tried to call Nancy Ann, but she was probably too far from the phone. No answer. I planned to have a big old word with KatieLyn when she got back. She needed to put that damn phone over for her momma to use. I'd told her time and time again to move the damn phone when she left. But finally, almost twelve o'clock and the phone rings.

"It was Berthy McAlister next door to Nan. She was screaming that the house was on fire. Took me a minute to realize she meant Nancy Ann's house, not hers. I snatched you out of bed and started running. Ebenezer came after us, in his pajamas, poor thing, waddling along barefooted. Three blocks away and I was hearing all this commotion. Sirens coming from all over town, getting so loud I couldn't think. And then I saw it."

Tears filled Nell's eyes, but she plowed on. "Oh, my good Lord, it was the worst thing I'd ever seen. Windows was breaking all over the house, and Nan's beautiful brocade drapes was flapping and twisting in the flames like they was alive. A wind was whipping all around and it seemed like the house

151

was burning up all at once. I never saw such a thing. The heat was so terrible I couldn't get close, couldn't even get into the yard, and I couldn't stop nobody to ask about my beloved Nancy Ann."

Nell dropped her head into her hand and tears fell.

Finally she raised her head up, her eyes tormented by the memory of that night, her mouth working to contain her grief. "The fire people were running too fast to notice that I was dying right there, not knowing where my sweet sister was. I was beside myself."

Nell stared off into the distance, her hands limp in her apron. The tears had dried on her cheeks before she continued.

"She was in there, helpless, in the bed. Left alone to burn to death was where she was, and KatieLyn had gone to a party. She didn't show up till nothing was left but a hollow house, smoking piles of ash, tottery brick walls. And puddles all over the yard." Her mouth worked and trembled with words too hateful to speak.

"I never saw my Nancy Ann again. They wouldn't open the casket 'cause she was all burnt to a crisp. KatieLyn carried on so at the funeral parlor, lots of people felt sorry for her." She shook her head. "I felt sorry for her about a minute, but when I thought about her leaving her mamma alone in that house, with no phone close to hand . . . in my heart I wanted to kill her. God forgive me, but if I'da had me a weapon, I'd have shot my niece dead and laughed while I was doing it.

"I hated her so much, and it wasn't only me. A lot of people judged her awful hard for what she did that night. I guess we didn't keep our opinions to ourselves in that little town, Jake. People shunned her. We shunned her, no two ways about it. So after a while, after she ran through most of her inheritance, she pulled up her roots—put you in her little red sports car and took off to Louisville."

Nell sat slumped over, her head resting on one hand. "She called me several times, mostly when she ran out of money. I sure didn't get to see much of you anymore. I guess, truth be told, I only took her phone calls and lent her money because I was afraid Nancy Ann might be looking down from heaven, wantin' me to treat her baby right."

Jake sat with her silently, both of them looking out at the night.

"I just miss my sister so much," Nell said, and silence held them still.

Jake finally spoke. "That's a terrible story." Nell nodded. No more words, no more beer or smokes. No consolation.

At last, she got up and started to go inside, but turned back toward Jake. "When you get old, you just get too tired to carry all that ugliness around. It's a heavy thing, hate is, and turns you bitter, eats at you all the time and don't do nothing to punish the one you're mad at. Couple years back, when we started listening to the TV preachers, I started praying to the good Lord to help me quit being so bitter, and He does help with that—most of the time."

She walked back to him and laid a hand on his shoulder. "I want you to try, Jake—if you can at all—try to forgive your mother for the things she done wrong to you. I think that may be what she's looking for. She's lookin' everywhere for a little bit of forgiveness and love. Try to do like Jesus says and forgive her, 'cause it ain't doing you a bit of good to hold onto those memories. Let's us both do it, okay?" Jake slowly reached up and laid his hand on hers. Then his head sagged over and his cheek rested on their hands.

"I don't know, Nell. Maybe. I'll try. Forgiveness is something we all need maybe."

After she made her way up to the front stoop and inside the trailer, Jake sat on through most of an hour, while sadness settled across his shoulders like a heavy blanket.

CHAPTER TWENTY-EIGHT: COLLISION COURSE

Milli's troubled eyes continued to haunt Jake, and he found himself wishing to see her, and talk with her. It had been weeks since he'd seen her. He wondered what she would think of Pete. He wondered why she had run off.

He started making time to walk his uncle Ebenezer around the trailer park, and Eb's big grin eased Jake's mind. While they slowly made their rounds, he thought often of the fire that had deformed his aunt's life—the fire that had left her with the burden of care for her brother, and no one to share it with.

Why does so much trouble come to the good, the innocents of the world? Why all the pain?

The question began to turn endlessly in his head, especially as it echoed down the deep well in his heart where he had been keeping the man on the side of the road. A human being—a man with a soul—dead because Jake casually ordered one more drink and failed to ignore his damned phone.

§

The sun had made its appearance, but it was low: a pale disk in the mist that drifted among the trees. Spring was near and the trees were budding, their branches swelling with sap and small leaves. Gravel skittered from beneath Jake's bike wheels as he leaned into the shortcut through the city park.

When he rounded the huge boxwood hedge on the corner, he nearly plowed head-on into a runner, but he swerved quickly and clipped the guy on one arm.

"Hey!" they both yelled in defiance, as the big man spun, caught his balance and began to dance backward, running in place, his voice changed to surprised recognition. "Well, hey there, Jake!"

Jake braked hard and circled back. "Pete! Sorry! Didn't see you behind the bushes. You hurt?" He stopped and stood astride the bike.

"Nah!" Pete shook his head, grinning. He was still breathing hard from his run and he leaned over with his palms on his knees to catch his breath. He peered up at Jake and said, "I was just thinking about calling you, man."

"Yeah?"

The preacher stood up again. "Yeah. How are you doing?"

Jake shook his head. "Well, just doing, I reckon. I've been thinking about you too, but . . ." His voice trailed off as he failed to find a meaningful excuse.

Pete nodded. "It's okay. No problem. Just glad to see you're still around."

"Oh, yeah . . . Still around." His lips shaped a thought, but he was helpless in the search for coherence and came to a halt, frowning. "Well, I tried to read the Bible some, but kind of bogged down."

"I imagine you did." Pete pushed his lips out thoughtfully. "I thought later, probably. With all you got going on, now would be a hard time to focus."

"Yeah, thanks, Pete. It's tough." Jake looked at the ground. "I guess I've gone backwards a little."

The quiet between them was stirred by the sound of emergency sirens on the main street.

"How about stopping by the office? I'm headed over there right now, and I'll put the coffee pot on."

Jake looked at him, hesitation and conflict clouding his thoughts, but somehow Pete's calm face and friendly smile loosened Jake's resistance, and he found himself saying, "Yeah. Okay."

§

Jake marveled as he climbed the ramp to the entrance at the rear of the little church building. The door gleamed with a glossy coat of black paint and a new brass doorknob set. As he looked around, he noticed the fresh white everywhere—on the wooden clapboard siding and the window trim—and even new black on the wrought iron railings. It seemed somebody had been working on the building since he had last hunkered down on the porch.

He opened the door and walked into a lunchroom where the clean smell of Lysol competed with fried chicken. Folding chairs were stacked neatly on two rows of long metal tables, and a stove and refrigerator sat at one end of the room, next to a sink and a set of worn metal kitchen cabinets. The floor gleamed with polish.

There was an open door at the other end, and Pete's voice rolled throughout the lunchroom, "Welcome. Come on back."

As Jake approached the doorway of the office, he peered into a small space with a window and a big, shiny mahogany desk, but no sign of Pete until his head and shoulders rose up from behind the handsome piece of furniture. It reminded Jake of their first meeting and the baby bottle, but this time the man held up a pink pacifier that looked extra tiny in his broad fingers. Jake heard the stirrings and fussy sounds of an infant out of sight behind the desk.

Pete sprang from behind the desk and came barreling toward Jake, saying, "Sorry, gotta wash this thing. Charlotte just dropped her off, and her rule is that God don't approve of pacifiers picked off the floor going into the mouth!"

Jake grinned, watching as Pete bent over the kitchen sink to wash the tiny pacifier. He returned, holding it aloft in two fingers, an embarrassed grin on his face.

"Where is she, the owner of that little whatchacallit?" Jake asked.

"Come on over here." Pete's face lit up as he pointed to the stroller be-hind his desk where a tiny infant, wrapped snugly in a pink-and-yellow blan-

ket, slept soundly, her breath blowing bubbles from the corner of her puck-
ered lips. Her skin was perfect silk and just the color of mocha latte, her hair
a cap of black curls. "Meet Kaleena."

Jake stared at sleeping perfection. "She's beautiful . . ." he muttered, unsure how to pitch such words.

"That's about the way I feel." Pete leaned over and tried to replace the
pacifier in her mouth, but the baby lips resisted and he carefully put it down
beside the blanket. The stroller seat had been laid down flat and the baby
seemed blissfully content, wrapped like a burrito in the bed on wheels, oblivious to the voices around her.

"Does she sleep a lot?" Jake asked.

"Real well during the day! Charlotte fed her before she dropped her off,
so I imagine she's down for at least a couple of hours, maybe three. Let's have
us a seat and talk awhile. How about a cup of coffee?"

"No thanks." Jake followed him out of the office into the kitchen area
and watched as he swung a couple of folding chairs off a stack, opened both
of them with a practiced jerk, and set them down at a corner of one of the
long tables.

Jake sat, rubbing at the tension in his neck and shoulders, while Pete
poured himself a cup of coffee. "Where you from, Jake?"

Jake shrugged. "Well, just recently, from Bedford Green."

"Yeah? Never been there. That's where Western State University is—
right? The Hawks?"

"Yeah, that's right. I was a student there."

Pete came over and straddled his chair, making it look just a little too
small. "Do you have much family there?"

"Just my father. My mother was kind of born with a dissatisfaction dis-
order, I guess you might say, and we moved a lot. Lived in apartments in
Louisville until she got herself in big trouble. When I was sixteen, she was
sentenced to three years for drugs, and signed custody of me over to my
father. I'd never met him before that, so he was a surprise—a *big* surprise.

But basically I've pretty much been on my own since . . . well, since I got on a school bus, I guess."

"Did you like school?"

There was a long pause before Jake said to the floor, "I felt safe at school. It was good not to get yelled at or hit, and every school I went to was better than being at home." He looked up, surprised to realize the truth of his words. "I guess you remind me a little of Mr. Phillips. He was math. I liked numbers and he liked me. We were friends for a little while."

He stopped there and studied the vinyl tiles on the floor. After a pause, he asked, "You ever visit Peewee Valley?" He tried to speak casually, but his voice trembled, and he shut himself up.

"Where's Peewee Valley?" Pete asked.

Jake shook his head and shrugged. "That's Kentucky's prison for women. Mom was there when I went to live in Bedford Green."

Pete watched him from above the rim of his steaming cup. "How did you end up here in Union Gate?"

"My great-aunt lives here, and my uncle. They took care of me when I was little. I guess, when I needed a place to go for a while, I knew she'd take me in. I owe them a lot." A clock ticked somewhere and Jake retreated behind lowered eyes, fiddled with a pack of gum, unwrapped a piece, and put it in his mouth.

Pete said, "I'd like to meet them sometime."

Jake stayed away somewhere in his thoughts, and after an awkward silence, Pete asked, "If you could be anything, have any kind of life, any kind of career, what would you do?"

Jake's eyes flew to Pete's face and then, staring out the window, he said. "I was going to be an astronomer."

"An *astronomer*? Whoa."

"I know. Weird, right? But it's funny . . . calculus, geometry, physics—all that—comes easy, and my astronomy professor at Western said I should consider becoming an astrophysicist." A flash of disappointment crinkled his eyes, and he shrugged again.

"Are you giving up on that idea?"

"Well, I reckon I've pretty much screwed it. I'm not going to be a prime candidate for grad school if I'm headed to jail for killing a guy." Again his eyes sought the sky through the back window and he frowned. "No, not just 'a guy.' No. His name was Harold W. Roebling. I looked it up, the newspaper account. I think a lot about him."

Jake swallowed hard and then recited, "'Harold W. Roebling, 73, a prominent local farmer and state legislator, husband of Louise Burke Roebling, was killed in a hit-and-run incident on Magadenz Road Friday night. Blunt-force trauma listed as cause of death. Any person having knowledge pertaining to . . .' etcetera, etcetera, quote, unquote."

He looked at Pete. "So. You were right, there is a family over in Bedford Green. Probably wantin' to see me in the electric chair, I imagine. I would, if I was them."

Pete shrugged. "Possibly. Though people surprise you sometimes. They don't always act the way you'd think. It's pretty likely, though, that they're in considerable pain."

The clock ticked on and Jake shifted in his chair, gripping and releasing the metal frame, until he finally spoke, "Most all my life, I been bent over double, just trying to survive. Never much thought I'd make it this far. Got in ever kind of trouble there is. Then, all of a sudden, it was like a door opened up in a high school math class." He paused, remembering. "Mr. Phillips, the guy you remind me of, pulled me out in front to work a problem on the board."

He struggled to navigate the flowing river of his thoughts. "The weirdest thing is that once I saw the idea that I might be good at something . . . and once I wanted to be someone, then I started looking around to see how other people lived, and later, after the scholarship got me into Western, I saw how my professor thought about his life. He just walked so different. He had confidence in himself. Didn't take drugs to feel good. That's what it was. He felt good all the time, I guess." Jake flushed and he rubbed his face with the palms of his hands.

"I wanted that: to have confidence in myself. Professor Greathammer had a friend at Ohio State, and he said that if I kept up the hard work, he probably could get me an assistantship to go to grad school up there. I never heard of that kind of opportunity. He had to explain it. Grad school. Wow." He breathed the words. "And Ohio State has one of the best astronomy departments in the country. Did you know that?"

Pete shook his head.

Jake had slipped down in the chair, his legs crossed at the ankles and his arms folded across his chest. His mind rambled across his life, and he was hardly aware of speaking his thoughts aloud, but the words kept spilling out.

"But now, when I wake up, all the hope is gone. There's just this sickness." He bit his thumbnail; his eyes roamed the room from under heavy lids.

Pete waited, and finally Jake blew a short laugh, pushing his head back. "I've tried to get drunk twice and can't. Tasted awful. Tried to pick up a girl, but she bailed. Everything that used to be an escape is closed off."

He turned his head slowly and looked squarely at Pete. "You know what I think? I think this God of yours has backed me into a corner."

He had come to the end of his words and just sat there, staring at nothing. "I think the man I wanted to be—that man would go back and face it."

Pete straightened, his eyes focused on the younger man's face as he waited for the next words.

Jake sat up and leaned forward, elbows on his knees, head bowed, but his voice was clear. "I think I have to go back there and turn myself in."

Then he lifted his gaze to Pete's face, his need written large in his own. "I don't guess you'd go with me, would you?"

CHAPTER TWENTY-NINE: THE SWING

The rusty chains holding up the front porch swing made a soft and rhythmic *screech, screech* as Milli and her grandmother swung back and forth in the peaceful hour before dark. The sun was setting beyond the sixty-foot sugar maple and the rosy sky lit their faces.

They had been going through boxes and trunks in the attic for most of the day, sorting the keepers from the discards, and before supper Milli had dragged three large trash bags down the steps and out to the road for pickup. After dinner, she helped finish up the dishes, and when Gran suggested they sit out front a while, she hung up the dish towel gladly and followed her out to the porch.

Both of them avoided looking at the SOLD sign in the yard as they swung back and forth.

Gran spoke softly, "Do you really know how much I love you?"

"Yes, but I love you to the moon and back!" They'd repeated the line since Milli was four.

After a time Milli spoke, her voice almost a whisper, "Please, let's just stay here, Gran. I'll look for a job and help with the bills. Maybe you could sell the bottomland, and we'd be happy right here in this pretty house."

Gran picked up her hand. "You will always be a precious part of my life, and you know that I will have a guest room available for you at Magnolia Terrace anytime you want to use it."

"But . . ."

"No buts, dear heart. I'm too old to manage this house anymore by myself, much less handle the farm chores. Hank will do a good job with this farm. It's the right thing for him and me both."

Gran unfolded the fist Milli had been unaware of making. "I'm a little worried about you though."

"Why?" A shiver ran down Milli's spine.

"I can't put my finger on it, exactly. I just have a feeling that something's bothering you."

Milli sat, feeling her hair blow against her cheeks as the breeze added lift to the swing's movement. The silvery white blooms of the old Henryi clematis nodded from the trellis at the other end of the porch, and she could catch the delicate scent of vanilla drifting on the light wind.

"Well . . . I just wish I could move over here near you. This is my favorite place, you are my favorite person, and I like myself more when I'm here with you. I will miss this farm so much."

"I know," Gran said. "Me too."

Milli had become very still, riding back and forth with her head down. The porch swing chains continued to groan into the stillness.

"Gran, I guess I need to talk to you about something . . ."

Screech, screech . . . screech . . . screech . . . Slower now.

Her grandmother spoke gently. "You know I'll always love you, no matter what."

Milli felt the knot inside loosen, and the familiar urge to confess thickened in her throat.

The swing came to a stop and Milli got up, went inside for a tissue, and came back out scrubbing at her face. She sat and after a moment her grandmother started the swing moving again.

The light had almost faded behind the tree when Milli said, "Billy Mac came home on leave at New Year's, and he—well, he called one night and, um . . ." She took a breath and spoke on the exhale. "I went out with him."

"You and . . . Billy Mac?" Disbelief was tucked under the words. Milli heard it, and from the corner of her eye she saw that Gran's forehead had creased into a worried frown over her glasses.

She nodded her head slowly. She knew that her Gran knew . . . *something* . . . and her heart sank.

From the darkness deep in the maple, a starling called to his mate and then repeated the notes.

"We're not just talking about going out for ice cream, are we?"

Milli's head had dropped to her chest and she shook it slowly.

"Are we talking about sex, Milli?"

Her yes was barely audible.

"Oh, *Lord*."

"I'm so sorry, Gran, please don't worry. It's all over now."

"Oh, honey, I just wish you had told me before this. How long, I mean . . . How long have you been involved with Billy Mac?"

"Well . . ." Milli sought the words. She couldn't possibly describe the long months it had taken the two of them to segue from friendship to playful teasing, and then into seductive games of experimentation and finally late-night consummations.

She turned her head to look through the window into the lamplit living room. Her grandmother's world was so different from hers. Simple. Filled with music and flowers and home-canned vegetables in the pantry. And love, quiet and strong and sure of what was right and what was wrong.

How could she tell Gran about the other world she lived in? The world where the TV pounded out the daily seductive message: freedom, sex, alcohol, and fast cars; where the family rooms racketed with noise and constant commotion, loud arguments, and laughter; where all of it seemed to circle her without including her—until the small hours after midnight when the door to her room opened and tall, good-looking Billy Mac slid through it, whispering her name, wanting her.

Milli shook her head at the curtains of Gran's house. She loved those rooms. The sweet peace inside seemed to call to her. She yearned toward the quietness where goodness was, where a silent voice spoke of grace.

Gran asked softly, "Help me understand. Do you think you are in love with your cousin?"

"No. It has nothing to do with love—not like you and Grandad, or Margaret and Dart, for that matter. I've seen two people love each other and it's not like that. It's . . ." Her head was bent and she stared down at her fingers, twisting them together, fidgeting. "I should have talked to you before now. I wanted to, but I couldn't."

She took a deep breath, "I . . . I just really loved his attention, Gran. It felt so good that he wanted me." She stumbled to a stop. Then she blurted, "It's a real miracle I haven't gotten pregnant." Her grandmother stirred. Without looking at her, Milli hurried to add, "Oh, we were careful and always used condoms, but still, Sally Marshall got pregnant, and she said they . . . well, you know."

She sighed and scooted down on the swing, twisting a strand of hair. When she glanced over, her grandmother's face was etched with the deep frown of loving concern that Milli knew so well.

"Gran, I felt like I was invisible at Margaret's and Gert's houses. I was so . . . well, by myself all the time. It seemed like nobody in the family ever really talked to me but him. I didn't have any friends at school. They seemed so silly, those girls. I just stayed to myself. Not that he ever spoke to me around the other kids, or anything. But when we were alone, he made me feel good, like I was the only one for him, like I was exceptional, beautiful even, and the secret friend who understood him. He never tried to force me except for one time—the first time—and he was really sorry. I could see that he was sorry; I believed him. After that, I could say yes or no to him—the mighty Billy Mac." She paused, and then added softly, "I guess I liked the power I had over him, Gran. That's a rotten thing to say, isn't it?"

The words gradually dissipated in the cool air, and the swing moved more slowly. Milli turned her head toward the road and watched a car's headlights sweep past the mailbox. She listened to the lonesome sound diminish with the increasing distance, before she saw her grandmother's face. "Oh, please don't cry, Gran. It isn't going to happen again, I promise. It's not that big of a deal."

"Oh, but it is, Milli. It is a great big deal." Gran felt in her pocket for her handkerchief, took her glasses off and wiped her eyes. Milli wished she could take her confession out of the air between them. Shame burned in her chest like a knife between her ribs.

"Listen, Gran, I am never, *ever* going to do it again. Please don't think I'm bad." And tears stood in Milli's eyes, burning.

"Sweetheart, I know you, and you're not bad. Not bad. I will never have a question about that. But I am terribly sad that I didn't know you were that unhappy and lonely. Am I to understand that you chose a sexual relationship to make yourself feel better? Is that it?"

"It wasn't actually something I chose to do, Gran. Not really." She, searching for words to explain. "It was more like, at first, I just loved the attention, the teasing. But then I . . . My body began to take over from my brain and I didn't want to say 'stop' anymore. I had no idea that, um, the urge could feel so strong. It was like I sort of lost my footing and fell into . . ." She stumbled along through images. "Into a place I couldn't stand up and climb out of, you know?" Milli sensed her grandmother's nod before she whispered, "It felt so good I lost track of what was right."

For a while they swung back and forth silently. Milli picked a clematis blossom.

"I tried to pray about it. Down deep I knew what we were doing was wrong—especially after we started to . . . you know, the serious stuff . . . And when I was away from him, I wanted to stop. I was disgusted with myself. I prayed for help, but it seemed like God was never there, or like He wasn't listening. The room always felt empty."

An owl sounded softly from a distant tree, a gentle comment in the night, and Gran sighed. She looked quietly into the darkness, and for Milli the moments seemed endless until Gran's words came again, spoken kindly, and with such compassion that Milli could feel the burn of tears welling again.

"I know just how that feels, Milli. I've been there too. But no room is ever empty when we pray—we have to know that. However, if we're holding on to something, unsure of whether we want to let go when we pray, then . . ." Gran hesitated before starting again, "Mmm." Gran's voice was soft and full of sadness. "Prayer. Such an earth-shaking thing, when we slow down enough to think what we're doing. Coming into the very presence of God." She took a deep breath. "And once we're there, we are literally asking something of the God and Maker of the universe."

There was a long silence. Despite the quiet, Milli felt as though she was being held warmly in a quiet room where someone important was coming.

"The thing is, Milli, I believe we must be *ready* to find God, *ready* for Him to find us. And ready for what He has to tell us. And when there is something in our lives that has hold of us in some powerful way, we aren't ready, and our ears, our hearts are closed to Him."

Gran turned her head and looked closely into Milli's eyes. "Fighting the war inside our souls between the part that yearns toward light and goodness, and the other side that loves darkness and finds delicious the thoughts and deeds we keep secret. That battle is harder than anyone is ever ready for. We can know scripture, and make all kinds of vows, but it is a war in the soul, my girl, and a terrible one."

For a moment Milli's eyes held, and then her lids fell, her eyelashes sweeping her cheeks. She nodded slowly. "You're right of course. It was more 'I want you to fix me, God, I think . . . but I'm not sure . . . maybe wait a while.' I guess that isn't prayer, is it?"

Again the sad smile, and Gran admitted, "Sweetheart, who am I to answer the biggest questions of our lives? But this I know: we are taught to pray. Always. And Christ teaches us to ask God to deliver us from evil. And then we are to obey. Correct?"

Milli nodded slowly.

"'For thine is the kingdom, and the power, and the glory.' He is so much more, so far beyond our understanding, that one poor prophet calling on the eternal God has stopped the world in its turning for a day.

"And that same God stoops to hold us as we fall, Milli, and He holds us as we lie where we have fallen, without strength. And then He helps us up again, so each day we can start again, washed and clean, forgiven."

Milli listened, turning a white clematis blossom in her hand, barely breathing as star after star appeared in the dark purple sky.

§

The next day was overcast and gloomy, a perfect day for sorting a room full of books into keepers and givers. Gran brushed her hands on her apron and asked, "How about a cup of tea?"

Milli had been quiet all morning and looked up with distant thoughts in her eyes, but Gran caught her hand and led her into the kitchen, where with the touch of a switch they were wrapped in warm lamplight. Gran clicked on the gas flame beneath the kettle.

Milli leaned back against the counter and folded her hands in front of her, watching her thumbs circle each other.

Gran kept an eye on her while the kettle muttered. "What time is your father coming Tuesday?"

"'Late' is all he said. 'After work,' so I guess he'll be here around eight."

"You think he'll want to spend the night?"

"No. He wants to get back. He sounded kind of bummed about having to come, but Aunt Gert is still down with the flu."

"When has Barley ever sounded cheerful about anything?" Gran rolled her eyes.

"Yeah." Milli grimaced. "Seems like never."

Gran's voice softened. "His life must be hard also, honey. He adored your mother. I'll give him that. Both of you have suffered without her, I know. I'll make a pecan pie for him Tuesday. He used to love my pecan pie and ice cream."

The kettle shrieked suddenly, startling them both. When Gran had poured herself tea and sweetened it, she said, "Let's sit down for a few more minutes."

Milli sat and leaned her elbows on the table, rubbing at the beginnings of the headache that usually followed a hard cry.

"Sweetheart?"

When Milli looked up, Gran was watching her with an expression of such love and sympathy that once again Milli felt tears threaten, though after last night, it was a desert wind that blew through her head. Gran came and sat in the chair beside her and put her arms around the narrow shoulders.

"Honey, this is not the end of the world. You have the rest of your life ahead of you. But, darling, you've got to take hold of it and steer it in a good direction. God expects you to use your gifts." The grip on Milli's shoulders was strong as Gran shook her slightly for emphasis. "Give yourself plenty of room to avoid Billy Mac in the future, and you will find the true and beautiful Millicent inside the gorgeous clothes you've been making this spring. There's a great girl in there that will have nothing to be ashamed of, you know."

Milli's head stayed bent over her chest as Gran walked back around the table to her place, sat down, and took a thoughtful sip of her tea. "Whatever happened to the idea of college and fashion design?"

Milli shook her head and looked out the window, where the gray day pressed against the glass. "Dad said he couldn't afford it, and cousin Mary Beth wanted me to help after her baby came." She shrugged. "Shit happens."

"Not necessarily, sweetheart. We're discussing the kind of life you're choosing for yourself and the way to go forward. I will not allow you to shrug and say 'shit happens.'" The twinkle in her eye softened her words, but Milli cringed slightly. Her Gran rarely spoke sharply, and Milli took it seriously.

"That kind of dismissal accepts defeat without making any real effort."

Gran shoved her tea away, sloshing a little into the saucer. "Milli, listen to me. You have several God-given talents, and being a loving babysitter is just one of them. Someone else can take over that job at this stage of your life. Right now, we need to look at your other options." Gran paused and seemed to bring a memory into focus. "Over and over since you were a little thing on the porch out there with your paper dolls, you have shown an amazing gift for art and fashion design. You are now over eighteen and no longer dependent on your father. When we close on the farm, I should have a little nest egg. You can have all or part of it if you will grab yourself by the straps of those combat boots and get busy."

Amusement tugged at the corner of her mouth, but Milli could feel a tiny gleam of something beginning to catch fire in her heart. Her mouth opened and closed twice before she said, "You think? Really?"

"I really do think."

"Well, how do I start exactly?"

"Get yourself upstairs on Hank's computer and start looking, girl. See what kind of design department UK has. Look at the Chicago art institute, while you're at it. Type in art and design schools, names of fashion designers you like—see where they studied, what their background is. Don't eliminate any possibility, and come back to talk when we've got something to talk about."

Milli stood and came around the table and hugged the old lady, whispering in her ear, "I love you to the moon and back, Granny!"

They chuckled, but Gran caught Milli's two hands in hers and said, "Don't forget to pray about this, Milli. We need the Lord's help—always, but especially when we're talking about restarting your life."

She released Milli's hands. "I'll finish down here; you skedaddle upstairs." Gran smiled as the boots thumped up the steps two at a time.

CHAPTER THIRTY: BRIGHTER MORNING

The next morning, the smell of frying bacon drifted through the house, and Milli hurried into the kitchen. "Sorry, Gran, I meant to be early. Am I too late to make the biscuits?"

Her grandmother glanced over her shoulder from the stove and smiled at her. "They're in the oven, honey, but you can scramble the eggs for me if you want to."

"Mornin', Uncle Hank!" Milli said as she slid past his chair to the refrigerator.

Hank, Gran's stepson, owned the farm adjoining his father's and lived about a mile down the road. When he had work to do on his dad's place, he was always in the kitchen early. He knew Louise could be counted on for a great breakfast. Today, he was immersed in the paper and just grunted a greeting to Milli. Three places were already set with the red-rimmed dishes and bright yellow napkins.

"Shred some cheddar into them, why don't you?" Gran suggested.

"Mm-mm, yeah," came from behind the sports section as Hank shifted in his chair.

As Milli worked, Gran looked over at her over her glasses, her eyes twinkling. "You look mighty chipper this morning, Miss Milli!"

Milli looked sideways at her and a smile spread wide. "I slept so well, Gran. I'm ready for a new day."

"Did you get on the computer last night?"

"No, not yet. I was trying to finish the short blue dress and . . ." She turned to Hank. "What's the password on the computer in the office, Uncle Hank?"

No answer came from behind the paper. Milli grinned over at Gran, intuiting the importance of the Kentucky Wildcats' basketball win by the size of the headline on the sports page.

Gran nodded in Milli's direction. "We're going to the finals!" she said, and by her twinkle, Milli knew Gran was as glad of the news as Hank.

Milli suddenly frowned. "Aw, Gran, I'm sorry. We were going to watch the regionals last night!"

Her grandmother's eyebrows rose above her glasses. "You think a ball game might in any way equal the importance of our time together the last couple of nights? Don't waste a thought in that direction, my girl."

Milli crossed the kitchen to hug her, the whisk still in her hand. "Love ya, Gran." The two women touched foreheads.

§

The game had been discussed, the bacon and eggs finished, and the coffee was almost gone when Milli asked, "When does the van come, Gran?"

"This Friday. Supposed to be here at eight!"

Hank said, "You sure have been a big help, Milli. Are you gonna come back and help me and Sue Beth move up the hill, week after?"

Milli's eyes flew to her uncle's to try to gauge his seriousness, but his chuckle was warm and reassuring. "Just kidding, hon. The boys are coming home and we'll get the transfer done in no time. When the kids moved out of our place and took all their stuff, Sue Beth and I weren't left with much to bring up here really. Especially since we're keeping a lot of Dad's furniture right where it sits. Most of it is an improvement on our stuff. Seems like four kids and six dogs kinda chewed up our things."

He looked over at Gran. "Now, we offered to move you, didn't we, Louise?" He turned a confidential look toward Milli. "But she won't let us move her piano, and I guess it's good she's gettin' help 'cause I tried shifting one of her boxes of books . . ." He nodded at Gran with a grin. "I reckon I'll be glad to see those hefty guys coming!"

"Is Sue Beth excited about moving up the hill?" Milli asked.

"Well . . . she's always loved this old house, but yesterday she was fretting a little about the dusting and cleaning of it. I think, too, she worries we're getting a little bit stiff for the stairs. But I tell her the house'll keep us young. And I can learn my way around a dust mop."

He picked up the last biscuit, throwing a questioning look at the two women. They both nodded and smiled. They'd been saving it for him.

He buttered and honeyed the biscuit, but held it a moment, resting the edge of his hand on the table and looking out the window. "Mainly, I just think Daddy would have wanted Susie and me to keep the place as long as we could, and with old Mac coming to tenant for me, I think we'll all be just fine."

Sunlight found dust motes in the air, and Milli watched them dance between herself and the window. *Seems like a death in the family tears an awful big hole out of the middle of things*, she thought.

The room was still as each heart wrestled silently. The sunlight lay in stripes and patches across the room. Hank spoke, his voice husky, "Milli? You'll come back to see us now, won't you?" He stood abruptly, awkwardly, biscuit in hand, and headed outside.

Gran smiled after him. "He's going to miss us. We'll have to come back real often, Milli."

PART THREE
CHAPTER THIRTY-ONE: KATIELYN CALLING

It was after nine and *Cars 2* was going full throttle in the dim front room of the trailer. Ebenezer had rocked forward in his chair, eyes riveted on a chase scene, mouth open in a wide smile, chin wet.

Jake was stretched out on the daybed, and Nell's old landline phone was right beside his head on the end table. If it hadn't been so near, he wouldn't have heard it ring. But he fervently wished he hadn't as he answered and his mother's voice jolted him wide awake.

"Jakey?" she asked in her husky drawl.

He fumbled for the remote and paused the movie, grimacing his apology toward Ebenezer.

"Yeah," he answered flatly.

"Where's Aunt Nell, honey?"

"She had to go to the store."

"She got you babysitting Uncle Ebenezer, kiddo?"

"I do what I can."

"Well, I'm glad you're helping your aunt Nell out, honey, but your momma needs you to help *her*. Why don't you come on back to Louisville and give me a hand around here—just for a while."

Jake, hunched over the phone, frowned at the worn places in the pea-green shag carpet.

"What's going on, Mother? You fresh out of boyfriends—or drugs?" His

173

voice dropped on the last suggestion.

"Now, Jacob. That's no way to talk to your momma. I'm sick, and I been having a hard time," she whined.

"So am I, Mother. Having a hard time, extra hard right now. But you always manage to help yourself to whatever you want. You don't need me."

"Now, Jakey." He could hear the tears in her voice, and he hated those tears, knew them well, had watched them fall all his life. He clicked the phone dead.

When the phone started ringing again, he jerked the clip from the phone jack and resumed the movie.

He sat and stared at the brightly colored cars, his hands trembling in his lap.

§

Later, Nell came through the door, a twelve-pack of Budweiser and a Walgreens bag dragging at one shoulder, and a smoking cigarette in the hand holding the door key. She stopped, her eyes roaming the room, a quizzical look on her face. Jake was sprawled on the daybed, looking at a magazine, and she saw that he had already helped Ebenezer to bed . . . but there was something . . .

"Hey." Jake didn't look up when he spoke.

"Hey, what's going on?" Nell had a way of waiting on answers that didn't allow for silence.

Jake shrugged.

"What," Nell persisted.

"Ah, well . . ." He sat up slowly and looked at her. "Momma called."

"I knew it! What'd she want this time?"

Jake flipped the pages of the magazine beneath his thumb. "She wants me to come back to Louisville and 'help out.'"

"Oh crap. She don't need your help getting into her kind of trouble.

What'd you say?"

"I said no way."

Nell sat heavily in Ebenezer's chair. "That's good. But she sure can take the starch out of you, can't she?" She reached for an ashtray and tapped her cigarette, took another draw, and stubbed it out, watching him as she blew a narrow stream of smoke down her shirtfront.

"You think people change, Nell?"

"Some can, if they want to. Most won't. Why? Did she sound different?"

"No. She started crying . . ."

"Oh yeah—she's an expert with the faucet handles, honey. Don't let her jerk your chain."

Jake nodded and turned a page.

Nell eyed him. "What's that you're looking at?"

"Oh, it's a *National Geographic*—big article on the Hubble Space Telescope."

"Oh." Nell worked herself up out of Eb's chair. "Well, how about a beer? Might go good with your stargazing."

Jake's nod and smile were not quite real, and before she went back into the kitchen with her purchases, she said, "Honey, don't let her get to you. Listen here to your aunt Nell. You've done grown up now. You've turned out a real good boy, maybe since you had to do your own raisin'. But she's done you enough harm for a lifetime, and you don't owe her a thing. Forgive her, forget her, and don't worry yourself about her, you hear?"

"Yeah, I hear you. Hard to do, though, give up on somebody."

"The thing is, Jake, a person has to really want to change theirselves in order to do it, and first they have to see the need. I mean, it has to be the most important thing in the world to 'em, because changing old habits is like trying to turn the tide—harder than that, sometimes. I been wantin' to stop smoking forever, but not bad enough, you know? I just don't see KatieLyn trying to change herself, do you?"

"No, not really."

"Drugs and the alcohol has just been too much of a everyday thing, and thinking only about herself is the habit that's maybe hardest of all to get shut off. So, kiddo, the best thing for any of us to do is stand back, be sad about it, but don't let her personal train wreck blow your life up too."

His eyes rode across the room to hers with his grief still in them, but he nodded and stared at nothing for a few minutes. Finally he stood and followed her into the kitchen.

Sliding into a chair by the table, he said, "Nell, could you sit down a minute? I need to tell you something else."

She frowned at him warily and looked over at Ebenezer's empty chair. "Eb's in bed?"

"No, he's in the bathroom, but he's headed that way."

She studied Jake. "He jittery tonight?"

"No, not that I could tell. He watched to the end of the movie and just sat there a minute or two, then announced he was 'g-g-going to bed.'"

Nell sent a fond smile in the direction of the bathroom and lowered herself into the chair across from Jake. "You sound just like him. Poor old feller."

"I know." Jake shook his head slowly. "If everybody was like him, wouldn't we have a fine old world? Life would just break out with simple goodness all over the place."

Nell studied the bony planes of Jake's face. "I reckon that's heaven, honey. Ain't happening round here—not anytime soon."

"Yeah." There was such sadness under his voice—always, but tonight especially.

The commode flushed, water ran, and Ebenezer shuffled into the narrow hallway and turned toward the living room. Without looking either of them in the eye, he sent his loose-lipped grin their way and said, "G-g-good bye."

Jake waved and Nell grinned. "Good night, Eb." They watched as he disappeared into his room and shut the door. Then he opened it again, and they heard his bedside light click on before he returned and closed his door the second time.

They both chuckled at the ritual. Going in and shutting his door meant he couldn't see, so every night he opened it again, found and turned on his bedside light, and closed the door again.

She shook her head. "Bless his heart."

When Jake was silent, she looked hard at him and saw other thoughts standing in his eyes. "What? What is it, Jake?"

"I need to . . . tell you something."

Nell's heart sank under a heavy dread. She waited.

"I'm going back." He swallowed. "Over to Bedford Green. Friday morning."

"Back . . . Why?"

"I have to turn myself in."

Nell shriveled, felt herself grow smaller. Her fears were becoming reality. "Why? What for?"

Jake's voice shook as he said, "Remember the accident? I told you . . ." His voice ran out, and when he looked to her for confirmation, she saw eyes hollow with anguish. She nodded. "The thing is . . . I killed a man."

Nell could feel the muscles around her mouth pull tight as she struggled for composure. "No. Oh no." Her head rang with shock as if a bell clapper had thudded inside her skull.

She jerked forward in the chair. "But it was an accident! You didn't mean to, right?"

His hand trembled as he pushed the hair off his forehead. "Doesn't matter. I'd been drinking, Nell. And I drove off. Left him there."

"Oh, God. No." Nell pushed herself up from the table. "This can't be right. Drinking? Were you drunk? You haven't touched the hard stuff since you've been here."

"I'm not sure, but I might have been over the limit. I had a couple."

Nell walked stiff legged to her rocking chair, but turned around and came back. She sagged back into the chair across from Jake and leaned forward, scowling. "Who saw you? How do they know what happened?"

"Nobody saw me. But I killed him, Nell, and I have to face it."

They sat in utter stillness with only the sound of wind and rain for company. His head was drooped and she couldn't find his eyes, so she asked in a small voice, "I don't understand. Have the police come for you?"

"No."

"Why? How?" She tried to form more words, but no sound came.

"I can't find my way around it, Aunt Nell, and it seems like I just have to go back and own up to it somehow in order to go on living." There was a long silence. Rain thrust against the window, hissing like a great paw raking the side of the trailer.

Nell took some time to come back to herself. "How are you going to get there?"

Jake raised his head. "I met a man, the pastor of a little church over on Maple and Broad—New Hope Church, I think it is." His eyes questioned her.

"Yeah, I know it." Nell frowned, bewildered. "Have you been going to that church? I thought you was at work all the time."

He shrugged and shook his head. "No, I met him, and I had to talk to somebody. He listened and I been back to talk several times. He's a real good person. He said he'd drive me over there."

She peered into his eyes.

"What?" he asked.

"You found Jesus over there at that little church?"

"Nah, nothing like that. I guess I found a good man over there though—seems like, anyway."

"He the one making you do this?" she asked, her face hard as stone, a determined tear in the corner of her eye.

Jake waived her off. "No, ain't like that."

Silent moments passed in the darkness. Finally she asked, "How did it happen?"

So he told her, and she could finally see the thing behind Jake's eyes that had been haunting him, tearing him from sleep with shouts and ferocious shaking. When he had told it all, they sat alone as the thunder diminished, dying away only to rise again to crash around the small metal home.

"I'm sorry, Nell, but I don't know what'll happen Friday. I thought I should tell you in case I don't come back right away." He glanced up at her but quickly looked back down, avoiding the pain in her eyes. "Listen, I've cashed my checks and been saving my money in a metal box under the daybed." He brought keys out of his pocket and began to wrestle a small one off the ring. "I want you to have any of it you or Ebenezer need."

But Nell reached out and closed her hand over his. "No. We're fine. Got along fine before you came, will again. I'll watch it for you though. It'll all be right here when you get out. And I don't care whether you want me to or not, but I'll be doing my best to pray for you."

He looked at her in surprise.

"I know. I'm awful new to the prayin' business, but I'm almost about to believe somebody's up there and it won't hurt to try to talk to Him a little bit—about you."

"No, it won't hurt." He ducked his head. "It won't hurt a bit. Thanks, Nell."

CHAPTER THIRTY-TWO: PETE'S STORY

Spring had arrived in Kentucky, trailing her spectacular train of bloom everywhere. The pale blossoms of the honey locusts lit the wooded hillsides, and some of the dogwoods were budding out in the unseasonably warm weeks. The houses and farm buildings were surrounded with forsythia bushes that waved great golden sprays in the wind.

Jake stared at the landscape flowing past him, but his dread of this day, this trip, had suited him with armor. He existed blindly inside a hard metal shell, and even a mass of brilliant phlox tumbling over a rocky bank didn't register in his consciousness.

Pete was dressed smartly in a turtleneck and sport coat. He looked over at Jake and asked, "You okay, buddy?"

"I'm okay—if you can call a dead man walking okay." He grimaced and fingered the worn leather of his jacket, beneath which peeked his Black Sabbath Tshirt.

Pete frowned. "I beg your pardon?"

"Oh, you know that movie about a criminal sentenced to death, going to the . . . Never mind, not funny."

"You know you won't be facing . . ."

"I know. I was just saying . . ."

After a minute Pete asked, "Do you want to stop for coffee? We're coming up on Bardstown."

"Not unless you want me to throw up in your nice car."

Pete chuckled. "No. No, that's quite alright. Baby Kaleena has already baptized this car several times. You don't need to do it again."

After another ten miles had unrolled behind them, and the sun had risen another notch, Jake asked, trying to be polite, "Where did you say your wife and baby were going?"

"My mom lives in Chicago, and she's been begging for so long to get her hands on the baby that Charley bought a ticket."

"They flew?"

"Yeah. Charlotte called last night and said Kalie slept the whole way. So they're snuggled up with Granny for five days. See? The Lord made a space for me to take you back to Bedford Green. He's looking after you, Jake. You just watch; something good will come of this yet."

Jake rolled his eyes as he turned to look at the passing landscape. All the flowering trees and brilliant greens might as well have been the sands of the Sahara for all he could see. He fantasized about asking Pete to let him out in Elizabethtown, but he hadn't brought enough money with him to buy a bus ticket to someplace far away, and the idea of robbing a convenience store had never appealed to him.

He had thought a couple of times about scrapping his "do right" plan and getting back in touch with his father, continuing his career as a drug dealer, but that idea always bounced away like a drop of water on a hot skillet. The money in it no longer seemed worth the loss of self-respect.

Finally, a question Jake had been turning over in his mind came to the surface. "You said once that you got on your knees to find God, and that it was a story I didn't deserve."

"Yeah. I remember that."

"What do I need to do to earn the story?"

Pete looked over at him. "Wouldn't you rather hear the one about the Baptist preacher and the rabbi?"

"No, I'd rather hear about what made you get on your knees. I've never known anybody I could talk with about God. I need to hear somebody else's story . . . Somebody that was looking for answers . . ."

The silence was long and Jake had almost given up when Pete said, "I've never talked to anyone else about this, Jake." His face was still and the twinkle of humor had disappeared from his expression. "I better warn you. Mine is not a pretty story."

Jake stared at the profile of the man that had shown him so much kindness, so much patience—and even some gentle affection. He was surprised by Pete's serious tone and something in him retreated, confused. But finally Jake said, "It might help me though. I can't imagine any story as bad as mine, and at least you've come through to a pretty sweet life, it seems like."

Pete glanced at him and nodded slightly. "I'd have to agree with you there. All in spite of myself. In spite of my *self*." He looked away again, his eyes focused on the road as he began to speak.

"Okay. Well, it started even before football. I grew up mad—with a bad temper, like my dad's. He left, but I had a good mom, and a saint for a grandmother who was there every day after school and literally scared me into good behavior most of the time. She was a force to reckon with." He smiled and shook his head. "Hoowee, look out for Gran and her ruler. Then it was a yardstick.

"Anyway, I played pretty good football in high school and got better in college. My coach called a scout or two, so when I went into the draft, I was picked to play for Denver. But that wasn't the best thing to happen to me . . .

"I met Charlotte my junior year. She was my biology tutor and helped me get an A in the class, and I was so in love with her that when my big opportunity with the pros came knocking, I dragged her to the courthouse and we got married. I didn't want to play ball without her in the stands, and to this day, she is the center of everything good in my worldly life."

Pete seemed to stall, and it took a little while before he started up again.

"But what happened was . . . I guess I started liking to hit too much. I had learned how to channel all the anger onto the football field. I can't describe the powerful rush of putting on shoulder pads, running onto the field and feeling like an animal inside. I had 'snarling, raging tiger blood' running in my veins. That's what a newspaper article said, and I was proud of it. Pretty soon I was starting on the offensive line, and when they told me which play, I knew who to take out. I never had to be told twice.

"I guess I fed on bloodlust because pretty soon I saw fear come into the eyes across from me, and no matter how hard they hit, I hit harder. I was vicious. Even my own teammates started avoiding me, and somebody always had to talk me down before we scrimmaged in practice. I let myself become a violent maniac and was proud of it. I broke a guy's leg during a game and don't even remember his name or what team he was on."

Jake stared across the car at the preacher, trying without success to see him as the fierce pro footballer he was describing.

Pete's nostril's flared as he drew in a breath. "It was mostly okay that first year, and I got named to the pro all-star team my first year. Made up for not getting a chance at the Super Bowl ring.

"Anyway, Charley and I had bought us a nice big butt-kicking house in a gated subdivision and I was pretty much king of the walk—I thought—but without a conscious thought, I had opened my worst self wide open to Satan, and he had walked in and made himself at home. In the weeks off, I felt all . . . kind of bound up in the suit you have to wear as a civilized man. You don't go up to strange guys in the street and knock their heads off unless you like the idea of yourself in a jail cell. So I had to let off steam on a punching bag every day in the basement and run hundreds of miles every week in the heat.

"We'd been trying to have a baby, and Charlotte wanted one so bad she would grieve for days out of every month when it didn't happen, but just when I was headed back to training camp, she conceived. We were . . ."

Pete's voice trailed off and Jake saw, even from the side, the anguish on the man's features. The words stopped and Pete shook his head. Then he seemed to draw his strength back together for the rest of it.

"Yeah, well, it was all good until one night . . ." He took a deep breath.

"Charlotte fixed spaghetti—my favorite. We were at the table and she said something. I have no idea what she said—maybe reminded me to use my napkin—just something simple. But like a shot, I flew into a rage and rared up, bumped the table and it slammed into her . . . It was a heavy oak thing and the edge caught her belly and knocked her backwards in the chair . . . and I was just standing there like I didn't even know where I was."

Pete's face was wet now, but he seemed unaware of his tears. His fists on the steering wheel were knotted muscle and bone and the car had slowed.

Jake stayed quiet, his eyes never leaving Pete's profile in the stark sunlight of early morning. Elizabethtown flicked by.

When Pete shook his head and picked up speed, he didn't look at his passenger, but after a deep sigh, he went on.

"She miscarried and it was horrendous. I got her to the hospital and she hemorrhaged for six hours. They had to give her two units of blood. Blood was everywhere in the labor hall; I thought sure I had killed her. She was my life, Jake. I knew I couldn't live without her.

"I think it was a nurse that led me down the stairs to the hospital chapel. I was not a religious man, Jake. My grandmother was, and Charlotte kept talking about finding a church we could go to, but I think that meanness had such a hold on me I just never thought about such things as God and religion. But when I went into that little chapel place with two fake stained-glass windows . . . I went down on the floor. I lay there on my face and cried out for help, Jake, and it was like I knew if some kind of something bigger than me didn't take over here I was going to lose everything that was important to me, and lose it because I for sure didn't deserve to keep it.

"It seemed like hours. I kept running upstairs to check on Charlotte, and running back downstairs to talk to God. I didn't know how to pray. I hadn't heard the Lord's Prayer in so long I couldn't think how it started, but something way down deep in me believed that God was in that little room, and I talked and cried and begged and made wild promises."

He chewed on his lower lip, frowning deeply at the remembering.

"Cops came and went, Coach, the owner, but I didn't even see them. I called my mother, though, and bought her and my grandmother airplane tickets. Charlotte didn't have any folks—her parents were dead—and she loved my "two mothers," as she called them. I knew they'd come, and she'd need them.

"Pretty soon reporters showed up, but I was not talking to anybody but the doctors and God. I just kept going back and forth, up and down the corridors, prayin' and beggin' and almost out of my mind. Finally, about daylight, I found a doctor ready to smile at me. The bleeding had stopped and they were moving her to a room in the intensive care unit."

Pete's face was wet, but a soft smile flickered at the corner of his lips. "I can't prove to you it was God saying yes to my begging. Nobody can ever claim to know God's will in a given situation, but I do know this: I was a different man after that night.

"Not that the rabid, homicidal maniac inside me just walked off the field and never reappeared. That's not true. I still have to fight him back now and then, but I honestly saw myself as weak in the presence of the evil inside me, and it frightened me to death. I knew that much, much more was at stake in my life than playing pro ball, and I began a serious search for God. Even if He came with little plastic stained-glass windows. That was going to be alright with me."

He looked over at Jake and gave a weak smile before returning his eyes to the highway, the black asphalt picking its way through the rolling countryside of south-central Kentucky.

"Seeing yourself as a failed man—or, as you put it so well, one who has never done a goddamned thing for somebody else—you begin to see a need for healing and forgiveness. That's often a big turning point in a life, Jake, and it seems to me that's where you are now. That's why I've been praying for you. I know that faith in God can make a light-year's worth of difference in a life."

Jake absorbed the silence, the sound of the tires against the road, for a while before he asked, "What happened with Charlotte?"

"Yeah. That was my next problem—whether Charlotte could forgive me, whether she could ever love me again. The doctors came in later that day and told us that because of the injury to her uterus, they didn't think she'd be able to have another baby."

Jake softly said, "Oh no."

"Yeah. And after we went home, for several months my momma and my grandmother lived between us. They moved in to take care of Charlotte, and they were like mother bears to her. None of the three of them were having anything to do with me. None of 'em—so disappointed in me they couldn't stand me in the room with 'em.

"I guess that was the worst period of our lives, but I kept up the prayin' and the team had me in anger management classes, and finally one night Charlotte asked Momma to let me come back to the bedroom so I could hold her and the only thing I could do was wrap her up tight in my arms and cry with her."

They came to the convergence of the parkway and Interstate 65 on the southern edge of Elizabethtown. Pete fell silent as he maneuvered through the interweaving lanes and pulled in behind a big rig.

"What happened then?"

Pete went on, "Well, I was no use to the Broncs—I couldn't hit hard enough anymore to save my career—and I was on big-time probation not only with Charlotte, the two mothers, and the team but also with God, I think.

"I kept on praying, getting on my knees any old where, asking God to help us. I needed God's forgiveness too. Seemed like I needed a miracle mighty bad."

He grinned. "I can look back and see the miracles now. First thing He did was help me out of football. Denver traded me, and we went to Pittsburgh, but my heart wasn't in it, and I started taking classes at the Bible college up there. I needed to learn something about this Jesus thing before I waded in over my head, right?"

Jake nodded.

"When Pitt let me out of my contract, I became a full-time Bible student, loving Him more and more the further I went.

"So—no doubt in my mind, God heard my prayers, Jake. One amazing day, my beautiful wife turned around and looked at me with love in her eyes again. Man, I felt like I had won the Love Super Bowl!

"He also heard me when I wanted to get loose from the violence in me and serve Him somehow. He heard me when I got accepted into the seminary, and He helped me study all the things I didn't know about Him. And God also had a great big hand in getting us the call to serve the little church in Union Gate. Then—great God almighty, by golly, and hallelujah, another big miracle happened—He sent us little Kaleena! We had been trying to adopt since the doctors said 'impossible,' and finally, after we moved to Union Gate, they found a little girl for us! I still can't believe it, that tiny little perfect girl! Thank you, God!"

Pete had been grinning ear to ear, but it faded as he glanced over at Jake, and said, "Oh, sorry. I forgot you're not quite with me on this just yet."

Jake stared out ahead at the road. "I sure would like to know if there is—someone—out there among the stars that we can't see, that does good things, creates worlds and babies, hears prayers, and everything . . . It's a big change for me, just to be wondering."

"Yeah, that's a big first step, for sure." Pete nodded.

Jake leaned his head back against the headrest and sighed. He remembered again where he was going and the sickness returned to his stomach.

"If God has really got hold of me like you said, you reckon He'd consider working a miracle in my case? Like maybe He would get me through this? Like help me confess it, and then help me with prison? I'm scared to death, Pete, I swear to . . ." His voice faltered and he swallowed back tears. "I'm just really scared."

"Well, I've been asking on your behalf. It's time for *you* to do the talking, I believe. I'll be quiet awhile."

Jake frowned. "Pray out loud?"

Pete glanced at him. "My thought is that He hears the silent words of the heart just as clear. Even the thoughts we can't wrap words around."

Jake struggled through the minutes that followed, repeating "God help me" over and over with every breath. But then, staring forward sightlessly, he said, "Pete?"

"Yeah?"

"I think we should try to find the Roeblings first, before we go to the police."

Pete nodded, expressionless. "All right. However you want to do it is fine with me."

Jake scooted another inch lower in the seat. "It's just that . . . if the police keep me, I won't get to talk to them except in court." He stared out at the high clouds—cheery, puffy clouds like children draw, bathed in early sunlight. His voice was so soft that Pete could barely hear him. "I wouldn't be able to tell her how sorry I am, in a courtroom, probably."

CHAPTER THIRTY-THREE: THE ROEBLINGS

They found the place with no trouble. The gas station had a phone book, and the Harold Roebling listing and address were clear. Pete asked directions, and after a tasteless lunch from the convenience store, they found the narrow country road, and Jake recognized its turnings with growing nausea. The numbers had faded on the mailbox, but the name Roebling was clear, and Pete turned his car into the paved drive. They stopped at the foot of three concrete steps and Pete turned to look at Jake.

The young man's eyes were so full of dread, and his breathing was so labored, that Pete reached out and put his hand on his arm. "Wait, Jake. Once I was very, very afraid, and I found this helped." He reached into the inside pocket of his jacket and pulled his small Bible out. He flipped it open easily, like it parted there often, and began to read, in a low voice, "The Ninety-First Psalm: He that dwelleth in the secret place of the most High shall abide under the shadow of the Almighty. I will say of the LORD, He is my refuge and my fortress: my God; in him will I trust. Surely he shall deliver thee . . ." and Pete's gentle, deep voice kept the sweet cadence of the psalm as Jake slowly, imperceptibly relaxed and began to breathe more deeply at the eternal weight and glory of the words.

A tall sun-browned man stood in the doorway of the barn and frowned, puzzling over the unfamiliar car in the drive. He waited and then began a slow, loose-jointed walk toward the back porch.

"He shall call upon me, and I will answer him: I will be with him in trouble; I will deliver him, and honour him. With long life will I satisfy him, and shew him my salvation." Pete closed the small leather-bound Bible and tucked it away, watching the effect of the words on Jake's face.

"Thank you, Pete." The eyes that turned to Pete were calmer now. "I hope . . ." He looked up at the house. "Lord, deliver me, just like You said."

The farmhouse stood tall, a two-story Victorian that had seen fresher paint and better days. It was imposing, however, with four attic dormer windows reflecting the afternoon sun. A deep porch spread across the front, furnished with an old glider, a swing, and wicker chairs plump with cushions. A large gray-and-white cat sat erect in a chair near the door, regally surveying the two men. As they climbed the steps, she stood, stretched slowly, and leapt to the floor, sweeping them with a disdainful feline gaze as she turned and stalked to the front edge of the porch.

Pete followed as Jake made his way across the gray planks, putting one foot in front of the other as though he walked to the gallows, numb to the marrow of his bones and blind to the cat, who slipped like silk beneath the railing and disappeared into the shrubbery.

He stood, paralyzed, until Pete nodded encouragingly. Slowly he raised his hand and pushed the doorbell, listened to the chimes.

Jake briefly hoped no one was home. But deep in the house, he heard the sound of a door being slammed and a voice calling unintelligible words. He swallowed back the rising nausea, and when footsteps approached, he made himself look up.

The lace curtains were pulled to the side and a face appeared briefly before a woman opened the door and stood behind the screen. She was short and soft around, with curly white hair, and she wore pants with a man's shirt over a flowered blouse. She held a rag in her hand, clearly not expecting company, but she smiled politely behind her wire-rimmed glasses. "May I help you?"

Again Jake struggled to produce words before Pete took pity on him and said, "We are looking for Mrs. Harold Roebling."

She nodded and her smile faded. "Yes, I'm Louise Roebling. But I can't talk about religion with you today. I have help with me, and we're in the middle of a ton of work. Besides, some of your folks came just last week."

"Oh no, ma'am. That's not it," Pete said hastily, and he looked at Jake and waited.

A tall, thin man in overalls appeared behind her, saying, "Louise?"

"It's fine. I'll be there in a minute, Hank." But the man stayed, openly curious about this pair of strangers at the door.

Jake realized they were an odd-looking combination. Pete had thought to dress well, in a turtlenecked sweater under a nice sport coat. He looked and acted like he deserved respect, and Jake was grateful to be seen with him. Under the eyes of the man and woman at the door, he knew his jeans and the Black Sabbath T-shirt under his scuffed leather jacket probably underscored his status as a lowlife. The sense of his guilt and wretchedness deepened, and he felt his face flush.

But he finally found his voice and said, "I'm sorry to bother you, ma'am, but could . . . I mean, can I talk to you about your . . ." He swallowed. "Husband?" It seemed to Jake that his voice echoed from some cave in him, where it was cold and dark.

Mrs. Roebling reacted with a slight step back, and she frowned as she said, "My husband is . . ." She stumbled into the fact. "Deceased. He was killed six months ago."

Jake's head dropped and he stared at the doorstep. "Yes, ma'am. I know."

When he finally looked up at her, sunlight flattened the lenses of her glasses, making her eyes invisible. He couldn't read her expression.

"Please, Mrs. Roebling, may we step inside a moment?" Pete asked. "We are so sorry to disturb you, but if you could spare just a few minutes, you would be giving this man a great blessing by listening to what he has to say. We won't stay any longer than you want us to."

She looked back and forth between them thoughtfully, then unlatched the screen and opened the door. "Come in."

Pete put his hand on Jake's shoulder, encouraging him, and Jake stepped over the threshold and into the large front hall. A baby grand piano stood in the corner beneath a stairway to the second floor, and stacks of sheet music lay on the piano bench. The heavy round table in the center of the room held a vase of tall white lilies. The two men blinked as their eyes adjusted to the dim light, and they didn't notice the slim figure of a young woman come in from the back of the house, drying her hands on a tea towel, until her voice rang a high note that spun in the air.

"Jake!" The name was filled with glad surprise and Jake knew her instantly, though she was just a silhouette against the sunlit kitchen behind her. She came forward quickly, and her huge welcoming smile lit up the hall. "Gran, Gran! This is my friend Jake! Remember . . . ?" Gradually, the strange tension in the room slowed Milli down and her smile flattened. "What, uh, what are you doing here?" she asked him.

Jake stared at her with confounded disbelief, stunned into a shocked, disorienting stillness, as if he had been struck in the face, hard and unexpectedly. After a long moment of registering the face of Milli Farley, he quickly turned to Pete in a seizure of panic. "No. Oh no—I can't . . ."

Pete stood like a rock outcropping in the room, and his eyes were full of peace. He nodded and the look that passed between them was almost, but not quite, audible. *I'm with you. Go on. You are doing fine.*

Jake heard the words without sound, and tears filled his eyes as he turned back to Milli. He shook his head slightly. "I'm so, so sorry. I *hate* this . . ." His agonized eyes turned to find the old woman staring at him with a frowning expression of dread and dawning suspicion.

She reached out a trembling hand and placed it on Milli's arm. "You . . . Harold?" She breathed out her husband's name in her question to Jake, and he answered with a weak nod. Gran's eyes closed and she nodded, her intuition confirmed. Milli took a sudden breath and slipped her arm around the bent shoulders.

"What the hell is going on?" came the bass voice of the man watching them, his frustration palpable.

"Hank, wait," Gran said quietly. Looking at Jake she turned slightly and gestured toward the tall observer. "This is my husband's son and my stepson, Harold Roebling Jr."

Jake felt emotions roiling inside him, worse than he could have imagined. Through the bedlam of self-accusatory voices in his head, he heard her gentle voice say, "Come on in, everyone. We all need to sit down. Collapsing won't help anybody."

Her stout little figure led the way into the front room, where tall windows welcomed the afternoon sun. Comfortable overstuffed furniture faced a tiled wood-burning fireplace, shielded by a brass fire screen. There were packing boxes sitting around, some scattered on the many-colored oriental rug, and empty shelves in the bookcases.

Jake stood stiff legged at the door until Gran gestured him toward a chair. When he got there, his legs folded abruptly and he practically fell into it. Milli sat next to her grandmother on the loveseat, holding her hand and the dishtowel.

Pete found a heavy Stickley chair that seemed to welcome his frame, and Hank went to stand alone, leaning against the doorframe. His wary suspicion of the two strangers was clear in his rigid shoulders and tightly folded arms. He had not perceived the exchange that revealed Jake's identity.

Jake looked at Milli for a second. For a heartbeat or two, Jake felt he might pass out, but very gradually a surprising sense of quietness seeped into him, as if finally, after months of fear, he had stepped from a high dive and plunged into deep water, where sounds were blurred and movements were in slow motion. He swallowed and looked at Mrs. Roebling. His heart was in his eyes and she could see his grief.

"I was . . ." He stopped. He took a breath. "I was driving the car . . ." He paused and swallowed. "That killed Mr. Roebling."

Gran flinched away from the information, gripping Milli's hand.

Hank jerked himself away from the door with disbelief dragging at his features. "What the hell?" He took a hard step toward Jake, bearing over him. Hank stammered for just a moment before his words, hard and sharp, broke through the air. "What do you think you're doing *here*? You are not welcome here, you son of a bitch. Get the hell out and turn your scrawny ass into the police department, 'cause I'm callin' 'em soon as you walk out that door!" The more he spoke, the angrier he got, and as he leaned toward Jake, he shook with the effort to control himself. "You left him, you coward piece of shit! *You left him like a dog in the road!*"

He raised his fist, but Gran stood up and reached out a hand. "Wait," she spoke crisply. "Wait, Hank. Wait. Let's just listen to what he has to say first."

Hank turned his eyes to Gran's. A muscle tightened in his jaw, but his arm dropped and he turned away, reaching for the handkerchief in his pocket, a disbelieving, distraught bystander again. Pete got up and went to stand beside him in the doorway, wordlessly offering sympathy.

Mrs. Roebling seemed smaller and frailer to Jake as she sat back on the couch, but after she straightened her back and gathered herself, she looked directly at him and nodded. "Can you tell us what happened?"

Jake took a deep breath and, staring at the oriental rug which lay between them, he started.

"The first terrible thing was, I had a few drinks. I thought it was two, but it might have been three. I was by myself when I left the bar, and I thought I was fine to drive, Mrs. Roebling, I really did . . . But anyway, I was right on that hill . . . when my cell phone . . . I looked down, and . . ." He wiped his mouth and his hand was trembling. "When I looked up, he was just right there in front of me." Jake reached to touch the bridge of his nose. He frowned and lowered his hand to his thigh where both hands trembled while he talked. "I guess I broke my nose on the steering wheel when I hit him . . . Blood was everywhere, and I was . . . so . . . confused."

Milli laid her head on her grandmother's shoulder, holding Gran's hand in both of hers, like it might escape.

Jake was unaware that tears were sliding down his face. "I thought, I hoped it was a deer. I stopped and backed up—but there was his shoe in the road . . ." Jake's eyes were wet glass. "And then I saw him over on the side, and he was dead." He shook his head.

"How did you know for sure he was gone?" Gran asked. "I've wondered whether anything could have saved him . . ." Her soft whisper trailed off into the still room.

Jake looked up at her. "No, I knew. His head was, um, broken, and the . . . the way the body was laying so flat . . . in the rain. It was raining. I forgot to say that . . ." He frowned deeply at the picture that haunted him, awake or asleep. "I'm sorry, but I just . . . I knew. There was nothing anybody could do."

When he began again, he spoke quickly. "I panicked. I was so scared. I'd been drinking, see, and I knew . . ." Jake felt shame rock him. "I went . . . I ran away."

Jake stopped talking, and the hum from the refrigerator seemed to intrude from two rooms away. "I will never stop hating myself for running away."

Hank was grinding his teeth and the muscle in his jaw jerked, while tears slid down his face.

Jake was bent so far over on himself that his face was almost invisible, but his voice leaked into the room. "I'm so, so sorry." He brushed his hand roughly against his wet face. "Most of all . . . I just wish I had stayed with him . . ."

Another long silence descended while Jake stared at the blurred pattern of rich crimson twisting in the Persian rug.

"Are you the one that called 911?" Gran asked.

"Yes, ma'am," he whispered.

"What happened to your car?" The question from the doorway was deadened by grief, and Hank cleared his throat before he added, "They said they searched and couldn't find it."

Jake turned toward him but couldn't look at the son of Harold Roebling. "I drove it to the quarry and rolled it off the edge, into the water."

There was a long stillness in the room, as though the dreadful finality in

Jake's words had to be handled and turned about by each of the three family members alone.

Jake became aware of the numb sensation—no hands, no feet, and underwater silence. More words came, and it felt to him as though someone else voiced the thought for him, and his mouth spoke, "I see him every single day, his shoe, his body . . ." His face crumpled as he sat there, rigidly holding himself still, facing himself and the family of the man he had killed. He was oblivious to the river of tears soaking his face.

At last, Gran picked up Milli's dishtowel and buried her face in it, her shoulders shuddering. Jake was aware of the movement but kept his eyes on the floor. Not one set of eyes looked to another in the room; each gaze found its own spot on the floor.

The cat walked into the room and stopped. She looked at each one individually and then leapt without effort into Gran's lap, where she curled into her longhaired tail and began to stare at Jake. Gran wiped her eyes once more and began to stroke the thick fur. Soon the room was full of a rumbling purr.

Finally, Gran raised her red-rimmed eyes to Jake's and said, "I want to thank you, young man, for coming. I know it took a lot of courage."

The simple kindness in the words completely broke Jake's heart and an audible sob escaped him. He dimly heard rustling and after a moment felt the damp towel being laid over his knee. Milli put her hand on his shoulder briefly before she returned to Gran's side.

It was a while before he could wipe his face and lift his head up, but he still couldn't look at the woman across from him.

Gran stopped stroking the cat and looked down at her hands buried in the fur. She said, "It helps me to know that you grieve for what you did. I can see it wasn't the act of a hard-hearted person, and I feel better knowing that you grieve for it. That is a sad fact, but a true one."

Hank straightened himself away from the doorjamb and came closer. His initial anger was damped by grief now, but tension was still visible in the lines of his mouth as he pulled up a straight-backed chair from near the wall and sat on the edge.

"I still want to know why you didn't go to the police," he said, his voice gruff and ragged.

The house creaked in a sudden gust of wind, and a shutter banged somewhere.

Jake nodded at Hank. "We are going there next, Pete and me."

Hank raised his eyebrows. "*Really?*"

"Yes, sir. Somehow, I wanted to come tell you and Mrs. Roebling first. I thought I might go straight to prison and not get the chance . . . to tell you."

Hank's shoulders seemed to relax a little. He stood and walked to the front window. He folded his arms and stared out onto the green lawn, silently watching the sunlight and shadows playing in the new maple leaves. A hush settled over the room, the wind coursing by the old lead-glass windows.

After a moment, Jake looked across at Milli. His eyes were clouded under a frown as he asked, "Was he your grandfather, Milli? You never mentioned anything about . . ."

"No." She glanced at Gran, who seemed lost in her own thoughts. "My grandfather Burke died while I was in junior high. Gran married Harold about three years ago. He was a widower in her church. Really good man though. I liked him a lot, and feel terrible for Gran."

Gran took a deep breath, exhaling with a sigh. Then, seeing Pete sitting quietly off to the side, she asked politely, "And who might you be, sir?"

Jake spoke up quickly. "I'm sorry, this is my . . . um," he stumbled, without a name for their relationship. "This is my good friend, Pete Andrews." He looked straight into Pete's eyes. "He brought me here. Kept me from giving up."

Pete smiled a little and said, "My name is Peter Andrews, Mrs. Roebling, and I'm so sorry we're meeting under these circumstances, but Jake came to my church over in Union Gate several months ago, and I've never met a more brokenhearted young man in my life. He seemed worth trying to help."

"You must be a preacher." Gran's eyes lit with warmth. "I thank you, Mr. Andrews, for helping me also. Not knowing what happened leaves a person full of terrible thoughts—but now . . ." She glanced toward Hank. "I don't see how we can look too hard on the young man for what was obviously an accident that has caused him great suffering also."

She paused and pursed her lips, her eyes looking back through the days and months to that night. She shook her head. "I tried to keep him from going out that night." She looked at Jake. "I have lived it over and over. You always wish . . . you'd done something different."

"Yes'm. I know." Jake held a question close inside of his chest; he didn't deserve any answers.

But Gran intuited his question, and answered it. "I'm sure you must have wondered where he came from, out on the road so late. He'd been down at Ben Robinson's, playing euchre. The Robinsons are old friends of ours, and they live down the road about three or four miles. A bunch of them get together every Friday night to play, and Harry loved to go down there when he could."

She sighed. "I told him the car was about out of gas, and he should take the truck, but the starter on the truck had been acting up, and he said he could make it down to Robinson's and back on fumes if he had to.

"The police said he ran out about a mile back and got it off onto a farm road. Evidently, the rain had pooled on the pavement along there, and they thought he had walked out on the road to come around it. They figured from the way they found him he was hit square on—killed instantly."

She looked at Jake. "He probably couldn't hear you coming. He was a little deaf." She stopped to wipe a tear, but went on with a clear voice, "It all seemed to make sense, but still, I thought they might just be trying to spare me, you know. You always hope there was no suffering . . . Now I think there probably wasn't, so you have taken away a great burden by coming today. I'm grateful."

Her eyes were beautiful and kind, and Jake felt a loosening of the bands around his chest.

"I wish I thought this sorrow could end right here for both of us," she went on, "but the truth is, we are both going to need plenty of the Lord's help to get on with our lives."

Jake nodded.

After a long pause, Gran spoke again. "My Harold was a good, rare man who held the truth in high regard." Her eyes found Jake's and held them. "And he would have been highly impressed that you came back here to tell us the truth of what happened."

Jake looked down, embarrassed.

Hank stirred where he stood leaning against the window frame. The anger had washed out of him with his tears, and now his eyes were simply sad as he looked at Jake. "I reckon she's right." He rubbed his jaw thoughtfully. "And Daddy—he served in the legislature after the parole board—he didn't think much of prisons, did he, Louise?"

She looked at him and nodded slowly, smiling inwardly at this son of the man she loved and admired.

Hank turned to the window again as if the sunlight out there was pulling him. Again a stillness settled over the room, and they all did their breathing and their thinking in separate fragile shells of humanity. Finally Hank spoke again. "Aw, hell, vengeance never much appealed to me, or Daddy either, for that matter. He wouldn't have wanted Jake to turn himself in, do you think, Louise?"

"No, Hank, I agree. He wouldn't have wanted that." She looked at Jake and then her eyes found Pete's. "I believe God's law is at work here, and I doubt any number of courts and lawyers and jails would be able to improve on the job the Lord's already done."

Pete pursed his lips and nodded, looking at her. The two of them recognized the kinship of faith in the other and acknowledged it with a smile.

Gran looked back at Jake. "Instead of turning yourself in to the questionable effects of prison, I believe the change in you is real, and I hope you will find a way to do exceptional things with your life—a way to do good things." She looked at him as he sat, head bent to the side, as though he had been slapped, frowning in disbelief, mouth slightly agape. "I believe you will. There is goodness in you. It's easy to see."

She smiled. "I'm rarely wrong about that. So will you keep in touch with me?" She glanced toward her granddaughter. "Milli will have my new address, and you can write to me, as often or seldom as you like. I will like to know how you get along."

Jake lifted his haggard face to hers and it was transformed by the wonder in his eyes. A flush rose across his bony jaws to his cheeks and he sat stunned. He shook his head and said, "No, wait. I didn't come to . . ."

"No. Seriously, Jake." Hank spoke firmly. "My dad would have wanted this. Go and be the best man you can be—in whatever you choose. Just accept forgiveness and walk into a new world. Live new. Start again."

When Jake looked over at Pete, he found a light in his face, and a tuck in the corner of his mouth that spoke his gladness. Hope, a transparent and shining thing, seemed to rise right through the room between them.

Then Jake breathed a "thank you" that Pete heard from twelve feet away without trouble—and without mistaking who was the One being thanked.

CHAPTER THIRTY-FOUR: RETURN

They were on I-65 heading north toward Elizabethtown. The hum of the tires and the sound of the air shushing past the windows had been their only companions for the past half hour. Pete's eyes were on the road ahead, and a comfortable silence filled the car as Jake re-trod the day, trying to make sense of the unexplainable.

Jake shook his head once, then again, without saying anything.

"What are you thinking?" Pete asked.

"I guess I just didn't know people like the Roeblings existed."

Pete nodded his understanding but remained silent.

Jake continued, "I'm still . . . I don't know, still in shock maybe. I should be thanking my . . ." He glanced quickly at Pete. "Guess you don't believe in lucky stars, do you?"

Pete smiled and raised his eyebrows in reply.

"Well, I am grateful. No." Jake hesitated. "'Grateful' isn't a big enough word to say what I feel, but I don't know what to do with it. I just feel sort of numb. Overwhelmed, I guess."

"I know." Pete's voice came to Jake like a warm hand on his shoulder. "I've thought a lot about forgiveness. Real forgiveness. It's so rare and so beautiful, and has everything holy in it. But I won't pontificate. I just pray I can be like my Charlotte, or like your Mrs. Roebling, when I need to find forgiveness for somebody else. That's the real Jesus at work, Jake. That's my Jesus."

Jake looked at him, thinking, then turned his head slowly, looking out his window toward the eastern sky. Evening draped the landscape with shadows, and the sound of the tires on the highway beneath them seemed to soften with the light.

After a time, Pete spoke again, his bass voice lending weight to the simple words: "'Find a way to do good in your life.' Isn't that what she said? That's no small task. But it's the way to move forward, seems like."

Jake nodded agreement and continued to stare out at the dusk. He watched the road a long time without saying anything. Finally exhaustion claimed him. His head sagged against the seat belt and he fell asleep.

§

Night had settled when Pete pulled into the gas station. The florescent lights above the tanks hurt Jake's eyes when he clambered out of the car, and he squinted at Pete, who was filling the tank. "I'll get it," he said, heading into the station, but when he got to the cash register, Pete had already put it on his charge card out at the pump.

They argued over it good-naturedly until Jake pointed out a steak house across the road.

The restaurant was crowded and they had to wait a few minutes for a table. Jake stood entranced by the lazy, rippling turns of the tropical fish circling in the tank by the door. The iridescent blue glow from the fish tank exaggerated the bony planes in Jake's face and the deep hollows around his eyes.

The hostess led them to a table on the other side of the tank and they looked over the menu, discussing their choices. After they had gotten their drinks and ordered, Pete asked, "How did you happen to know the granddaughter?"

Jake looked down, unwrapping his silverware. "I met her the day I arrived in Union Gate. Her name's Milli. Did I introduce you? Everything that happened this afternoon is kind of blurred in my mind. She told me on the phone she was at her grandmother's in Bedford Green, but I could not believe it when she came walking out of that kitchen. There are a hell of a lot of grandmothers in Bedford Green!"

Pete waited as Jake's attention wandered to the angelfish floating past him.

When he came back to the moment, he suddenly blurted, "I almost fell for her, back around Christmas." He frowned down at his hands. "Well, I guess I *did* fall for her," he admitted in a rush of words. "But she left, and now that she knows what I did . . ." His eyes were full of regret as he shook his head. "Un-fucking-believable. Oh, sorry, Pete."

Pete raised his eyebrows above a wry grin. "Three years in the NFL? I believe I'm familiar with the expression. Used it myself on occasion."

Jake grinned at Pete. The waitress arrived with their drinks and breadbasket, and as they ate, they talked about Kentucky basketball and the game on television.

§

Later, as they were rolling east along the Bluegrass Parkway in the dark, Jake's voice warmed the darkness, "Pete?"

"Yeah?"

"What do you think about the way things happened?"

"Well . . ." Pete hesitated. "I've been thinking about it—"

"You think I should maybe go to the state police?"

Pete glanced over at him but returned his eyes to the moonlit roadway shining out ahead of them.

Jake watched a glowing green exit sign approach until it flashed by his window.

When he looked over at Pete, the man was frowning. "Maybe . . ." He shook his head. "But I'm not sure. It seems to me, the two people most affected by what you did forgave you freely and completely. That is no small thing they did."

Jake rode along, feeling the road beneath them, staring up at the stars.

Pete added softly, "It seems to me, like Mrs. Roebling said, you brought your confession to a higher court, and were given grace. I don't see that societal punishment could change anything. You are a different man than the one who hit Mr. Roebling." He paused. "But as always, my advice is to pray about it. Ask the final judge of all things if there is more for you to do."

Jake nodded and smiled. "I'm beginning to feel familiar with that suggestion."

Miles passed, and Jake continued to watch the sky.

He turned his head and looked at Pete. "Thank you, Pete. Thank you for everything you've done for me." He paused, frowning. "It's really amazing. I don't remember ever before . . . seeing how good people are to me, you know? First Aunt Nell opened her trailer to me, and Milli spoke out for me back there, and you . . . taking all your time and going all this way . . . And *now*, the Roeblings . . . Talk about unbelievable! Not a reason in this world for any of you to be so good to me."

He dropped his head back against the headrest. The moon was silvering the road ahead of them, and his searching gaze found Orion in the space reserved for it from the beginning.

"You should meet Aunt Nell, and old Ebenezer," Jake said.

"Bring them to New Hope with you."

Jake turned and gave Pete a long look. "Maybe I will."

CHAPTER THIRTY-FIVE: PACKING AND UNPACKING

Gran came into Milli's room with a neatly folded sweater, warm from the dryer, and Milli put it on top of the clothes in her suitcase.

"Thanks, Gran." Milli wrapped her arms around her, held the hug for a few heartbeats before letting go. As they looked at each other, Milli's eyes welled with tears.

"No, no, sweetheart. Don't do that." Gran pulled a tissue from a box nearby and wiped at Milli's cheeks. Then she turned away to wipe her own eyes and busied herself folding a pair of jeans. When she looked up, Milli was watching her.

"I just really, really want you to be happy at that place, Gran."

Gran patted her back. "Magnolia Terrace? Now stop worrying, Milli; I'm going to be just fine. We talked about selling the farm long before Harold was killed. This move was inevitable, honey, and his death just moved it forward a little. The truth is I'm looking forward to a simpler life, with no vegetables to can this summer." She chuckled.

Milli searched Gran's expression and found clear eyes looking back at her, so she finally nodded and rolled a brightly patterned silk scarf into a small bundle. She tucked it carefully into a corner of the bag.

"They come tomorrow for the piano?" Milli asked, making her question cheerful.

"About nine tomorrow morning. I asked a lot of questions, but they assured me they have moved hundreds of old pianos. They will even send a man to tune it after it has 'settled in' for a few weeks."

Milli smiled at her. "That piano has been your big shiny baby a long time, hasn't it?"

Gran nodded, her lips compressed in a wry smile. "It has. A lot of children have learned to play on it, and teaching them has taught me a lot, kept me young—well, young-*ish*." She looked at Milli with a grin. "I was surprised that none of my ducklings quit. I know the parents are happy not to have to drive so far out in the country, but still . . . I guess I thought several of the serious ones would start looking for someone younger." She looked at Milli with a sudden twinkle. "Mrs. Fields, the Magnolia manager, was enthusiastic about little ones coming and going in the afternoons, and the piano will be off in the sunroom, so it should be fine . . . Most of the residents seem the tolerant sort."

Milli raised her eyebrows.

"Oh, I believe I'll enjoy it, Milli, once I've settled down. Don't waste your energy worrying, you hear?"

Milli smiled and sat down on the edge of the bed, pulling Gran to a seat beside her. "I was thinking that if I decide on UK, Lexington will be almost an hour closer to you."

"So have you made up your mind? I thought you were interested in Chicago."

"Well, yeah, I was till I added up the expense. I just thought UK's design school looks pretty impressive, and it sure is more affordable. I could commute back and forth from home, and actually finish there with a degree, not just taste the big time for a semester or two and have to come home."

Gran nodded slowly. "But, Milli, I have to ask: is Lexington going to be far enough away from Billy Mac?"

Milli's eyes narrowed and she nodded as she looked into Gran's eyes. "I am done there, Gran, thanks to you. Somehow, telling you about it and seeing your face made me realize how pathetic and awful it was. I just feel purely disgusted with myself, and I promise I'll be able to make a clean, clear break the next time I see him. *If* I see him again."

Gran couldn't hide her concern. "I believe you mean that. But I also know how much strength it takes to end a relationship with an overpowering personality . . . It isn't a matter of flipping a switch, honey. He'll still come home, and he'll still try to keep it going between you."

"No, really, Gran. I promise I can do it. I've thought so much about it over the past days—and planned what to say." Milli shook her head. "I'm keeping my eyes on the future. I want you to be proud of me. And me to be proud of me."

Gran's bony fingers picked up Milli's hand and squeezed it with surprising strength. "Bravo, my girl, bravo!"

Gran leaned forward to get up from the edge of the bed, but Milli put her hand on her arm.

"But wait, Gran, there is one more thing . . ."

The old lady sat back and nodded encouragement, but Milli hesitated, biting her lip. "I've been wanting to talk a little more about Friday . . . about Jake and Pete and the . . . confession, I guess you'd call it." Gran nodded and Milli asked timidly, "How are you feeling about it now?"

Gran turned her eyes to the window behind Milli, where the afternoon sun was dipping in and out of cloud bundles and a light wind was flicking the new leaves back and forth. She took a deep breath and sighed. "We've been so busy I haven't had much time to think how I feel. It did occur to me to wonder whether we did the right thing." Her eyes returned to Milli's. "I even mentioned it to Hank. The question of, What if he repeats the crime? haunts me a little. But Hank doesn't second-guess himself—just like his dad. Once those men make a decision, they rest with it. So I've been sleeping fine. I think I'm still just relieved. It is really good to know what happened, somehow."

After a thoughtful pause, Gran went on in a voice bearing mild surprise. "That tormented young man kind of got to me, I must say. Seemed to me he couldn't have felt much worse about what happened if Harry had been his father! I've been on jury duty when we handed down guilty verdicts that resulted in big prison terms, and you could look in some of those eyes and know they only felt sorry for themselves. They were heartless, but Jake wasn't like that. I found myself wanting to . . . well, to comfort him."

"I know, Gran, he kind of had that effect on me when I first met him. I could tell something terrible had happened to him. I mean, he had a kind of damaged look, and I was a little leery of him at first. But he was interesting and . . . and kind. He seemed to like me, but he kept me at a distance, so I was intrigued. After just a short time, I got totally relaxed with him. We talked a lot. Almost every week. I looked forward to it, because he seemed to . . . really listen and understand me. And his story was sad. He had a hard life growing up, Gran. But he wants to be somebody real . . . um, smart and important."

Gran studied the wallpaper and then turned to look directly into Milli's eyes. "I really hope Jake can become the man he wants to be. There's great potential there. You can see in his face how hard he's had it, but I've known people who were able to change direction, especially if God gets involved in the effort."

Milli nodded, her mind elsewhere, chewing on her thumbnail. "I feel like I really need to see him when I get back home, Gran. I need to apologize for the way I left, and for not answering his calls."

Gran nodded and looked away to the spring rain that had begun to pepper the window. "If—or *when*—you do, tell him . . ."

"What?"

Gran looked back at her. "Tell him I'm praying for him."

Milli looked at her, her heart in her eyes. "I will, Gran. Pray for me too?"

"Absolutely. Every day.

CHAPTER THIRTY-SIX: GROCERY AISLE

Jake saw the toddler drop the sack of cornmeal. The mother had turned away for something on the opposite shelf, and the little guy leaned out over the edge of the basket and dropped the two-pound bag, cackling when it burst and sent white grains flying ten feet down the aisle. Jake stopped what he was doing and went to get the broom and outsized dustpan.

"I'm so sorry," the mom said when he returned.

"No, no, you're fine. No problem." She pushed the cart away down the aisle, and he grinned to himself at the baby's wide-eyed surprise as he had looked up at Jake.

He was sweeping up the last bits when a voice came from behind him. "How much do they pay you for sweeping?"

A crooked grin crinkled one cheek, and his eyes were smiling when he stood to look at her.

"Hey, Milli!"

"Hey, you." Her black hair swept one cheek as she cocked her head. "The kitchen at my house needs sweeping."

"You pay more than Kroger's?"

She grimaced. "Guess not. Maybe supper, if you're lucky . . . ?"

For an awkward moment they looked at each other, their smiles gradually failing them, until he bent to brush the last of the cornmeal expertly into his wide dustpan. She waited until he stood, holding the pan carefully, before she said, "I tried to call. You lose your cell phone?"

"No. Pitched it. Don't need one. Saving my money."

"What for? You want a new bike?"

He shook his head. "Nope. Going back to school, I hope. I'll be in serious need of a car."

"Really?" Her eyes lit with her smile and she pulled her hair behind her ear. "Oh, I'm so glad . . . You going back to study astronomy?"

"I sure hope so. I've applied to UK and I think they'll take me with no problem, but I'm still trying to figure out whether the scholarship will transfer from Western."

Milli smiled warmly. "I'm so glad for you." She hesitated, then said, "I think I may be going to UK too."

He was unable to suppress the crooked grin which spread over his face. "No kidding?"

Jake saw his supervisor pass the end of the aisle.

"I better get back to work."

Milli put out her hand to brake his turn. "Can we have coffee sometime?"

"Uh, well . . ." He looked at her and knew she sensed his reservations.

"Listen, Jake." She spoke quickly. "What you did last week for my grandmother was amazing, and I want to thank you. I know it must have been really hard. And I know I should have kept in touch when I left town, but I really would like to talk it all over, and maybe—be friends again?"

He looked at her anxious face and felt the hardness melting.

"Yeah. I guess . . . Okay. But I don't get off till ten. Is that too late?"

"No, that's perfect. McDonald's?"

§

As Milli carried her soda toward him between the booths, he figured out what had seemed different about her. It was the way she was dressed. She looked beautiful in her slim-fitting jeans and black V-neck sweater, black high-top sneakers on her feet. Her chin-length hair was smooth and sleek and well cut.

"You're looking a little like Johnny Cash," he commented with his grin well tucked into his cheek.

She stopped short with a confused smile.

"Sorry, I just figured out you're dressed like, cool. Well, cool for somebody who likes black."

She laughed as she slid in across from him. "Well, thanks. I guess." She looked at him seriously then, and her gaze grew introspective. "I guess I've just come back here . . ." She pursed her lips. "I don't know—a more serious person, maybe. But maybe I went too far."

"No, no, you look nice. But I really liked that pink ballet skirt."

Neither of them smiled as they looked at each other, then down at the table. Milli said, "I almost couldn't find you. I've been to Kroger's three times in the last two days."

"I couldn't find you at all, back in January. I tried to find your aunt Gert's house from the phone book." He let his frustration into his voice.

"How did you know to look there?"

"You told me that was where you stayed most, but she was gone too . . ." He paused, looking at her, watching her discomfort. "I was worried—that is, until you answered your damn phone and gave me the brush-off. Then I stopped worrying about you and said, 'Okay. I'm done.'"

Milli's eyes widened with hurt and Jake looked down at the table.

After a breath, she said. "Can I tell you? Would you mind if I tried to explain?"

Jake shrugged. "Be my guest."

"Well, you know that last day we met at the library?"

Jake nodded.

"Well, that night something happened. Something really bad." Her head was down and her hair did a pretty good job of hiding her flushed face. "I can't talk about it yet, but it was bad. I talked Gert into taking me over to

Gran's. I was planning to go in a few weeks, anyway—to help her pack and get ready to move." She shook her head. "But anytime something's really wrong, I run to her like a little kid." She raised her head. "I'm trying to grow up, Jake, I really am, and it's hard. And I'm so sorry I didn't let you know where I was going . . ." Tears threatened to spill, and she blinked them back.

"Like I told you before, it seems like there are two people mixed up in me," Milli said with slow care. "And I believe both of them are equally strong." She raised her eyes to his face as she said, "I think sometimes about becoming a nun."

"A *nun*?"

"I know—I'm not even Catholic. But I imagine living in bright, clean spaces with every day divided into singing and prayer, and loving God with my whole self, living with sisters who all love God and each other and live in silence. I guess I'm thinking of the contemplative order of nuns in a book I read at Gran's. It was a big book of photographs and I have looked at those faces, at that place, over and over and over. They seem so peaceful." She smiled and her face was tender. "Every part of me is pulled toward that life."

Jake sat listening, watching her face.

The softness faded as she went on, "But then, when I come back home, even when I start back home, Dad or Gert or Margaret—whoever comes to get me—they all like the same kind of pop rock and the music starts pounding and the other life crowds in, and it's like I sink into the craziness and the noise and I . . . forget the God part of me. It's like I wash out to sea . . . and I do things I wish I didn't." She stared out at nothing and Jake waited, watching her mouth tremble. "I think I *have* to decide who I am.

"But the worst part of January was that I feel like I really stepped in it with you. Ruined something special that was . . . maybe beginning to happen."

He gaped at her.

"What?" Her eyebrows lifted anxiously as she saw the look of incredulity on his face.

He shook his head, amazed. "Did you think that way, really?"

She gave a sad little nod. "I did, kind of . . . Didn't you?"

He looked at her from under his brows, and finally gave an almost imperceptible nod. "I guess." His heart was banging around beneath his ribs. "But I'm pretty sure I'm past it now."

"Yeah. That's okay." Her voice was muffled, but he could hear the sadness.

"I've got to go back to school if I can," Jake said. "I reckon all I have room for right now is just a friend."

She nodded. "That's good. I can deal with that, and I promise never to make a mad dash like that without letting you know. Good friends don't do that."

"Yeah. They don't."

"I promise."

A long moment stretched thin between them until Milli took an audible breath and Jake looked up into anxious eyes. "Maybe I should tell you . . ." She hesitated but then went on as if propelled by an irresistible force, "I lied to you that day, kind of . . ."

But suddenly he reached out and gently laid his finger across her lips, stopping her words. "No, I don't need to know. I was lying to you too back then, pretending nothing was bad wrong. That was then. This is now. Let's go from here. Let's start again, and we'll promise to never lie to each other from tonight on. Okay?" His eyes were earnest. "Friends?"

Milli's smile bore so much relief that Jake could barely stand the dazzle. She nodded, and with a low voice she said, "I promise, friend." And her tongue slipped along the lips he had touched.

They sat quietly together, equally glad to share the warmth and the clatter of the room around them, feeling affection and, more than that, *possibility* wash back and forth between them. They finished their drinks and still stayed.

Jake finally broke the silence. "I think about your Gran—wonder about her. Do you think she's sorry she forgave me?"

"Not at all. Oh, she gave me a message for you. I almost forgot."

Jake stared at Milli. "She did?"

"She just told me to say she is praying for you, for you to become the man you want to be. And I'm sure she is doing that with a true heart. She takes prayer very seriously."

Jake shook his head slowly. "She's amazing."

"I promised her that I'd keep looking for a church to go to here. I think I'll visit your friend Pete's church this Sunday. I liked him."

Jake's eyes found hers and he nodded. "Huh." He nodded again, his mouth pursed in thought. "Good idea. I think I'll join you.

CHAPTER THIRTY-SEVEN: NEW HOPE

Ebenezer pulled himself up the steps by the handrail, one at a time, chewing his underlip with the effort. He wore his blue necktie under his shirt collar, looped once in front. Nell came one step behind him, her hand out as though she could help, push, support. Jake had led the way, and Eb reached toward him, closing pudgy fingers around Jake's strong ones, and his damp face folded into a broad smile as he reached the top.

The singing had started and when Jake pulled open the door, the sound seemed to spill over them. He took a quick breath to center himself.

There were no instruments, no organ: just a bunch of people singing, but the sound was big in the simple sanctuary. Jake saw Milli's dark hair and he steered Ebenezer and Nell toward her wooden pew, where he sat awkwardly between them. She stopped singing to smile and supply each of them with a hymnal from the racks on the pew in front of them. She was clearly familiar with the customs of church attendance, which were arcane mysteries to a guy who'd never before been inside a sanctuary.

Jake stared down at the lines blindly, overcome by self-conscious embarrassment. He glanced past Nell at Milli, who was singing now, with more enthusiasm than melody, and an amused smile tugged at his mouth.

When Nell had gotten wind of this visit to Pete's church, she had invited herself and Eb to come along, and now their bodies on either side of him anchored him to the pew. He could feel his nervousness dissipate.

As the music filled him up, he looked at the notes and the words written beneath, and he read the words without understanding many of them.

Nell joined the chorus on "We're marching to Zion, beautiful, beautiful Zion," her hoarse smoker's voice surprisingly sweet, and Eb's smile broadened from ear to ear. He began to rock, his easy motion bumping against the seat back slightly, until Nell reached over Jake to lightly touch Eb's thigh and he stopped.

Jake looked around at the mix of people. He was surprised that all but a few seemed to be really singing, with all of themselves, even the little ones—and there seemed to be a lot of little ones. Several were peering over the pew backs at the newcomers in Jake's pew, until tugs from parents faced them front again. There were many old folks, and most of the congregation was black, but a number of other skin colors were mixed in.

Jake looked for Pete and spotted him, sitting on the front pew, head bowed. He also looked for Charlotte, with the baby he had met, but there were several possibilities, so he gave up and began to look at the songbook. Ebenezer had begun to "sing," his tuneless voice out of sync with the others. Jake noticed a woman glance back at Eb, but her smile was friendly, and she nodded as she returned to her book. He stopped himself from wiping the drool from Ebenezer's chin.

As the congregation sang a cappella, the song leader took hymn numbers called out from the pews. The next one was number eighty-nine: "Show Pity, Lord." Jake turned the pages of the *Old School Hymnal* he was sharing with Eb, and when the people began to sing, he immediately recognized it with a shiver that ran down his spine. It was the hymn he had heard on the church steps so many months ago. Now he read the words as the voices joined in a minor key a grieving, haunting sound:

Show pity, Lord, O Lord forgive,
Let a repenting rebel live;
Are not Thy mercies large and free?
May not a sinner trust in Thee?

216

My crimes are great, but don't surpass
The pow'r and glory of Thy grace;
Great God, Thy nature hath no bound,
So let Thy pard'ning love be found.

The old and young voices seemed to him to be joined in one great, longing plea, and uninvited tears came to Jake's eyes.

Yet save a trembling sinner, Lord,
Whose hope, still hov'ring round Thy word
Would light on some sweet promise there,
Some sure support against despair.

And there, in a small church, in a small town, on an ordinary Sunday, Jake saw a glimpse of glory. Surrounded by neighbors, strangers, and kin, wrapped in a hymn sung by unexceptional voices, the phrases and the tune and the harmony and the sunlight in the windows that bathed the room in gold—all the colors of skin, the shapes and sizes of human beings all gathered into one living, seeking moment of extraordinary power—he felt the earthly become divine, where a sweetness, a solemnity, a transcending kind of joy came close to rapture.

His life seemed to him as a moment in time, without weight. A peace filled him, a joy that brought with it a small, brilliant thing called hope.

He knew that here, in this small and simple sanctuary, the inarticulate longing in his soul had found rest. Here was the experience he had longed for without knowing what he had lacked: the feeling of love given and received without question, and the sense of belonging to something infinitely larger and more important than himself.

He felt himself very close to shining.

EPILOGUE

When she saw him coming, Milli stood from her aluminum chair and grabbed Bobby with one hand as he hopped down the steps. Jake slid the bike sideways in the gravel drive and left it against the wire fence. "That was quick!" She was laughing as she picked up the tot. "You must have found a shortcut."

He leaned forward, hands on his thighs to catch his breath. "Well, good news is hard to go slow with."

"Wait, wait." Bobby was squirming to get away, so she went to close the gate and set him on his feet before she turned her smile on Jake. "Tell me," she urged. "What's happened?"

"Letter came today. I got a full ride—tuition and books!"

The glow in his face was contagious and Milli leapt at him. Before he knew what was happening, she was in his arms. They rocked around the yard in a clumsy waltz, laughing together until they broke apart.

"Jake! This is fantastic! I'm so happy for you!"

"Can you believe it?" He grinned at her, full and running over with the possibilities opening in front of him. "UK gave me the Foster Scholarship and added a grant to it from the state. So I can be a full-time student in the fall." He shook his head in disbelief. "It's beyond amazing."

"Come on. Let's sit down." Milli led him to the concrete steps and they sat down, with a suddenly self-conscious space between them.

"I was thinking on the way over," Jake said, "that I haven't written to your grandmother yet, and now I really have great news to tell her. I also should write Professor Greathammer. How are you at editing letters?"

"I'm pretty good, especially letters to Gran. It's easy if you don't try to act all formal and educated." They laughed. "What'd your aunt Nell say?"

"She doesn't know yet. I got the call at the store . . . Want to go over there with me and break the news?"

Milli looked at him with all the happiness in the world on her face, and just nodded. "Wait for me?"

§

Jake and Milli walked toward the trailer, laughing. They didn't pay attention to a dirty old sedan parked between Nell's place and Charlie's.

"My aunt Nell is the best—well, next to your Gran." Jake's eyes twinkled. "But if she's gotten herself upset about something, she's liable to come up with swear words like you've never heard. I've learned a few new ones from her."

Milli chuckled. "Wow. New swears. Like what?"

"Oh, she says 'hell-o-Peter-Rabbit'—stuff like that."

Milli's head rocked back with laughter. "'Hell-o-Peter-Rabbit?' *What?* Where did that come from?"

"Damned if I know." He grinned as he fished the key out of his pocket. "But now, you met old Eb at church. He's also the best. Never swears because he's happy all the time!"

He got the door unlocked and stepped back to usher Milli through. He stepped in behind her.

And came to an abrupt halt.

The woman was sitting at Nell's table with a baby on her lap. It took Jake a few seconds to recognize her. She was skin and bones held up by spite. Her once beautiful face was a peculiar shade of yellow and her hair was dry. Sunken eyes still flashed with life, but the rest of her looked cadaverous. She surveyed Milli and Jake, and then she smiled, lips pulling skin flat over jutting cheekbones, revealing the gaps where two teeth were gone.

"Hey, Jakey."

"Mother. What are you doing here?"

"No 'hello'? Not going to say 'How are you, Mom?'"

Jake just stood, stunned and blinking.

Sensing the tension, Milli started to turn back to the door, but Jake gripped her arm and held on.

"Milli, this is my mother, KatieLyn." His voice halted, and his eyes, full of dread and confusion, flew to Nell, who sat motionless in her rocker.

After a moment, Nell appeared to shake herself alive and said, "Well, come on in, Jake, Milli. You all sit down. My niece was just telling me her news. Guess you need to hear it too, Jake."

Jake continued to stand, looking back and forth between Nell and his mother. He could feel the blood rising in his face.

The awkward silence stretched while Milli smiled at the baby, who regarded her solemnly from his seat in KatieLyn's lap. After what seemed to Jake an hour, Milli broke the tension. "What's his name?" she asked politely.

Jake shook his head, mute, and KatieLyn's mouth pulled tight in her sad face. "Since Jake don't seem to remember his little brother's name—it's Samuel. We call him Sammie." She picked him up and nuzzled his neck. She looked over at Nell. "He's Skinny's baby."

"Ah, and where is Skinny?" Nell asked in a voice loaded with irony.

KatieLyn's eyes dropped back to the baby. She struggled to control her voice. "Oh, you know I can't keep a man interested very long, Aunt Nell."

The baby began to wriggle and fret.

"May I?" Milli asked, and at KatieLyn's nod she took the baby into her arms and sat down, loosening the soft wrap, murmuring to him, cuddling him. He quieted, and Ebenezer smiled happily at the two of them, while Milli laid the tiny boy down in her lap and began to make playful little faces at him. He smiled at her in wonder.

Jake looked at his mother, frowning. She had been thin when he passed through her apartment six months ago, but now she was gaunt and had changed color.

"Is something wrong with you?" he asked, frowning and awkward.

She looked at him without expression. "I guess you could say that. I seem to have managed to wreck my liver among other body parts. Doc says I got maybe a year."

Jake stared at her with his mouth open. One hand reached, found the back of a kitchen chair, and he sat down.

Milli's entertainment kept the baby spellbound, and for a length of time the room was silent.

Finally KatieLyn spoke again, "I decided, since you couldn't come over to Louisville, I'd better get myself over here to see you all while I still could. My friend Kitty brought me. She's out in the car. I'm not supposed to drive anymore." Her voice held traces of the self-pity he was so familiar with, but as he watched, the rigid self-control slipped out of the sick woman and her shoulders slumped. "I'm sorry, Jake. I don't blame you for not coming." She seemed genuinely exhausted.

Nobody spoke or stirred. The clock on the back of the stove clicked through many seconds.

KatieLyn seemed to gather strength to look at Nell. "I know I owe you, Aunt Nell. I owe you money and a lot more of everything than I can ever pay back. I know that, and I'm sorry about it." Her voice had become raspy, dry, and thin. She shook her head. "I don't know why exactly, but I've just never been any good at doin' the right thing. I know it and wish it was different. I always meant to do better . . ."

Her voice seemed as pale as her face. "I wadn't no good to Momma. I sure do wish I could tell her how . . . sorry I am—so I'm just telling you." A tear slipped out. "Aw, Nell, I shouldn't have left that night. I've always known that, and I despise myself for it. That fire has damn near haunted me to death. You know? I never minded prison. It just seemed like where I belonged. I couldn't never get past that fire, Nell."

Nell's face had crumpled as she listened, but she said nothing.

KatieLyn sat staring at the floor. Then she seemed to remember the baby and she watched him waving his arms and gurgling at Milli. The sadness in her eyes was so heavy Jake could feel it across the room, and all the bitterness in him broke up like a glacial mass shedding ice into the sea. When she looked at Jake, his defenses were down, and the sympathy in his eyes made tears slide down her face. With a broken voice, her eyes sinking to the floor at Jake's feet, she said, "I wadn't ever a good momma to you, Jake, but I been tryin' harder with little Sammy. Seems like I kinda been trying to make it up to you, by loving him extra hard. Stupid, hunh?" She looked around vaguely until her gaze returned to Jake.

"You sure have turned out real good, Jake. I'm glad. I had no idea about Roger, honey, and that's the truth. Your father told me he'd gone straight and I believed him. Duh . . . Still stupid after all these years—but I thought you'd be better off there than with some strange court-appointed somebody. I'm awful sorry about sendin' you there, Jake. It was just recent that I heard he had you sellin'. Man, when I found that out . . . Well, never mind." She frowned and shook her head. "You know it all came down on him, don't you? The feds moved in and cleaned up Bedford Green, and looks like old Roger and his buddies are all gonna be tucked up in the pen for a while."

Her voice trailed off as one hand scratched at the other absently. Then she dug in her purse for her cigarettes. "Ain't supposed to be doin' cigs either, but hell, what's the point . . ." She lit one and looked over at Sammy, as if remembering his tiny lungs. KatieLyn pushed herself up with difficulty and went to the trailer door, took a couple of drags, and flicked the butt outside.

Then she came and sat on a chair next to Jake, looking into his eyes. She started to speak and then bit her lip and stopped. He watched the tear slide down over the bones in her face. "I got no excuses, honey. I just got all screwed around in my mind. Seem like all I could think about was getting high again, partyin' somewhere, tryin' to forget ever'thing I did so wrong. I wish you'd forgive me, but you prob'ly can't, and that's okay too."

Jake's heart was pounding. He avoided looking at her, but finally he said, "I guess . . . You probably did the best you could."

She reached out and touched his cheek. "Thank you for saying that, honey."

Nell grabbed a box of tissues, and Jake and KatieLyn each took one with a fluster of embarrassed laughter.

After KatieLyn wiped at her eyes, she looked over at Milli. "He raised hisself, he really did, and turned out to be real smart. Real smart." Her querulous, suffering eyes returned to Jake. "I wonder where those smarts came from, Jakey. Maybe you know the Lord better'n I do, but I think you better be thanking Him for getting you along through all the awfulness you went through with me. Thank Him ever day, Jakey!"

Milli spoke up. "He got a big letter yesterday."

Each head turned to look at her.

"Yeah? What about?" KatieLyn looked at Jake.

"They transferred my scholarship to UK, so I'm going back to school in the fall—for free."

KatieLyn seemed to jar with the news, like she'd been knocked a little backward, like some plan of hers just went off the tracks, but she said. "That's just great, Jake. You sure do deserve it!" Her eyes moved to Milli. "And a pretty girlfriend—good with kids! Everything's turning out real good for you, ain't it?" There was no trace of irony in her assessment, and neither Jake nor Milli corrected the "girlfriend" word, both of them carefully avoiding looking at the other.

KatieLyn seemed to have shrunk down into the chair, and the heel of one hand rubbed at her side absentmindedly, before she started scratching her hand again. She seemed to still be searching her mind for something she wanted to say, still needing the right words to express her regrets. But her eyes fell on Ebenezer, smiling his innocent smile at her, his eyebrows over the close-set eyes locked together in perpetual sympathy.

"Ebbie, darlin'," she said, "You sure are still the sweetest old thing. I do hope I never hurt you. I need to apologize to most ever'body I know, but you always been too sweet to get any of my meanness thrown at you."

But Ebenezer wasn't looking at KatieLyn anymore. His eyes were on Sammy and his face was shining with his wide goofy grin.

"You want to hold him, Ebbie?" KatieLyn asked softly. Eb nodded eagerly, so Milli brought the baby and laid him carefully across the fat outthrust arms. Eb lifted him up and rubbed his nose on the baby's belly, eliciting a bright chortle from the little guy. He did it again, and the baby's laughter filled the trailer, and for a blessed moment, the heaviness was washed away, and all of them were smiling.

"Well, I'll be damned. Look at that." Nell spoke softly. "He used to do that to you, Jakey . . . all those years ago!"

"I remember that!" KatieLyn said, but her voice broke and her eyes filled again. She nodded toward her baby. "That is the worst thing about this deal." Tears spilled. "I can't hardly stand to let go of sweet Sammy. He's not a bit sick. After they found all what was wrong with me, they ran tests on Sammy, but said he's sound as a dollar. I thank the good Lord for that, anyway."

"What are you going to do with him?" Nell asked in a gentle voice.

KatieLyn shook her head, tried to pull herself together. Finally, with a crack in her voice, she said, "He has to go to the state, I reckon. His daddy left us when I got sick. No forwarding address, of course. Ain't nothing to do but give him to the welfare ladies." There was desperate hope in her voice as she sought to encourage herself. "He'll be okay. They said maybe some good people will adopt him. Well, unless . . ." She trailed off, looked around the room, at the shoes of each person present. Finally, her eyes settled again on the floor in front of her. "He'll be all right."

After a long silence, in which the stove clock clicked away the seconds, KatieLyn wiped her eyes, pushed herself up, stood with a hand on the back of the chair for balance, and brushed the thin hair back from her face. "Well, come on Sammy-wammy. Time to go on now." She grimaced briefly as she lifted him out of Eb's's arms. But she stood for a moment, holding the baby close and saying to Eb, "Thank ya, honey. You're a jim-dandy babysitter. You too, Milli."

KatieLyn sent a quick, shy glance to Jake and then to Nell before she looked down at the floor. "I just wanted you to know I'm sorry . . . real sorry for . . . for all the stuff . . ." She shrugged. "For everything." Then she went to the door, and stopped there, head down. Nell labored up out of the rocker, opened the door for KatieLyn, and took her elbow as they walked to the car.

Jake felt his heart pounding in his ears. His mind flailed back and forth between protest and assent. *Do good in your life*—Gran's words—and almost without thinking, he rose to his feet.

He looked at Milli, and when she looked back at him, her eyebrows rose over calm eyes.

"I could help you," she said.

He nodded, bit his lip to hold something back. A calm settled over him and he lifted his chin. Milli followed as he went out to the car. Sammy was wailing in his car seat, his face red and wet with mucous around his nose. KatieLyn bent to wipe his face and give him his pacifier, and when she stood, she looked at Jake with an expression of surprise that gave way to a mix of love and sorrow that broke his heart.

"It's okay, Mom." He took her in his arms and let her cry awhile as Milli looked on and Nell joined her. When KatieLyn pulled away to wipe her face, he said, "When the time comes, I'll make sure Sammy is well cared for. I'll be there. Family, right?"

The look that came into KatieLyn's eyes was so full of hope and gratitude that her poor ravaged face was transformed, and once more, like in his visit to Pete's church, Jake saw that there was a place and a time where this world could shine.

THE BEGINNING

CAROLYN BELL YOUNG HISEL

Carolyn Hisel, 1989
Photo: Lucy Massie Phenix

Carolyn Bell Young Hisel (1942-2017) was a native of Lexington, Kentucky, where she lived most of her life.

Better known for her luminous visual art, which has been exhibited throughout the eastern United States, Carolyn also wrote light-infused fiction, expressing her deep faith and probing spiritual inquiry in both realms.

In her own words, her work posed "questions about virtue and evil, guilt and innocence, the meaning of suffering and loss, redemption, revelation, love and transcendent joy, hope and despair." Her creative output was informed by a tender awareness of human frailty and an enduring fascination with those moments when we recognize the truth about ourselves and those in which we apprehend the transcendent.

Carolyn sought the holy light she glimpsed in the world around her, despite the reality of the darkness, a quest echoed by her protagonist in *Close to Shining*.

Did you love this book?
Take one minute right now to share an honest review on Amazon or Goodreads. Just one sentence helps readers find books they'll love.

If you enjoyed *Close to Shining*...you'll love:

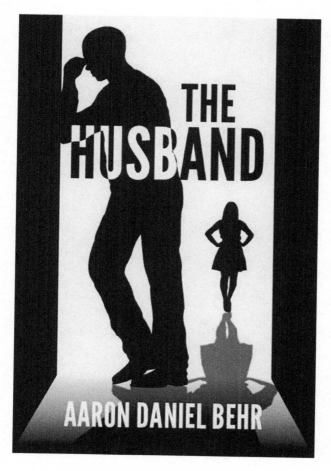

Loser. Thug. Abuser. Stupid. Worthless.

Insults play on repeat in The Husband's brain. He has been bullied and abused. An affair by The Wife, the one person The Husband loved the most, leaves him standing in a dark basement with a homemade noose around his neck.

As The Husband struggles silently through the anguish of betrayal and divorce, he turns inward to face a host of past tormentors, and confront The Creator. One way or another, The Boy inside him will stop the pain.

Available from book retailers everywhere!
Find it on Amazon or ask for it at your local bookshop.

Made in the USA
Monee, IL
23 January 2022

89660500R00132